TANK & FIZZ

THE CASE OF THE TENTACULAR TERROR

TANK & FIZZ

THE CASE OF THE TENTACULAR TERROR

LIAM O'DONNELL

MIKE DEAS

ORCA BOOK PUBLISHERS

Library and Archives Canada Cataloguing in Publication
O'Donnell, Liam, 1970–, author
Tank & Fizz: the case of the tentacle terror / Liam O'Donnell;
illustrated by Mike Deas.

Issued in print and electronic formats.
ISBN 978-1-4598-1952-8 (softcover).—ISBN 978-1-4598-1953-5 (pdf).—
ISBN 978-1-4598-1954-2 (epub)

I. Deas, Mike, 1982–, illustrator II. Title. III. Title: Tank and Fizz.
IV. Title: Case of the tentacle terror.
PS8579.D646T362019 jC813'.6 C2018-904880-8
C2018-904881-6

Simultaneously published in Canada and the United States in 2019
Library of Congress Control Number: 2018954086

Summary: In this illustrated middle-grade novel, fifth in the Tank and Fizz series, a goblin detective and technology-tinkering troll get tangled up with a sea creature, a dangerous band of kobold pirates and a blaze fairy who may be up to no good.

MIX
Paper from responsible sources
FSC® C016245
www.fsc.org

Orca Book Publishers is dedicated to preserving the environment and has printed this book on Forest Stewardship Council® certified paper.

Orca Book Publishers gratefully acknowledges the support for its publishing programs provided by the following agencies: the Government of Canada, the Canada Council for the Arts and the Province of British Columbia through the BC Arts Council and the Book Publishing Tax Credit.

Design by Jenn Playford
Illustrations and cover image by Mike Deas
Author photo by Ail Sonderup
Illustrator photo by Billie Woods

ORCA BOOK PUBLISHERS
orcabook.com

Printed and bound in Canada.

22 21 20 19 • 4 3 2 1

To my family, friends and readers who
joined me on all these adventures.
Thank you.

—Liam O'Donnell

For the readers of Tank and Fizz.
—Mike Deas

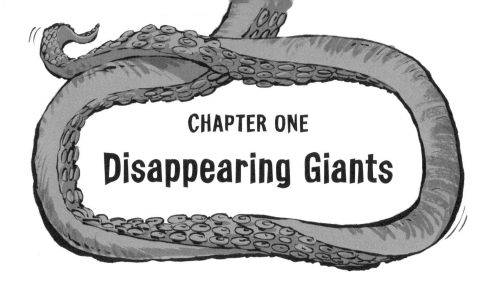

CHAPTER ONE
Disappearing Giants

The second ship vanished at midnight.

I was three choco-slug cookies into an unhealthy breakfast when I heard the news. A cargo ship bigger than Gravelmuck Elementary was missing from Fang Harbor. It had simply disappeared without a trace. It happens to my homework a lot, but it shouldn't happen to a massive ship made of metal and machinery. It had *mystery* written all over it. And that's my favorite kind of writing.

The name is Marlow. Fizz Marlow. I'm in the fourth grade, and I'm a detective. I'm also a goblin. Green scales, cute fangs and an adorable tail. The whole package. You cool with goblins? Good, because there are a lot of goblins and other monsters in my hometown, Slick City.

The moment I heard the news, I grabbed another cookie and hopped on a city bus heading to Fang Harbor. It was the weekend, which meant I had no school and nothing to do (except for a pile of unfinished homework, but who wants to do homework when there's a mystery to solve?). As the bus rolled through my neighborhood, I tried to wrap my head around the disappearances.

It started a week ago, when a cargo ship loaded with home appliances, furniture and other boring stuff sailed into Fang Harbor. The next morning the ship was gone. There was no record of it leaving the harbor and definitely nowhere it could be hiding. It had simply disappeared. It was the top news story across Slick City and all the way to the Dark Depths deep beneath Rockfall Mountain. The police had no clue where the ship had gone or even how it had vanished. And now it had happened again.

I got off the bus and walked the last few blocks to the harbor. Well, I tried to walk.

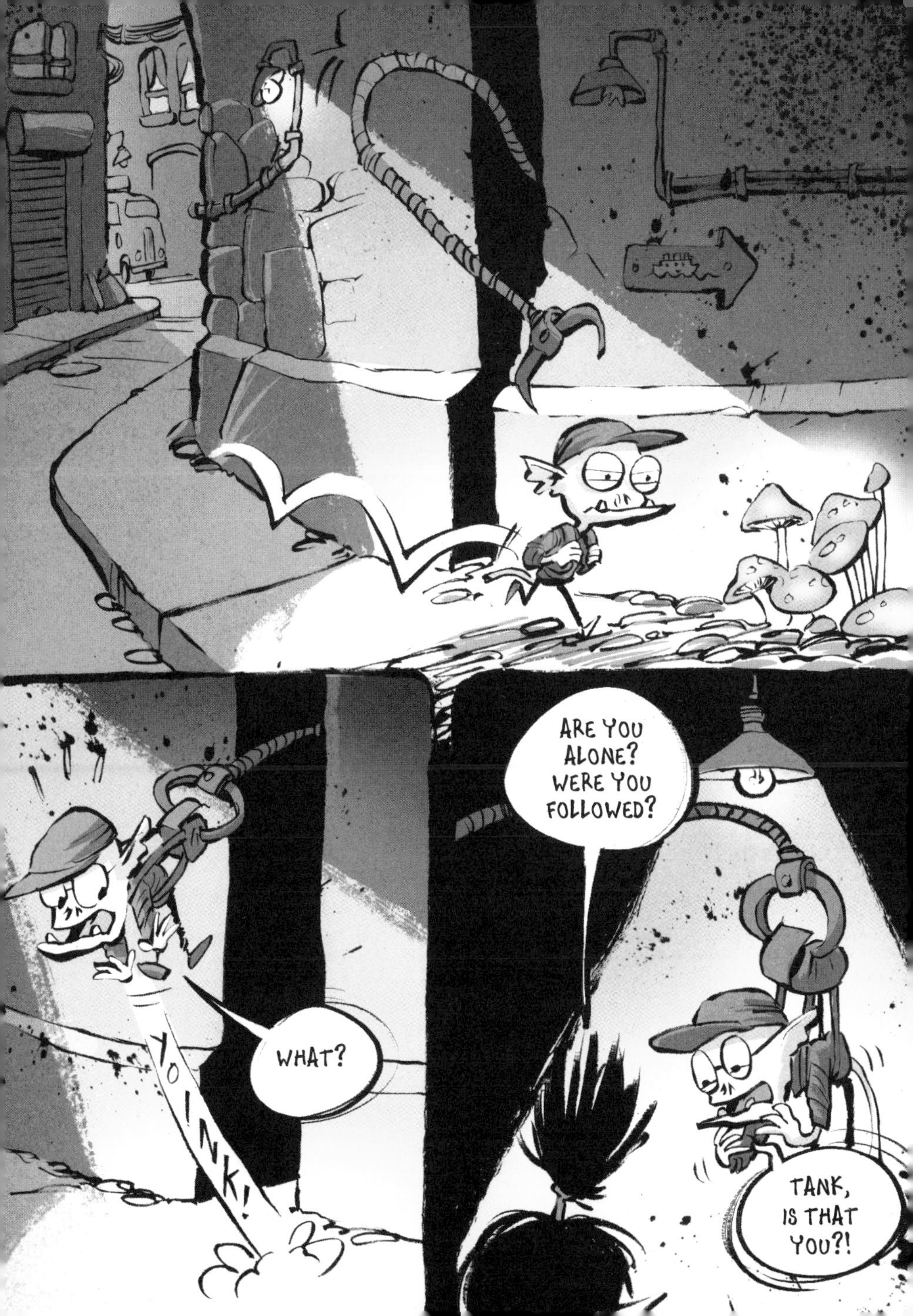
YOINK!
WHAT?
ARE YOU ALONE? WERE YOU FOLLOWED?
TANK, IS THAT YOU?!

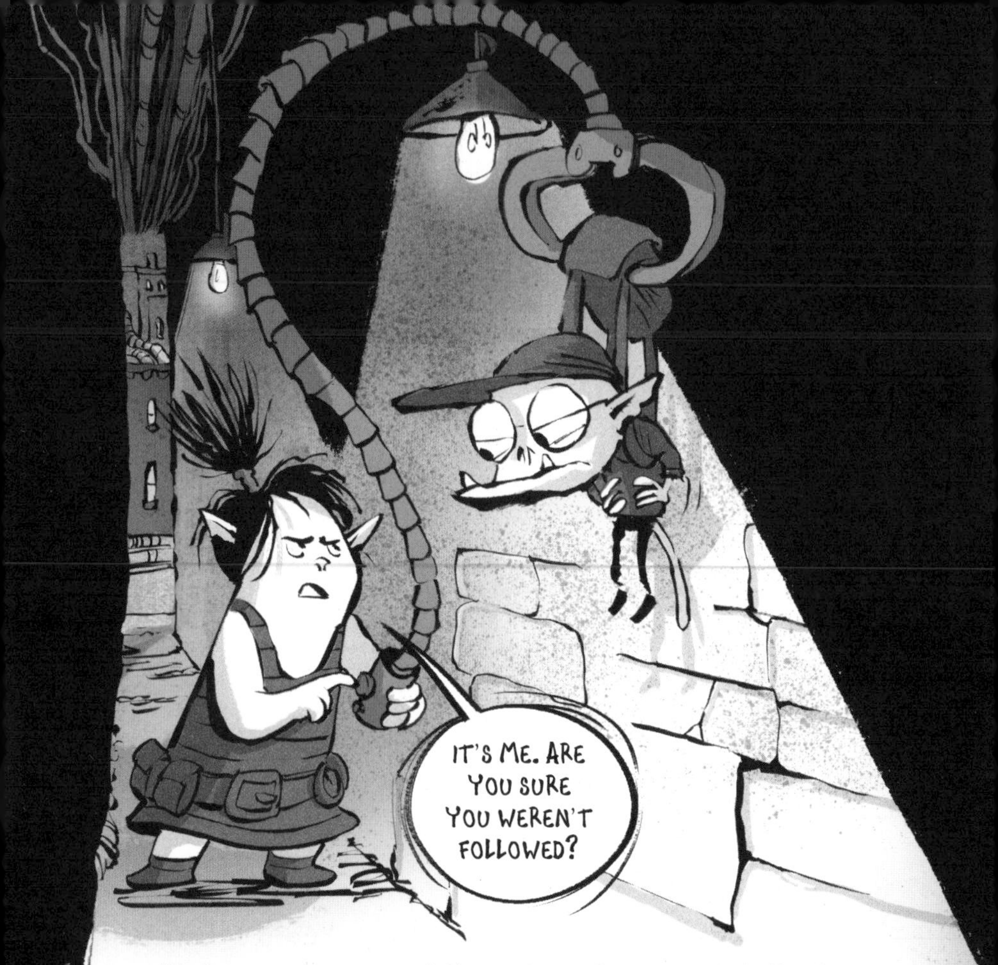
IT'S ME. ARE YOU SURE YOU WEREN'T FOLLOWED?

"Of course no one followed me," I snapped. "Why would anyone tail a fourth-grade goblin?"

"Because they think the goblin's best friend's mom stole those ships."

Tank stuffed her articulated grabber into her tool belt and sniffed like she was about to cry. Her full name is Tatanka Wrenchlin, but only her mom and a few teachers call her Tatanka. Everyone else calls her Tank. I call her best friend, detective partner and the smartest troll I know. Like all trolls, Tank loves tinkering with technology. From circuit boards to turbo-induced thingamajigs, she can fix just about anything that's put into her green hands. But from the frown on her face now, it looked like Tank was facing a problem even she couldn't fix.

"Now I know why you stopped me," I said.

Tank nodded. "My mom isn't answering her phone. What if they've already arrested her? And they're looking for me now?"

"That's ridiculous!" I said. "Your mom is the harbor master, not the police chief. She's not responsible for stopping crimes like this."

"Tell that to the news." Tank sniffed.

She had a point. With no clues and no answers, the media were desperate to find someone to blame. As the monster in charge of Fang Harbor, Janaka Wrenchlin, Tank's mom, was that *someone*. As harbor master she oversaw all the ships that came into the Slick City port. That was good enough for the TV stations, daily papers and news sites to pin the blame on her. When the first ship vanished, her face had appeared on the evening news and in the papers. Now that another ship had vanished, things could only get worse for Tank's mom.

Tank held up her phone. "Look who just jumped into the blame game."

On the screen was the face of the most sinister monster in Slick City. Bald head, beady eyes and fangs more crooked than a politician. In fact, this monster *was* a politician. Mayor Grimlock, leader of Slick City, ogre most likely to steal lunch money from a lost first-grader and also the biggest bully on the hottest gossip social-media site, Mobsplainr.

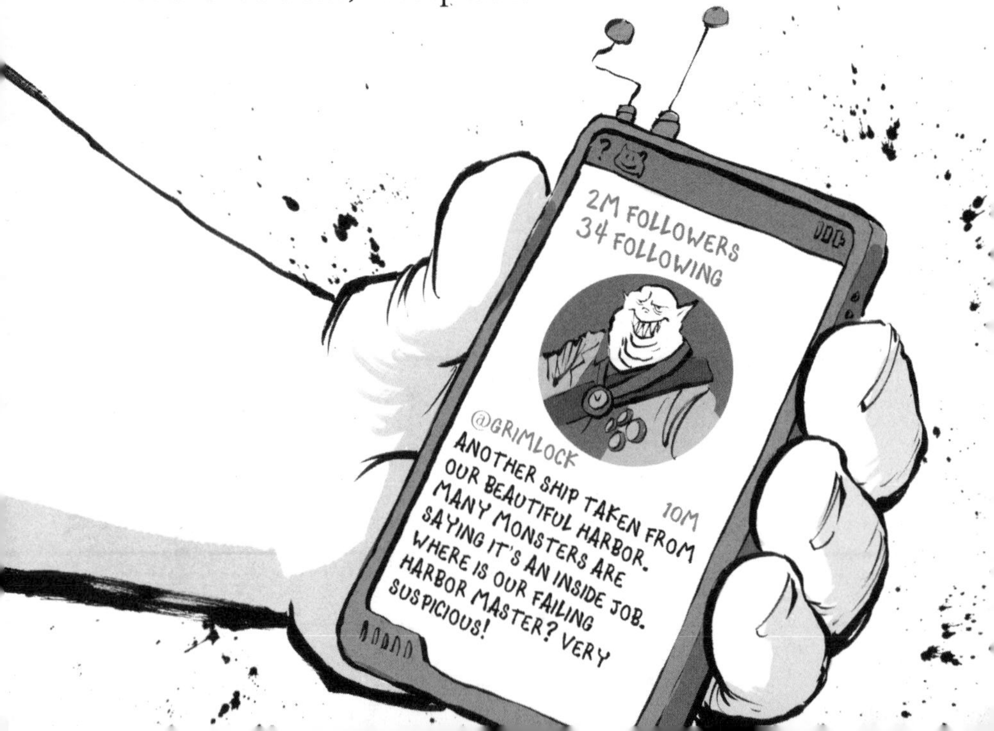
2M FOLLOWERS
34 FOLLOWING
@GRIMLOCK
10M
ANOTHER SHIP TAKEN FROM OUR BEAUTIFUL HARBOR. MANY MONSTERS ARE SAYING IT'S AN INSIDE JOB. WHERE IS OUR FAILING HARBOR MASTER? VERY SUSPICIOUS!

"What a jerk!" I growled.

"A jerk with power," Tank said. "One word from him, and my mom will lose her job. She could even be arrested! I have to find her!"

"Let's get to the harbor."

Getting to the harbor was no problem. Actually seeing Tank's mom was a different story.

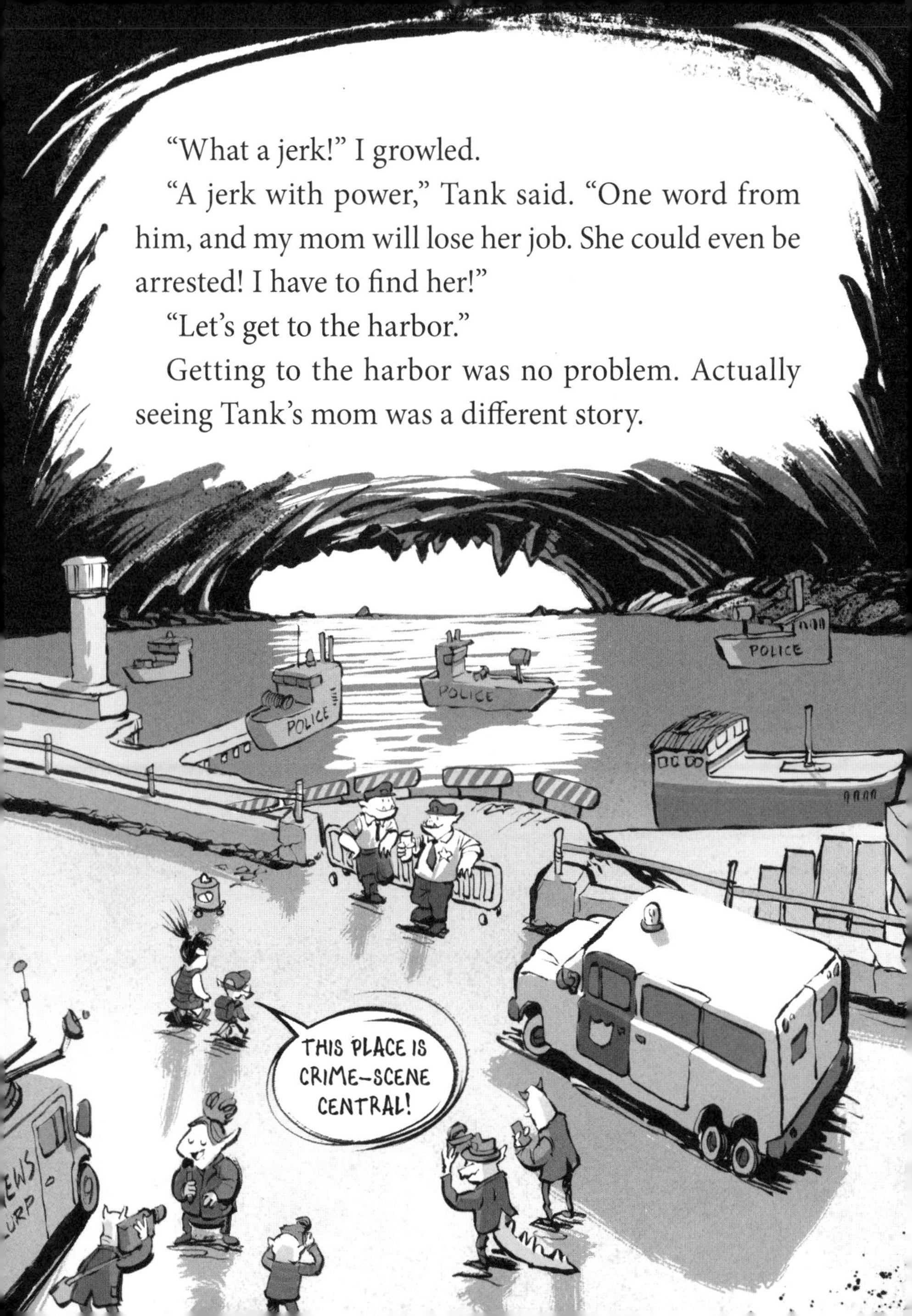
POLICE
POLICE
POLICE
POLICE
THIS PLACE IS CRIME-SCENE CENTRAL!

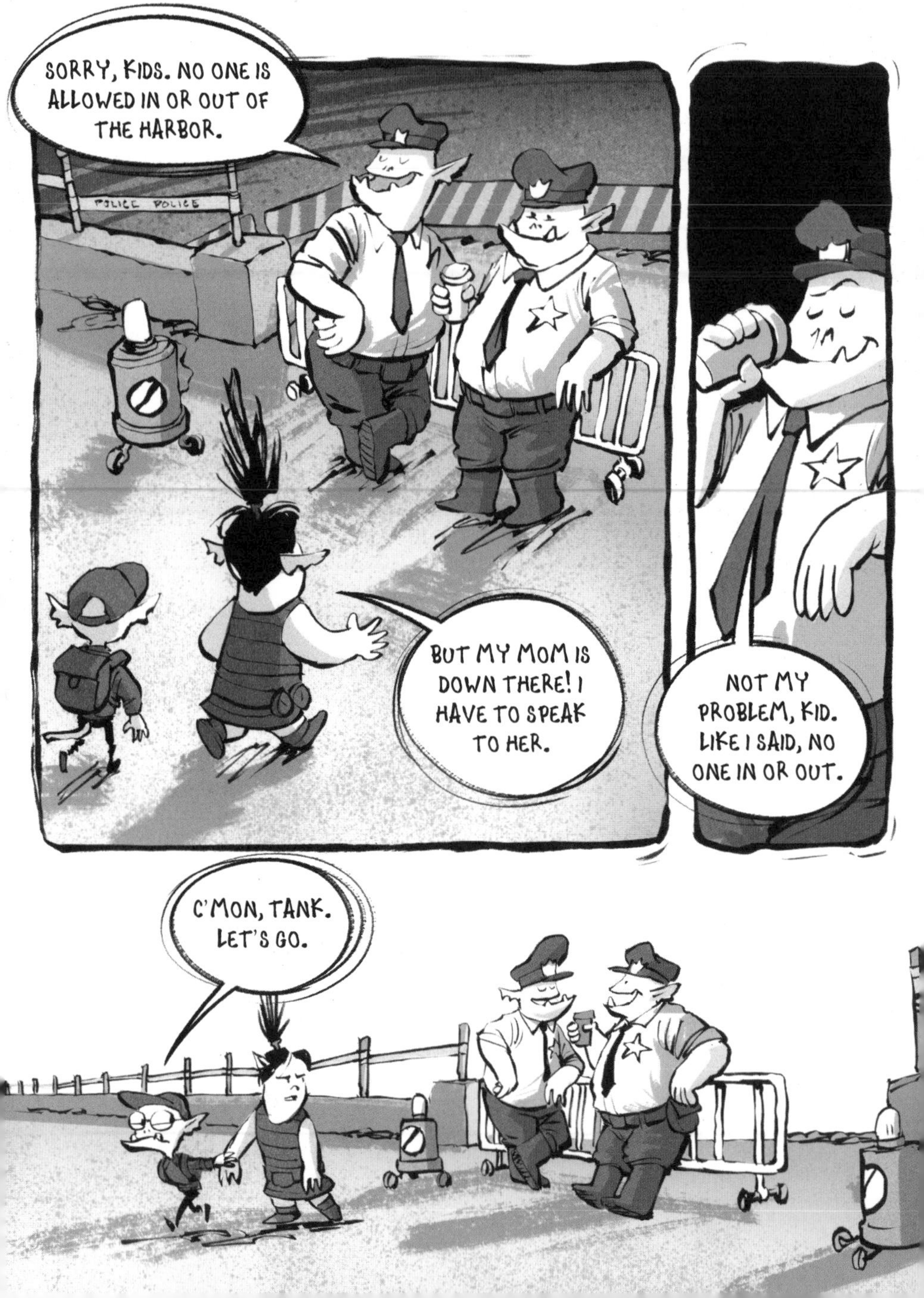
SORRY, KIDS. NO ONE IS ALLOWED IN OR OUT OF THE HARBOR.
POLICE POLICE
BUT MY MOM IS DOWN THERE! I HAVE TO SPEAK TO HER.
NOT MY PROBLEM, KID. LIKE I SAID, NO ONE IN OR OUT.
C'MON, TANK. LET'S GO.

We left the police to their very important job of denying mother-daughter reunions. Tank's ears drooped like a pair of wilted snaggleruff leaves.

"They'll take my mom away, and I'll never see her again." She moaned.

My friend's head drooped just like her ears, and she rubbed her eyes. It takes a lot to make Tank cry. She's as tough as they come and stronger than any of those slouch-spined police officers.

Something bad was happening down on the harbor, and Tank's mom was going to get blamed for it. I didn't know what had happened to those ships or if we could stop Mrs. Wrenchlin from taking the fall. But I was sure of one thing—I was going to help my friend. We were going to find out who had stolen those ships.

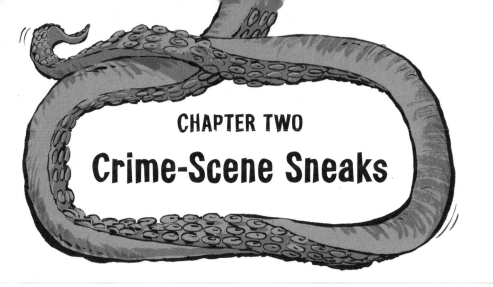

CHAPTER TWO
Crime-Scene Sneaks

Tank stared down the hill to the water's edge.

The boardwalk along Fang Harbor was normally busy with monsters enjoying the view. Today it was packed with police. Teams of forensic ogres dusted for paw prints and claw marks, while more cops rode with the Harbor Patrol tugboats across the choppy water.

"We have to get down there and speak to my mom." Tank's brow furrowed. "Somehow."

"Fizz Marlow! What are you doing here?"

The voice made me jump like a surprised toddler. In fact, the voice had been making me jump, in a good way, since before I was a toddler.

"Mom!" I ran to where my mom stood with the other reporters near the gate to the harbor. "What are you doing here?"

"I was asking you the same thing," my mom said. "I'm here covering the disappearances for the paper. Didn't I leave you at home with a healthy breakfast and homework to finish?"

"Um, well, I heard about the second ship and…"

My mom rolled her eyes. "And you couldn't resist investigating. Always on duty, aren't you, Mr. Detective? Okay, you can do your 'sleuthing,' but don't get in anyone's way. Hi, Tank. I'm sorry about the way the press is treating your mom. I know she has nothing to do with all this."

"Thanks, Ms. Marlow."

At the gate to the harbor, the slouching police officers jumped to life as a sleek black limousine approached. The reporters huddled around the gate took photos and moved closer to the car.

My mom pulled a notebook from her pocket and headed to the car.

"Got to get back to work. Don't stay too long. Be home for dinner!" she called over her shoulder.

The driver's-side window of the car silently slid open

to reveal a goblin in a black cap behind the wheel. The goblin said something to the police officer, who nodded and waved to his partner to open the barricade.

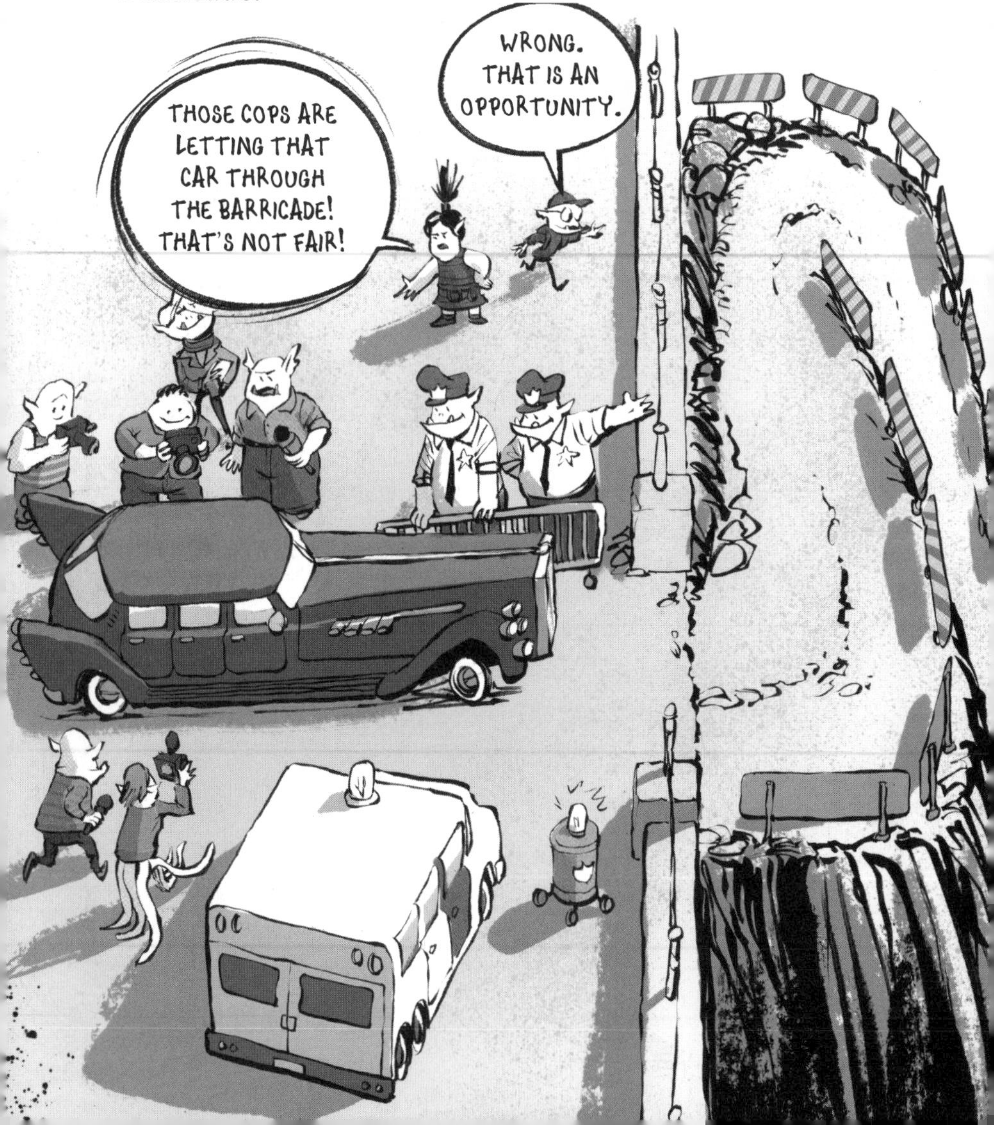
THOSE COPS ARE LETTING THAT CAR THROUGH THE BARRICADE! THAT'S NOT FAIR!
WRONG. THAT IS AN OPPORTUNITY.

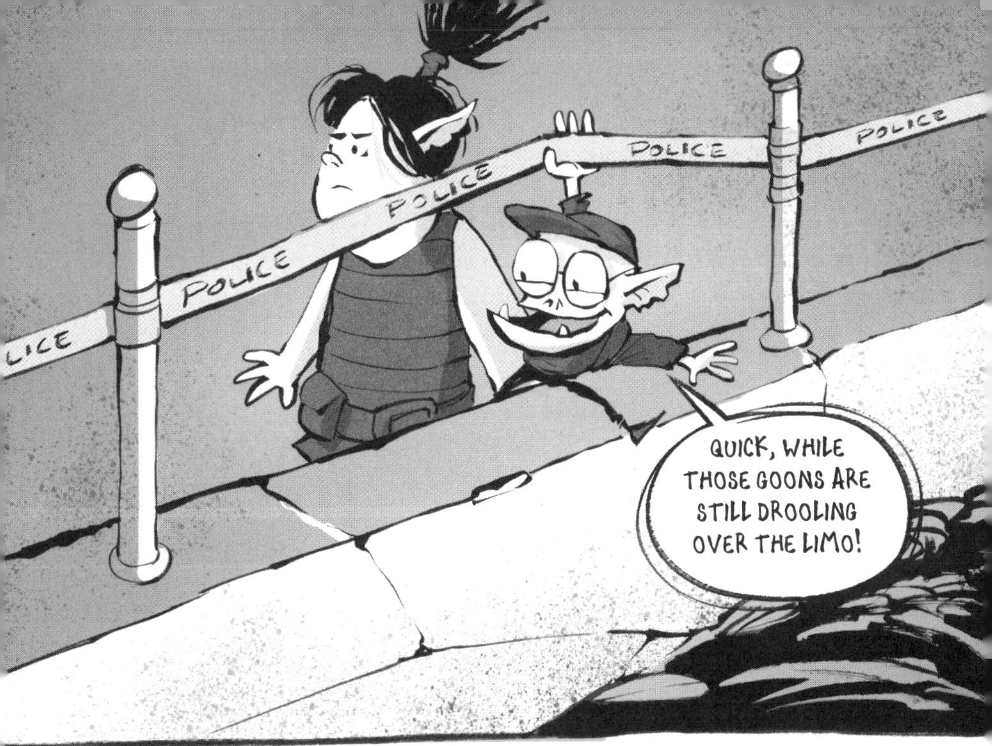
LICE
POLICE
POLICE
POLICE
POLICE
QUICK, WHILE THOSE GOONS ARE STILL DROOLING OVER THE LIMO!

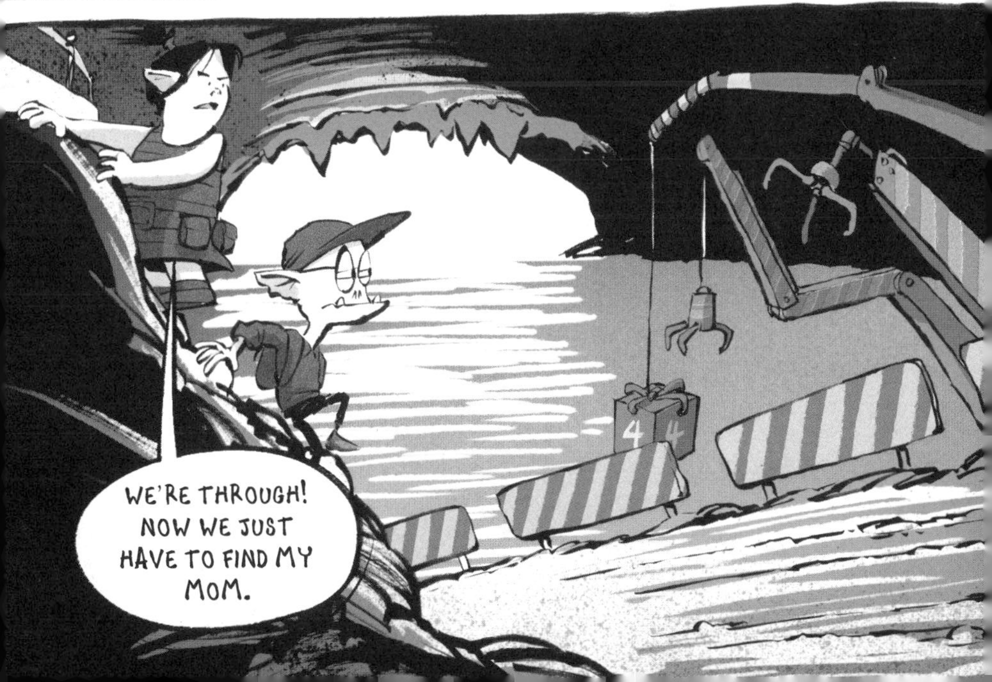
WE'RE THROUGH! NOW WE JUST HAVE TO FIND MY MOM.
44

We got to the boardwalk and stayed out of sight. Farther along the walkway stood a squat stone building. A tower with large windows rose out of the middle of the building and overlooked the harbor.

"That's the harbor master's office," Tank said. "I bet she's in there."

She took a step forward, but I pulled her back.

"Wait," I whispered.

The black limo had made its way to the water's edge and now drove slowly along the boardwalk toward us.

Tank's eyes narrowed. "Vehicles aren't allowed on the boardwalk. Why can they do that?"

"The answer is on the front fender," I said.

Tank read the limo's license plate and rolled her eyes. "SlurpCo. What is someone from the biggest company in Rockfall Mountain doing here?"

"The news said it was another SlurpCo cargo ship that vanished," I said. "Maybe they're here to make sure it gets found—and fast."

The SlurpCo limo rolled past us. The windows on the car were completely black. I couldn't see who was inside. No doubt sitting in the backseat was some bigwig monster with bad hair, bad breath and bad taste in ties. Everything that came from SlurpCo was bad.

But without the company, Slick City and the rest of Rockfall Mountain would be in big trouble. Every day, monsters throughout the mountain depend on products produced by SlurpCo Industries. The company drills deep into the rocks for the goopy slick that runs all our machines. Their factories make the phones and other gadgets we all stare at. Their farms grow the food we eat. And every week, their massive cargo ships arrive in Fang Harbor, loaded with more stuff that we monsters rely on. Tank and I had come snout-to-snout with their corrupt executives before. It was not something I wanted to do again.

The limo stopped in front of the harbor master's office. The wrinkly goblin in a black jacket and cap climbed out of the driver's side and shuffled to the car's rear door. A second later the door to the harbor master's office flew open. Tank's mom came barreling out and stormed over to the limo.

YOU CAN'T PARK HERE!

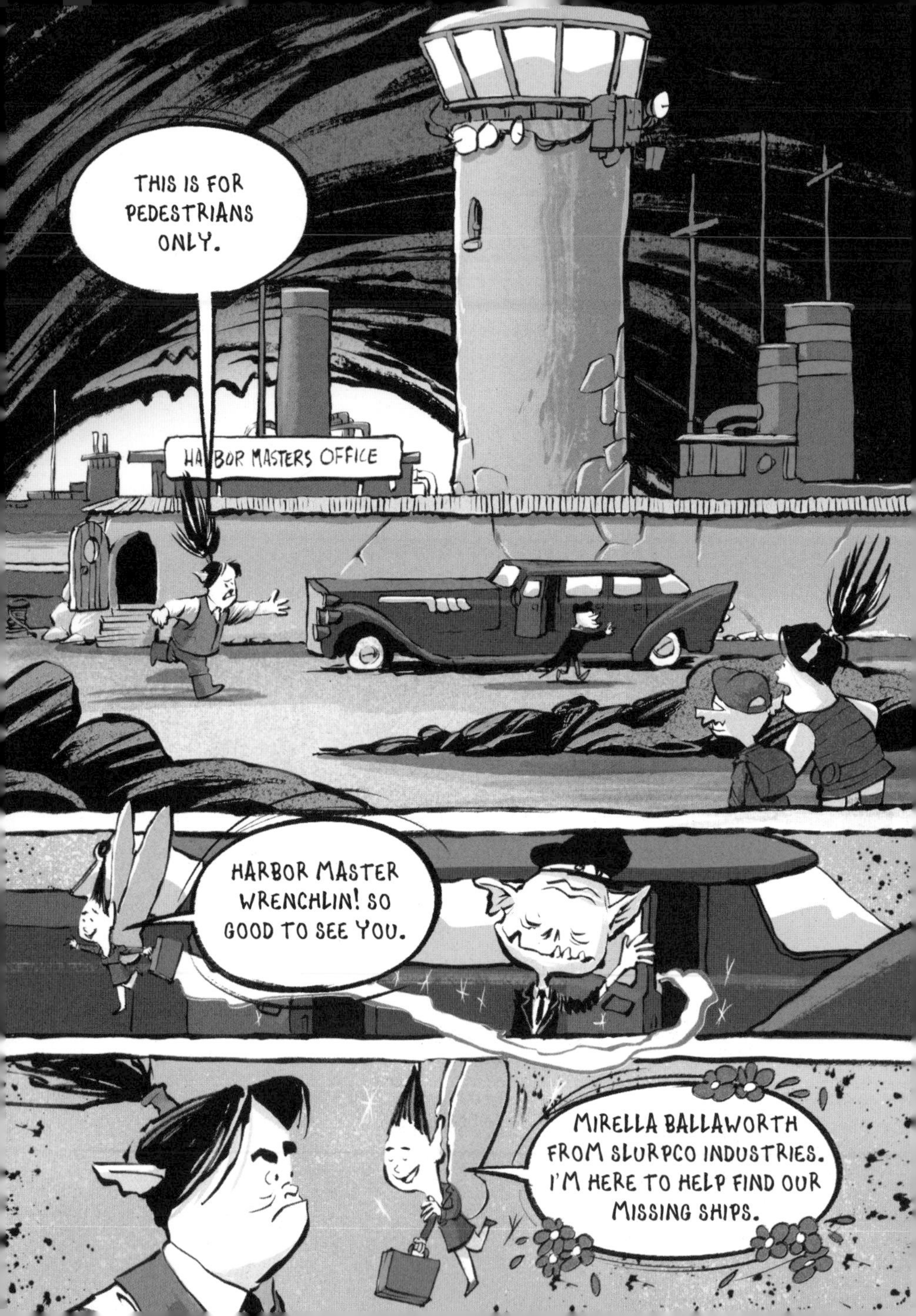
THIS IS FOR PEDESTRIANS ONLY.
HARBOR MASTERS OFFICE
HARBOR MASTER WRENCHLIN! SO GOOD TO SEE YOU.
MIRELLA BALLAWORTH FROM SLURPCO INDUSTRIES. I'M HERE TO HELP FIND OUR MISSING SHIPS.

Mrs. Wrenchlin scowled at the small blaze fairy hovering in front of her.

"It's such a pleasure to meet you." Mirella Ballaworth's words bubbled like she was singing a children's song.

"That still doesn't mean you can drive your car along the boardwalk," Mrs. Wrenchlin snapped.

"Ms. Ballaworth can park her car wherever she likes." The gruff voice sent a chill down to my tail. A slouching ogre in a rumpled overcoat stood on the steps of the harbor master's office.

"Detective Hordish!" I whispered.

"What's he doing here?" Tank moaned.

Detective Hordish was as pleasant as a bag of old gym socks. We had helped the police detective solve a couple of big mysteries in the past, but he still treated us like a rash that wouldn't go away. If he was here, that meant he was leading the police investigation into the missing ships. And that meant we had better stay out of sight.

Hordish shuffled down the steps and over to the limo. "I received word from Mayor Grimlock himself that Ms. Ballaworth is permitted to assist in our search for the missing ships."

"Assist us?" Mrs. Wrenchlin's brow furrowed. "Why does the mayor think I can't do my own job?"

"I completely understand, Harbor Master." Mirella's words dripped with sweetness. "But please remember that SlurpCo Industries is the real victim here. We've lost valuable cargo, and we'd like to help in any way we can."

Mrs. Wrenchlin glared at the blaze fairy. "SlurpCo Industries has been trying to take control of this harbor for years. You'd like to put me and my colleagues out of our jobs and replace us with your bots."

"It would be more efficient," Mirella chimed. "And save the city money."

"It would be more dangerous," Mrs. Wrenchlin growled. "And it would line the pockets of your bosses and the politicians they bribe."

Detective Hordish stepped in between the two monsters. "Why don't we put aside our different views and move this inside?"

"Fine," Mrs. Wrenchlin said.

"A wise suggestion, Detective." Mirella flew a tight circle around the other monsters. "Before we do that, perhaps we should say hello to your other guests."

Mrs. Wrenchlin looked around. "Other guests?"

"Yes." Mirella chuckled and looked in our direction. "Hiding in the shadows over there."

My scales stood on end. Beside me, Tank gasped.

"Children, come out from there," Mirella called. "I'm sure Tank would like to see her mother."

Tank gulped. "Busted."

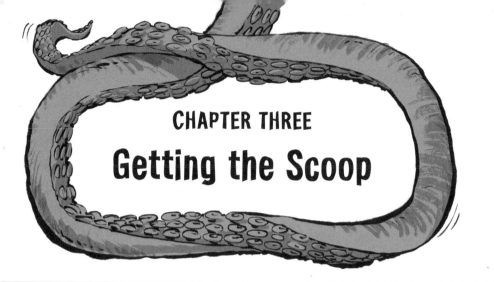

CHAPTER THREE
Getting the Scoop

The tiny fairy had busted us big-time.

We stepped out from our hiding spot. Tank rushed to her mom and hugged her.

I looked at the blaze fairy. "How did you know we were there?"

Mirella smiled. "Fizz Marlow, I'm from SlurpCo. We know everything about everybody. It's what we do."

"I was wondering when you two would show up." Detective Hordish scowled. "Get inside."

"You don't want us to scram? Stay away from this mystery?" I said.

Detective Hordish sighed. "Would you listen to me if I did?"

"Probably not."

"That's what I figured," Hordish said. "Get inside. And stay out of the way."

***

Tank's mom led us into the harbor master's office and to the control room at the top of the glass tower. The large windows overlooking the harbor wrapped around the open room. A row of computer terminals sat against one wall. Lights flashed and small screens blinked, tracking the movement of all the boats on the water below. A sharp-eyed troll sat at the control panel, speaking quietly into her headset to one of the tugboat captains bobbing along on the harbor.

Mrs. Wrenchlin stood in front of a large screen that hung on the back wall. "I can fill you in on what we know."

I grabbed a seat near the screen and got comfortable. My scales tingled with anticipation. All that was missing was a bag of popped slugcorn. Tank pulled up a seat beside me.

"Try not to look so happy," she whispered. "Remember, my mom's job is on the line."

"Sorry." I wiped the grin from my snout. "But we're finally going to get the scoop on the missing ships."

Mirella Ballaworth buzzed once around the room and perched on top of a filing cabinet near one of the windows. Detective Hordish slouched into the room and stood beside Tank's mom. The ogre cleared his throat before speaking.

"This recap of what we know shouldn't take too long because we really don't know much," he said.

"Don't be so hard on yourself, Detective," Mirella chirped from her perch. She peered out the window to the harbor, where the harbor patrol and the police were combing the chilly waters for clues. "Your monsters are doing a wonderful job."

Detective Hordish pulled at the collar of his wrinkled shirt. "Um, thank you, Ms. Ballaworth."

"Please call me Mirella, my dear," the blaze fairy cooed. "We have no time for stuffy formalities. We have ships to find!"

"Very well, Mirella," Hordish muttered. The screen behind him lit up and displayed an image of two cargo ships. He waved a meaty hand at the screen. "These are the vessels that have vanished. Both are SlurpCo cargo tankers and both disappeared in the same way."

"What do you mean 'the same way'?" I asked. "The papers said you had no idea how they disappeared."

"We don't always tell the press everything we know," Hordish said with a smirk.

"A brilliant strategy, Detective!" Mirella flew up from her perch and hovered near Hordish. "You don't want the culprits reading about your investigation on the front page of the *Rockfall Times*."

Hordish nodded. "Exactly. So, here's what we do know." Something buzzed in the detective's coat. He fumbled through his pockets with his big hands and pulled out his phone. He looked at the screen and frowned. "It's Mayor Grimlock. I better take this outside."

Detective Hordish shuffled out of the control room. Mrs. Wrenchlin stepped forward and pointed to one of the ships on the screen. "That is the *Empire Star,* the first ship to disappear. She pulled into the harbor late in the evening last week. She carried a cargo of small appliances—toasters, vacuum cleaners, that sort of thing. She set her anchor for the night so the morning shift of dock workers could unload her. She didn't make it to the morning."

"Yes, but exactly what happened?" Mirella buzzed

closer to the screen and hovered next to Tank's mom. "I read your report of the incident, but quite frankly, I simply don't understand how it is possible."

"None of us do." Mrs. Wrenchlin sighed. "It's probably easier if we just watch the video from the security camera."

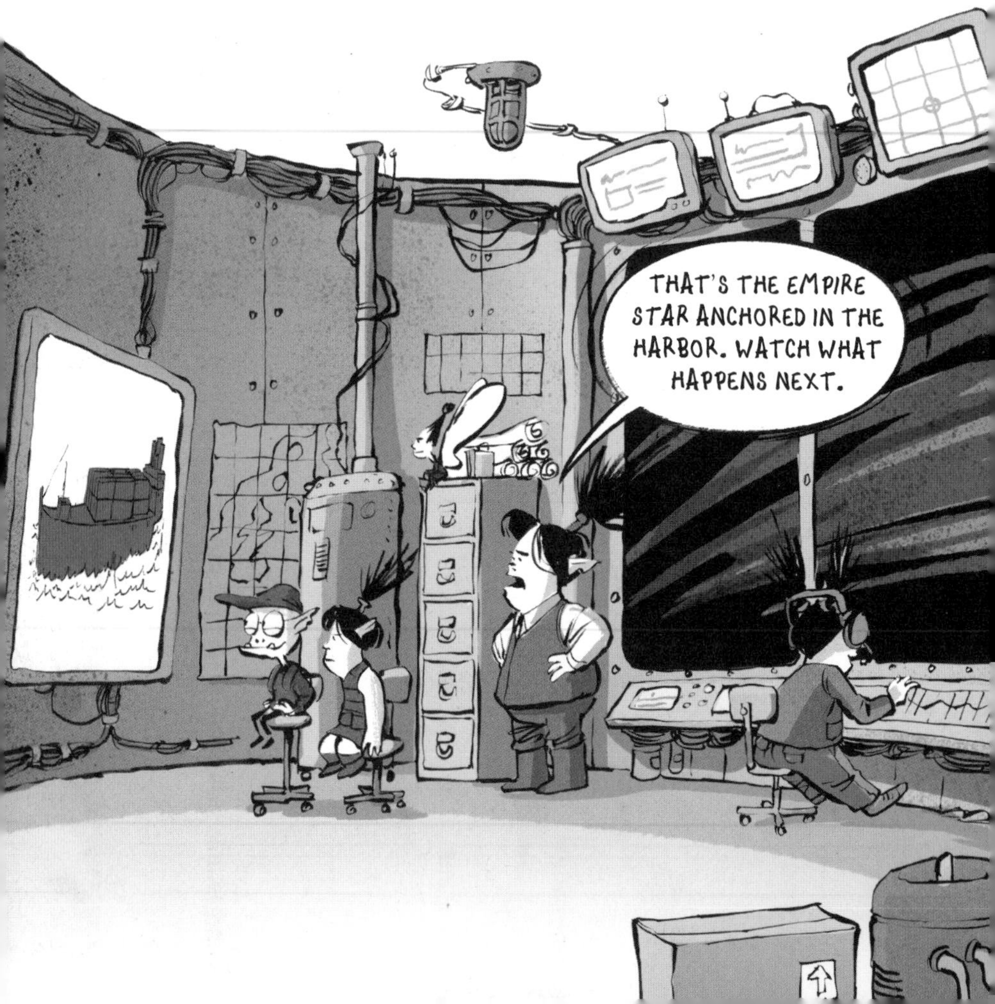
THAT'S THE EMPIRE STAR ANCHORED IN THE HARBOR. WATCH WHAT HAPPENS NEXT.

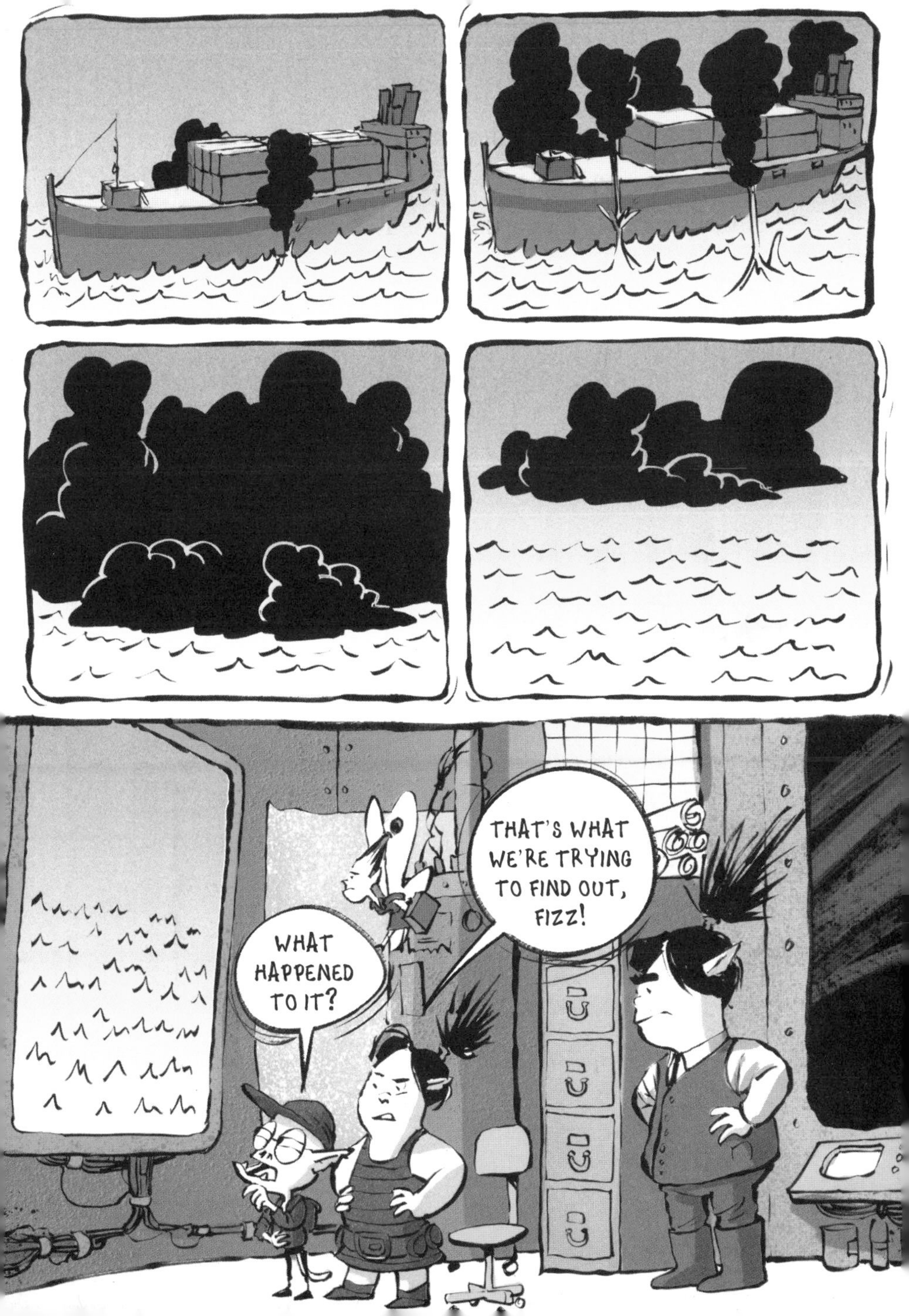
WHAT HAPPENED TO IT?
THAT'S WHAT WE'RE TRYING TO FIND OUT, FIZZ!

"I know that." I glared at my detective partner. "I was just, um, thinking out loud."

"What a curious way for a ship to disappear." Mirella flew closer to the screen. "What of the ship's crew? Were they taken too?"

"They were found on the beach, unconscious and with no memory of what had happened," Mrs. Wrenchlin said. "The theft happened at night, so most of the crew were already asleep. The ones who were awake remembered seeing the black cloud appear, but nothing after that."

"Very curious." Mirella studied the screen for a moment before spinning to face Mrs. Wrenchlin. "What theories does the Harbor Patrol have?"

"None that make sense," Tank's mom said. "It could be something in the water causing the mist. It could be thieves operating somehow from within Slick City. It could even be pirates from outside the mountain. We just don't know. Hopefully Detective Hordish can help narrow down suspects. We've analyzed the video, but all we can say is that there must be something in the mist that affected the ship."

"That much is obvious." Mirella narrowed her tiny eyes. "SlurpCo needs our ships back. We cannot afford to lose a single crate."

Mrs. Wrenchlin smiled at the buzzing blaze fairy. "The Harbor Patrol is working hard to find the ship, Ms. Ballaworth."

"Mirella, please! We are all friends here," the SlurpCo executive said in a singsong voice.

"I've doubled the night patrols on the water, and we've had a team of divers searching the harbor floor," Mrs. Wrenchlin continued. "So far they haven't found anything. We showed this video to senior wizards at the Shadow Tower, but they can't confirm what created the mist. They will be sending a team of wizards later today to investigate further."

"And what of the second ship, *Nolan's Edge*?" Mirella asked. "How did it disappear?"

"In the same way," Mrs. Wrenchlin answered. "One week to the day, and at the exact same time."

She tapped the screen, and security-camera video of the second ship appeared. We watched the video in silence. It followed the same pattern. A SlurpCo cargo ship floated in the water, minding its own business, when suddenly the water around it began to bubble. A black mist rose from the water and engulfed the entire ship. And then, as quickly as it had come, the mist disappeared and the ship was gone.

"So two ships vanish, and you have no idea, no clues and no suspects?" Mirella said. "I see why Mayor Grimlock is losing patience with you, Harbor Master."

Mrs. Wrenchlin crossed her arms. "Between the Harbor Patrol and the police department we will find out who is behind these disappearances."

"You better hurry," Mirella snapped. Her whimsical laugh was gone. In its place was the stern words of a monster used to getting what she wanted. "Another SlurpCo ship arrives in Fang Harbor this evening. We don't want to lose that one too."

"Actually, Detective Hordish and I had just come up with a plan for that ship when you arrived," Mrs. Wrenchlin said. "If you agree to it."

"What sort of plan?"

"Both ships vanished in the middle of night. We think the thieves, whoever they are, will strike again tonight for the third ship. This time we're going to be ready. We'll have police officers and the Harbor

Patrol standing by, ready to act at the first sign of trouble."

"Are you talking about a stakeout?" Tank asked. She looked to me, her ears perked up.

Mrs. Wrenchlin smiled. "Yes, it's a stakeout. But don't even think about asking to come. It's late at night. Both you and Fizz will be at home in your beds."

She silenced Tank's protests with a single look. My friend's ears flopped. There was no way her mom was going to let her go on that stakeout. It'd be the same story with my mom.

I didn't really listen as Mrs. Wrenchlin explained the details of the stakeout to Mirella. I was too busy making plans of my own.

Whatever it took, Tank and I would be at that stakeout.

CHAPTER FOUR
Stakeout Spies

The glowshrooms around Fang Harbor cast their pale light across the water.

The third SlurpCo cargo ship, *Wave Dancer*, floated in the middle of the harbor like a silent giant. The ship's crew had been removed earlier, so now the ship lay empty except for the dozen or so shipping containers filled with SlurpCo products. Near the edge of the water Detective Hordish and a small army of police officers waited in a flotilla of Harbor Patrol boats. With them was a contingent of wizards from the Shadow Tower. The school of wizardry rarely got involved with anything that happened outside the tower. This time, though, the possibility that the thieves were using magic to conjure the cloud of black mist that engulfed the ships had them interested. Tank's mom watched over it all from the harbor master's control tower.

Despite Mrs. Wrenchlin's earlier warnings, she eventually agreed to let Tank watch the stakeout from the safety of the shore. Since we didn't have school in the morning, it only took an hour or two of pestering. Tank is a good pest. I'm not so shabby myself. It took less than half an hour of nagging to get my mom agree to let me tag along. We had just slipped down to the water's edge when a shadow on the water appeared.

"Here she comes," Tank whispered.

The shadow drifted closer.

"Are you sure it's her?"

"Of course it's me, Fizz!" a familiar voice called out from the water.

"Aleetha!" I cheered as loudly as I dared.

The shadow revealed itself to be a small rowboat carrying a lone lava elf, our pal Aleetha Cinderwisp. She used to go to school with us, but now she's studying to be a wizard at the Shadow Tower. That's where all the elves go to learn magic. She goes to classes just like Tank and I do, but has some pretty weird subjects. Who ever heard of getting an A in History of Magical Mishaps? That's a thing apparently.

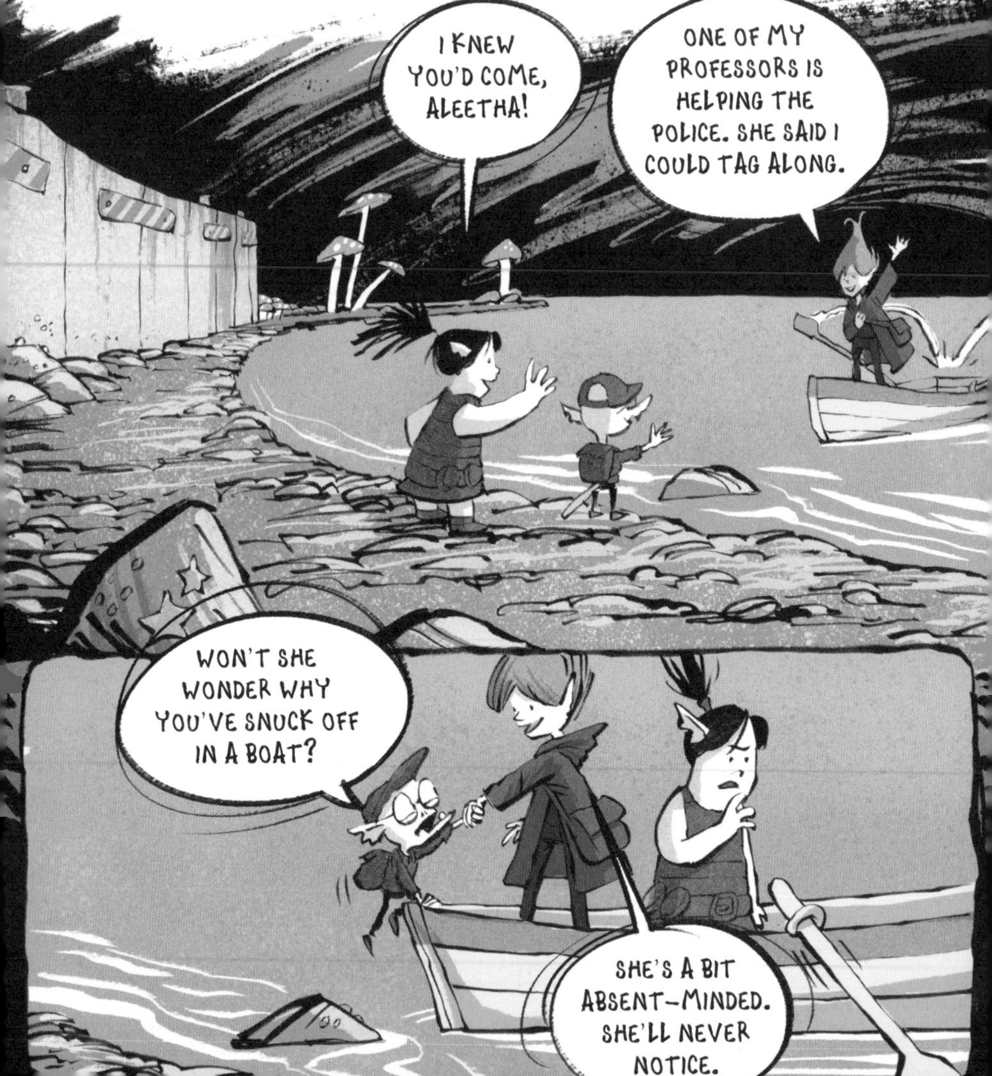
I KNEW YOU'D COME, ALEETHA!
ONE OF MY PROFESSORS IS HELPING THE POLICE. SHE SAID I COULD TAG ALONG.
WON'T SHE WONDER WHY YOU'VE SNUCK OFF IN A BOAT?
SHE'S A BIT ABSENT-MINDED. SHE'LL NEVER NOTICE.

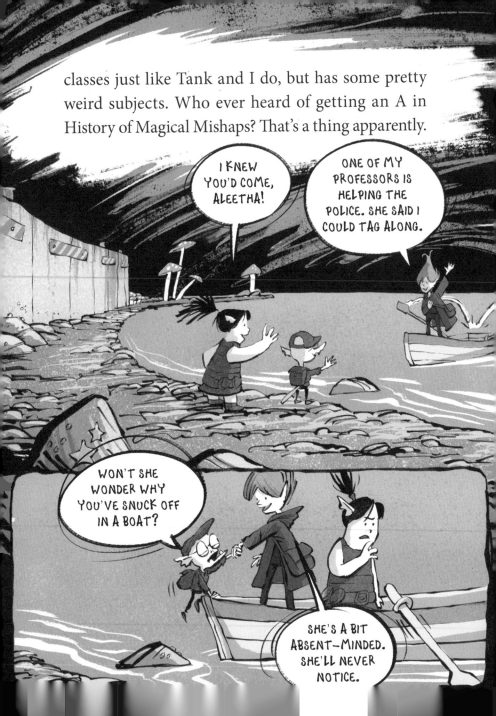

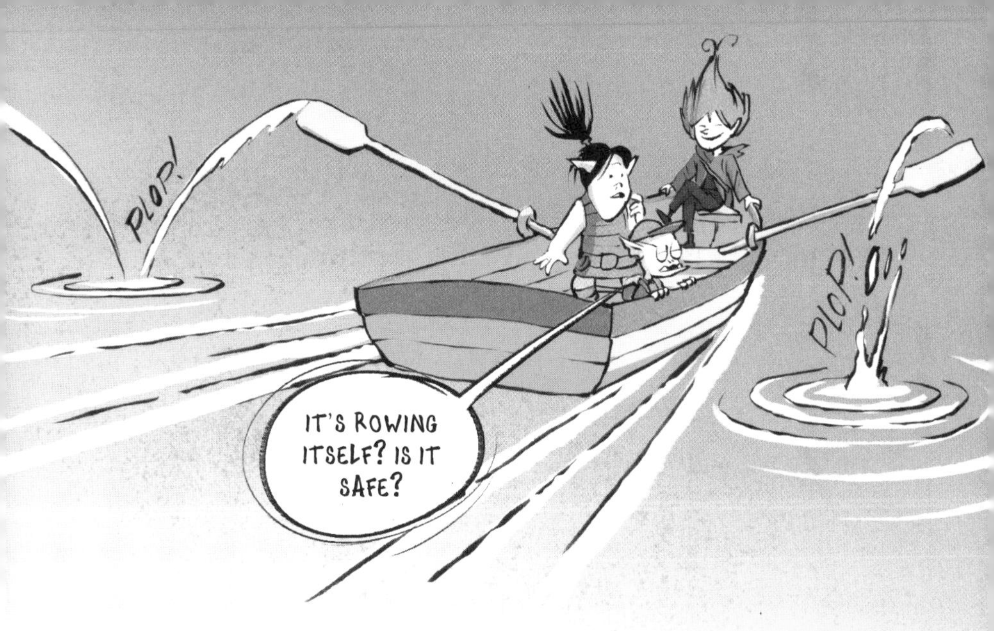
PLOP!
PLOP!
IT'S ROWING ITSELF? IS IT SAFE?

"Relax, Fizz," Aleetha chuckled. "It's a real boat. It's just powered by magic. You'll be fine."

The oars of the small boat slowly paddled us toward to the *Wave Dancer*. Tank scanned the water.

"What happened to the other boats?"

"They're around here somewhere," Aleetha said. "The wizards have them cloaked in an invisibility bubble to avoid being spotted by the thieves."

I nearly fell out of the boat. "Really?! The Slick City police are using magic? I thought they banned using that stuff in their investigations."

"Times are changing, Fizz." Aleetha grinned. "I think we had a hand in that."

Every monster in Slick City knows to stay clear of magic. Magic is unreliable, unpredictable and downright dangerous. Only elves like Aleetha are comfortable with the arcane arts. Trolls, ogres and goblins like me are happy to use technology to get stuff done. And all monsters know never to mix technology with magic. Putting those two together is a great way to fry your scales and blow up your neighborhood.

When we were closer to the *Wave Dancer*, Aleetha whispered a word of magic and the oars lifted out of the water. Our little boat slowed to a stop.

"This is close enough," Aleetha whispered.

We bobbed on the water in silence, waiting for the thieves to arrive. After a few minutes something did show up, but it wasn't the ship stealers.

Next to us, a dozen Harbor Patrol boats had suddenly appeared. They formed a wide circle around the *Wave Dancer*. Police officers stood on the decks of each boat, watching the cargo ship.

"Where did they come from?" I hissed.

Aleetha cursed. "We drifted into the invisibility bubble. Now we're invisible too."

"That's good, right?" I said.

"Not really," Aleetha muttered. "Invisible can see invisible, which is why we can see them."

"And they can see us," Tank whispered. "Let's just hope they don't notice our little rowboat."

All eyes were on the cargo ship in front of us. Well, almost all eyes.

Three boats away, one burly ogre in a rumpled overcoat glared directly at our little vessel. Detective Hordish practically fell over the railing of his boat when he spotted us. We'd promised him we'd stay out of the way and watch from the shore. Now he'd caught us far from the shore and very much in the way. The ogre barked an order to one of his officers, and soon every monster on the boat was looking our way.

"I think we've been noticed," I said. "Aleetha, get us out of here before we become Hordish's catch of the day."

"Good idea."

Our oars dropped back into the water and magically began rowing us away from the cargo ship. Suddenly the water around us began to bubble. The sight of the bubbling water drew Hordish's attention away from us and back to the *Wave Dancer*.

A dark mist appeared on the surface of the bubbling water. It grew into a thick cloud of smoke around the cargo ship. Aleetha stood at the front of our tiny rowboat. She thrust her hand into the dark cloud swirling around us. It sparkled purple at her touch.

"We were right," I said. "It's magic."

"You got it, Fizz." Aleetha studied the mist with narrowed eyes. "This has been created by some kind of spell."

As the smoke surrounded our boat, my head grew heavy and my vision blurred. Through the gathering cloud, I could just make out Detective Hordish. He wobbled on the deck of his boat, nearly falling over. Next to him, one of his officers collapsed. Hordish waved his arms madly, ordering the other Harbor Patrol vessels to pull back. I liked his thinking.

"There's something in the smoke." I struggled to get my words out through the growing fog in my mind.

The water beneath us began to churn. Bubbles burst through the surface and rocked our boat. I held onto the gunwale with both claws, wishing I had stayed home and done something more enjoyable, like finishing my homework.

The dark cloud now completely surrounded us. Tank sat in the bottom of the boat. She rubbed her eyes and struggled to stay awake. Waves splashed over the side of the boat as the bubbles turned into gushing geysers of water.

A heavy thud sounded against the bottom of the boat.

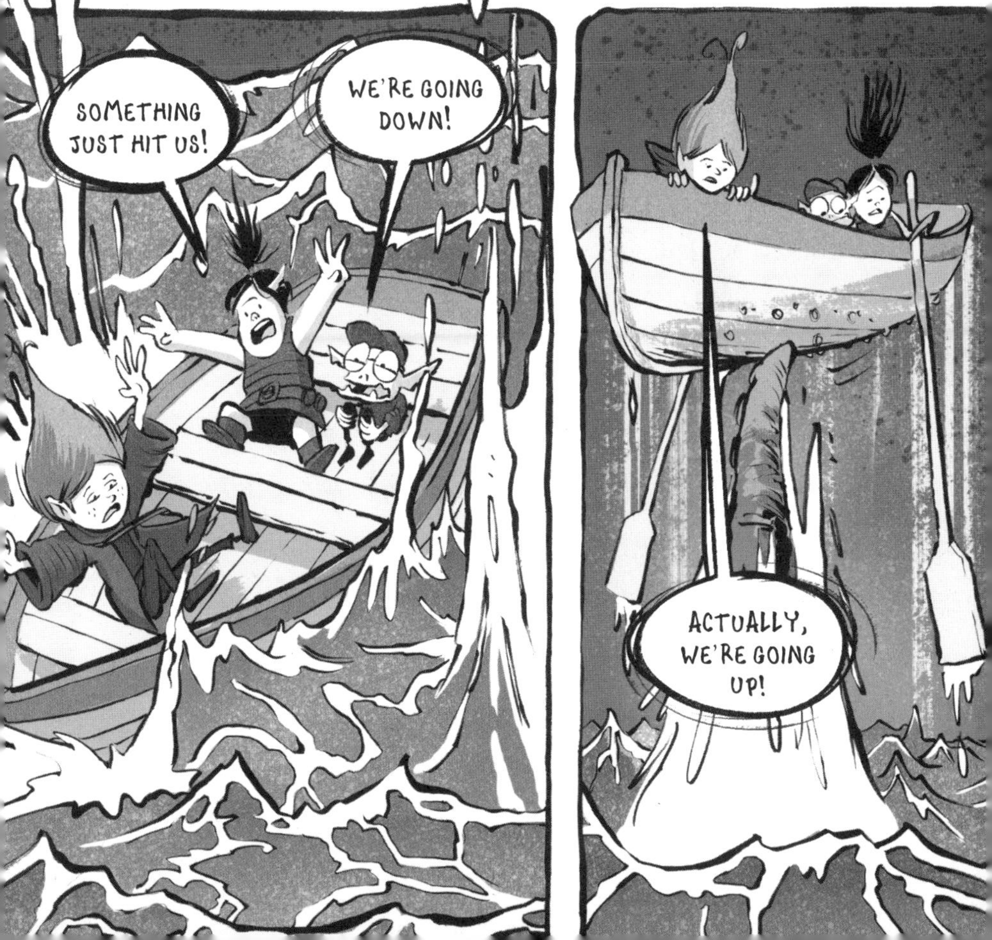
SOMETHING JUST HIT US!
WE'RE GOING DOWN!
ACTUALLY, WE'RE GOING UP!

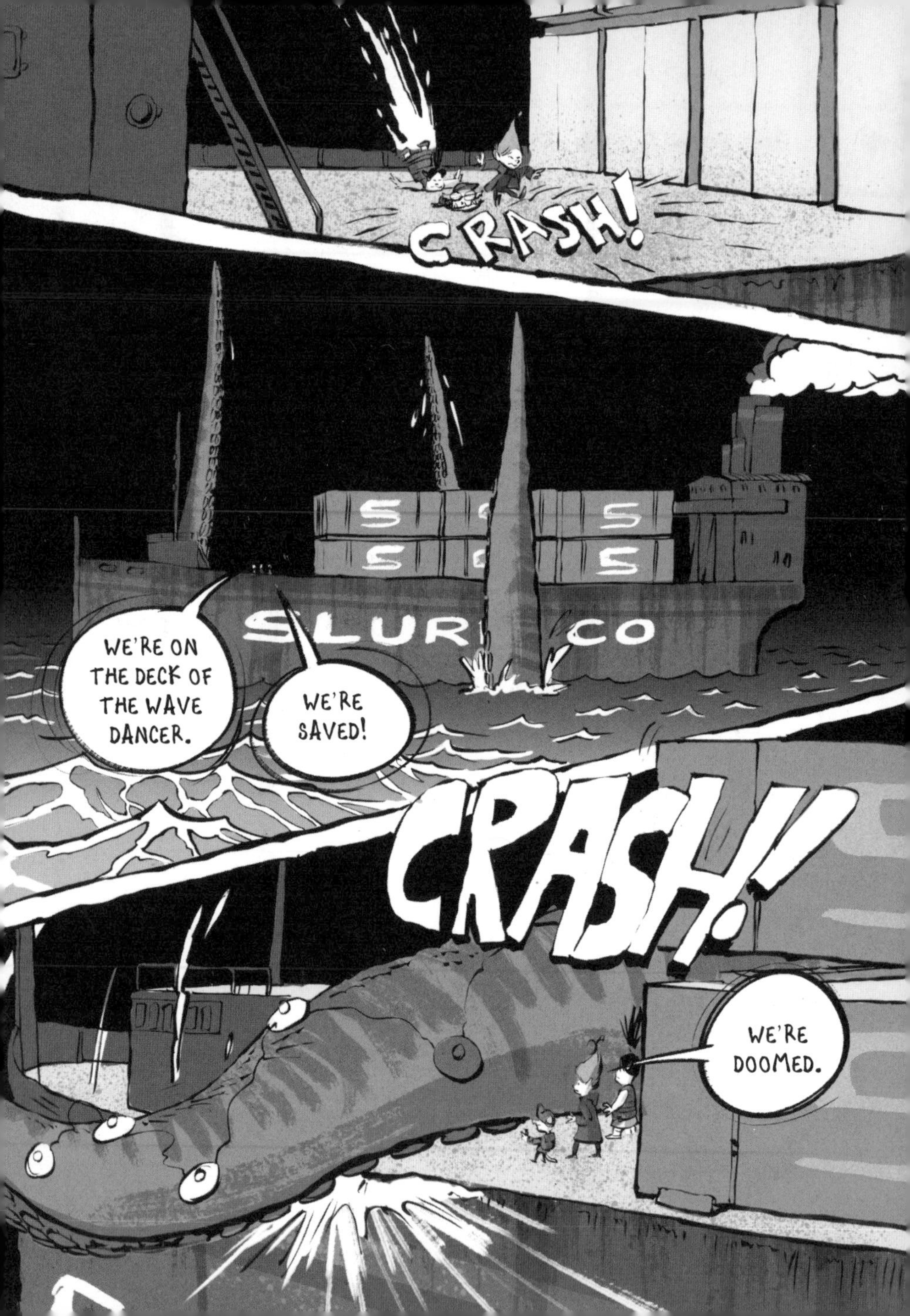
CRASH!
SLURCO
WE'RE ON THE DECK OF THE WAVE DANCER.
WE'RE SAVED!
CRASH!
WE'RE DOOMED.

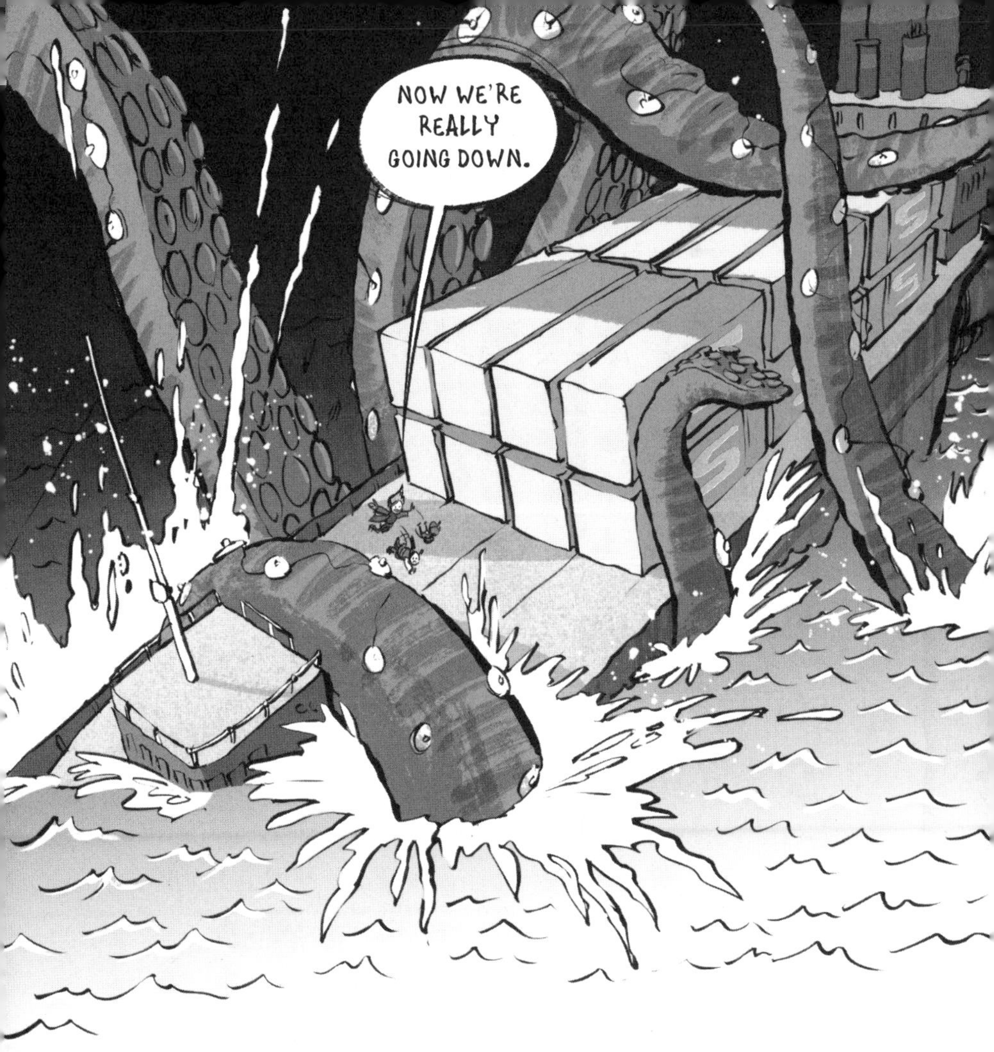
NOW WE'RE REALLY GOING DOWN.

Whatever had grabbed the *Wave Dancer* now lifted it out of the water and tilted it like a salt shaker. The three of us slid down the deck, tumbling toward the churning waves of Fang Harbor. We'd come to catch the ship thieves, but now we were sunk.

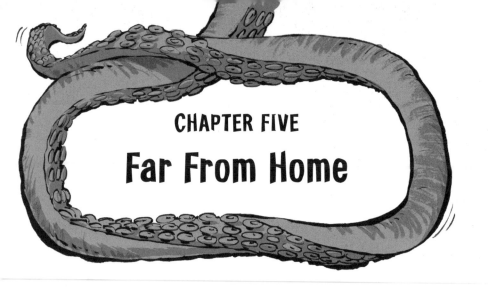

CHAPTER FIVE
Far From Home

I landed with a *splat* instead of a *splash*.

My body crashed into something solid, squishing my snout, bending my tail and shaking my brain. Tank and Aleetha landed beside me. Somehow we had missed the water and stayed on the deck of the *Wave Dancer*. The whole ship was tilted at a sharp angle.

Suddenly the ship's massive hull groaned like it had a toothache. The world around me moved. My stomach lurched into my throat. Water whooshed high into the air on all sides as the ship's massive hull splashed back into the harbor. I wobbled to my feet.

Tank sat up and rubbed her head. "Have we landed?"

The cargo ship rocked from side to side. Aleetha poked her head out from under her cloak.

"What happened?" she groaned.

Tank jumped to her feet, suddenly alert and eyes wide. She pointed straight ahead.

"*That* happened!"

On the far side of the ship, a thick, slimy snake slithered across the deck. Except it wasn't a snake. It was the largest tentacle I had ever seen. Living in a mountain full of monsters, I'd seen my fair share of tentacles. From the octo-ettins who were my class-mates to slabbergrabbers who hung from the rocks and snatched food out of the claws of unsuspecting tourists, tentacles were as common as tails and usually about as big. This tentacle was different. It was as thick as an ogre and as long as the mudball playing field. It had wrapped itself around the *Wave Dancer* like a child grabbing a toy. A shiver ran through my scales at the thought of the size of the creature who commanded such strength.

"That thing just grabbed the *Wave Dancer* right out of the water!" Aleetha said.

The tentacle slid across the deck as the monster released its grip on the ship. Tank had her phone in her hands and snapped photos of the retreating tentacle. She looked up from her screen.

"There's more to that monster than just tentacles."

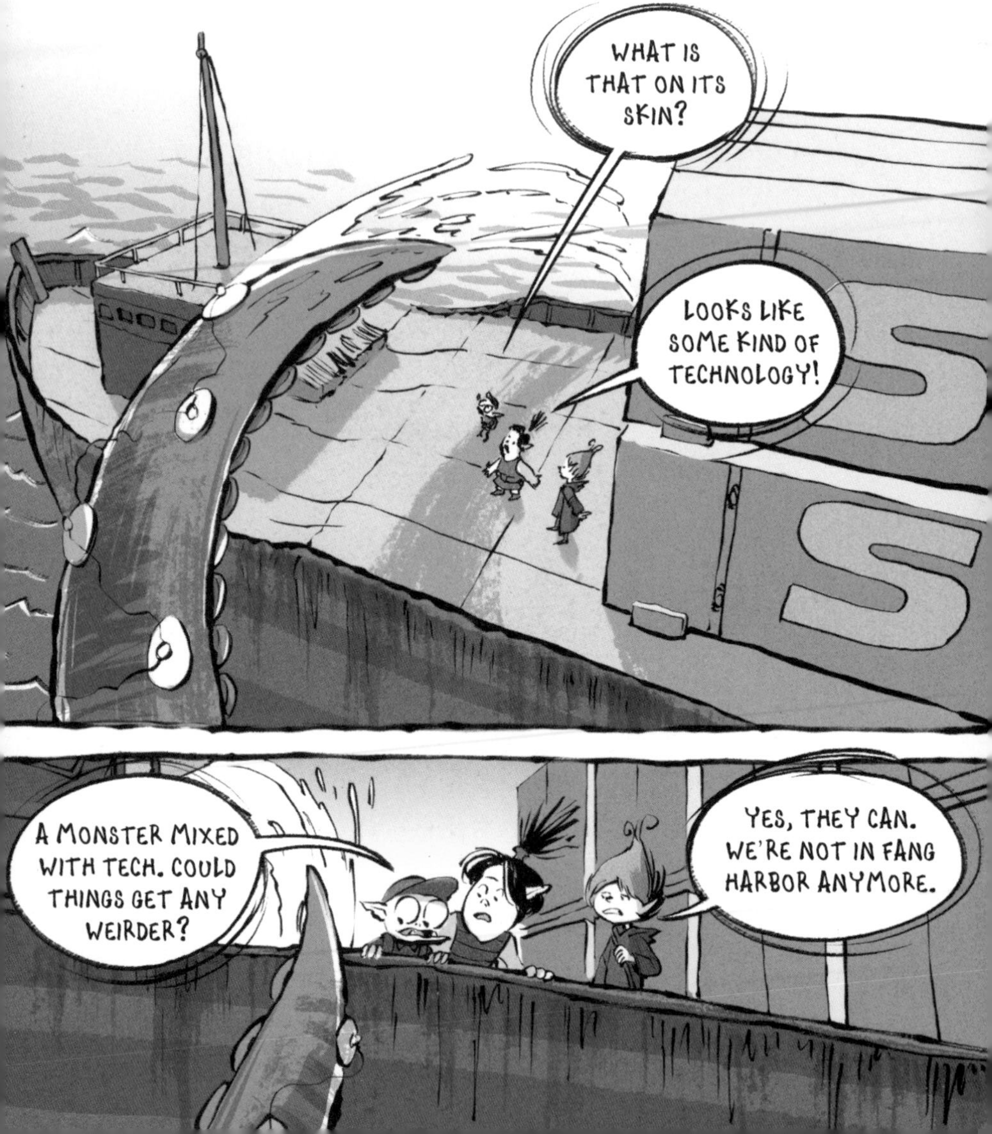
WHAT IS THAT ON ITS SKIN?
LOOKS LIKE SOME KIND OF TECHNOLOGY!
A MONSTER MIXED WITH TECH. COULD THINGS GET ANY WEIRDER?
YES, THEY CAN. WE'RE NOT IN FANG HARBOR ANYMORE.

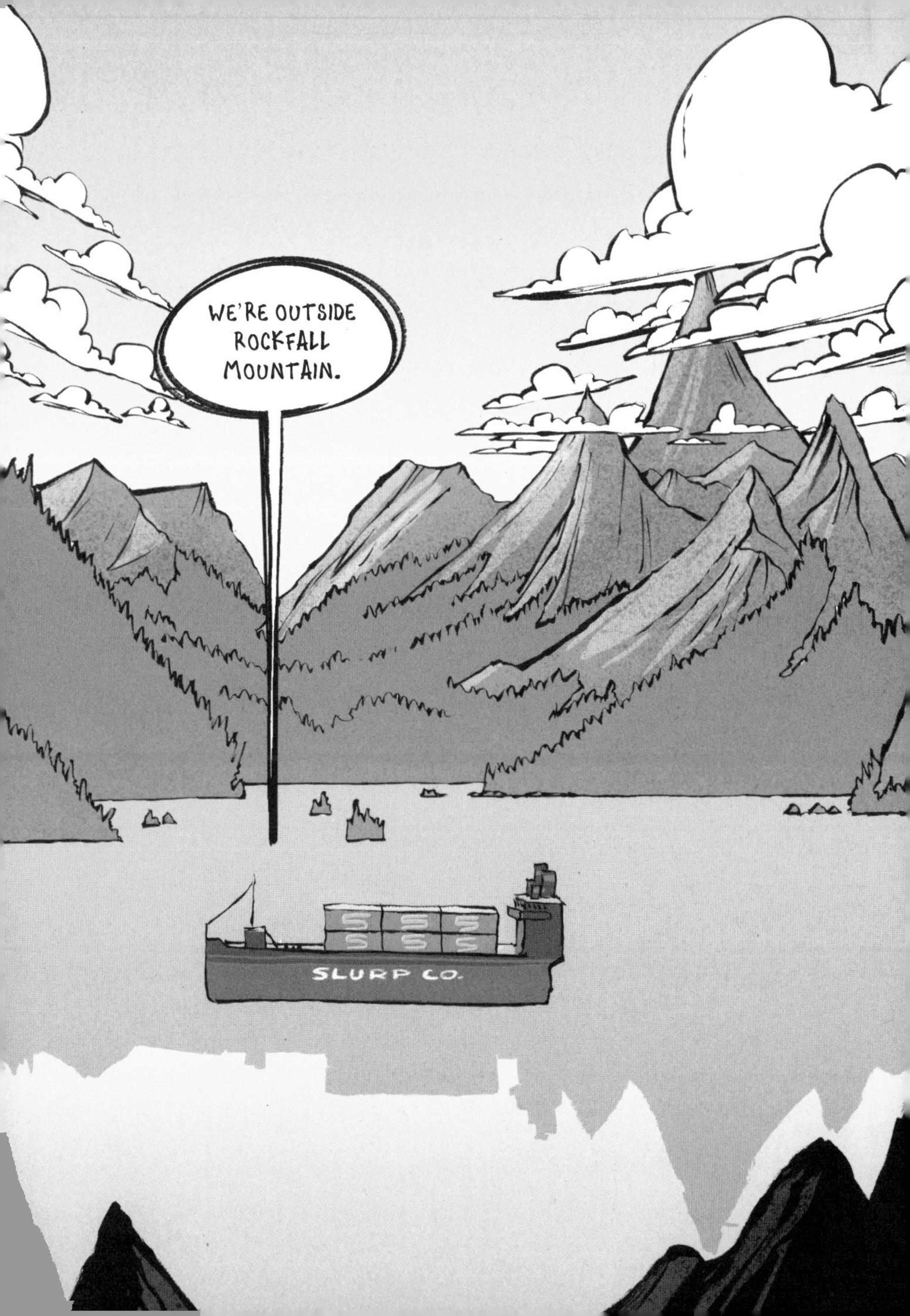
WE'RE OUTSIDE ROCKFALL MOUNTAIN.
SLURP CO.

The roof above us was a brilliant blue. Puffy white balls of smoke drifted across it overhead. A blindingly bright circle of light shone down on us. Somewhere deep in my brain, the name of the light bubbled up.

"The sun." I shielded my eyes against the brightness. "And those white things are clouds!"

Most monsters live their entire lives without ever leaving the darkness of Rockfall Mountain. That included the three of us. I had briefly glimpsed the world beyond the mountain once before. It was only for a few seconds, and I was still safely inside the mountain. Now, water stretched as far as I could see. In the distance a line of rocky cliffs loomed on the blue horizon. We were definitely not in Slick City anymore.

Tank stared at the sky, her jaw hanging open. "How? Where?"

"My thoughts exactly," I said. "Where are we, and how did we get here?"

Aleetha shook her head slowly. I'd never see her look so confused. "As far as I can tell, this ship has been moved from Fang Harbor and dropped somewhere outside the mountain."

"With us tagging along as stowaways." Tank pulled her phone from her tool belt and frowned. "There's no signal! I can't send a message home."

My scales ran cold. Together, the three of us had been to the top of Rockfall Mountain and all the way down to the Dark Depths at the very bottom. It had been terrifying, dangerous and nearly fatal, but at least we'd been *inside* the mountain. Rocks and darkness were what we knew. Now, we were surrounded by blue sky and brightness. This was another world, and it was more terrifying than any beast I'd faced before.

A shadow fell across us, blocking out the sun in the sky. A ship as tall as Slick Stadium loomed over us. Three thick masts rose from the deck of the wooden ship. A patchwork sail hung from the main mast. It billowed in the gentle breeze that drew the ship alongside us. From the top of the tallest mast flew a black flag with white skull emblazoned on it.

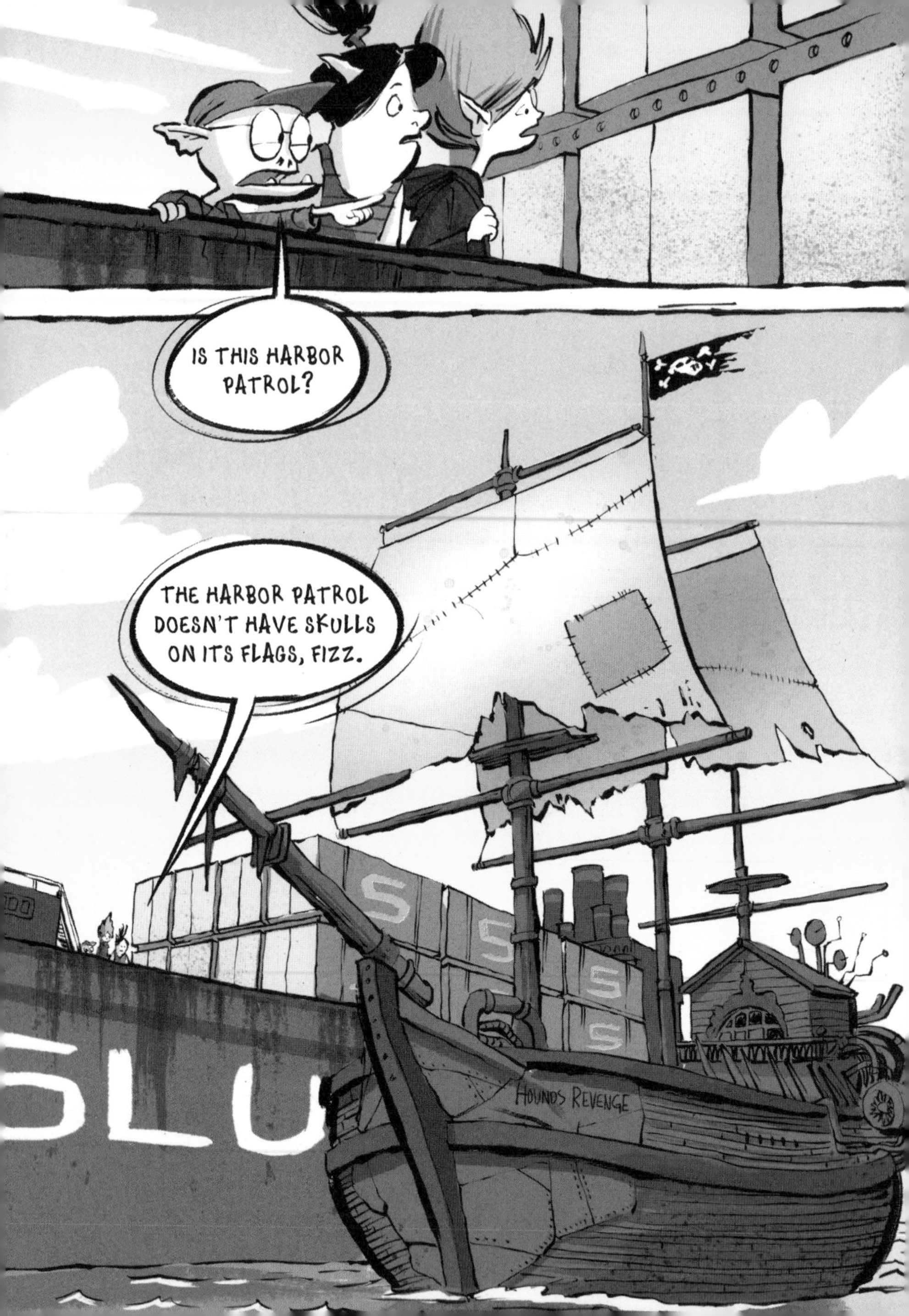
IS THIS HARBOR PATROL?
THE HARBOR PATROL DOESN'T HAVE SKULLS ON ITS FLAGS, FIZZ.
HOUNDS REVENGE
SLU

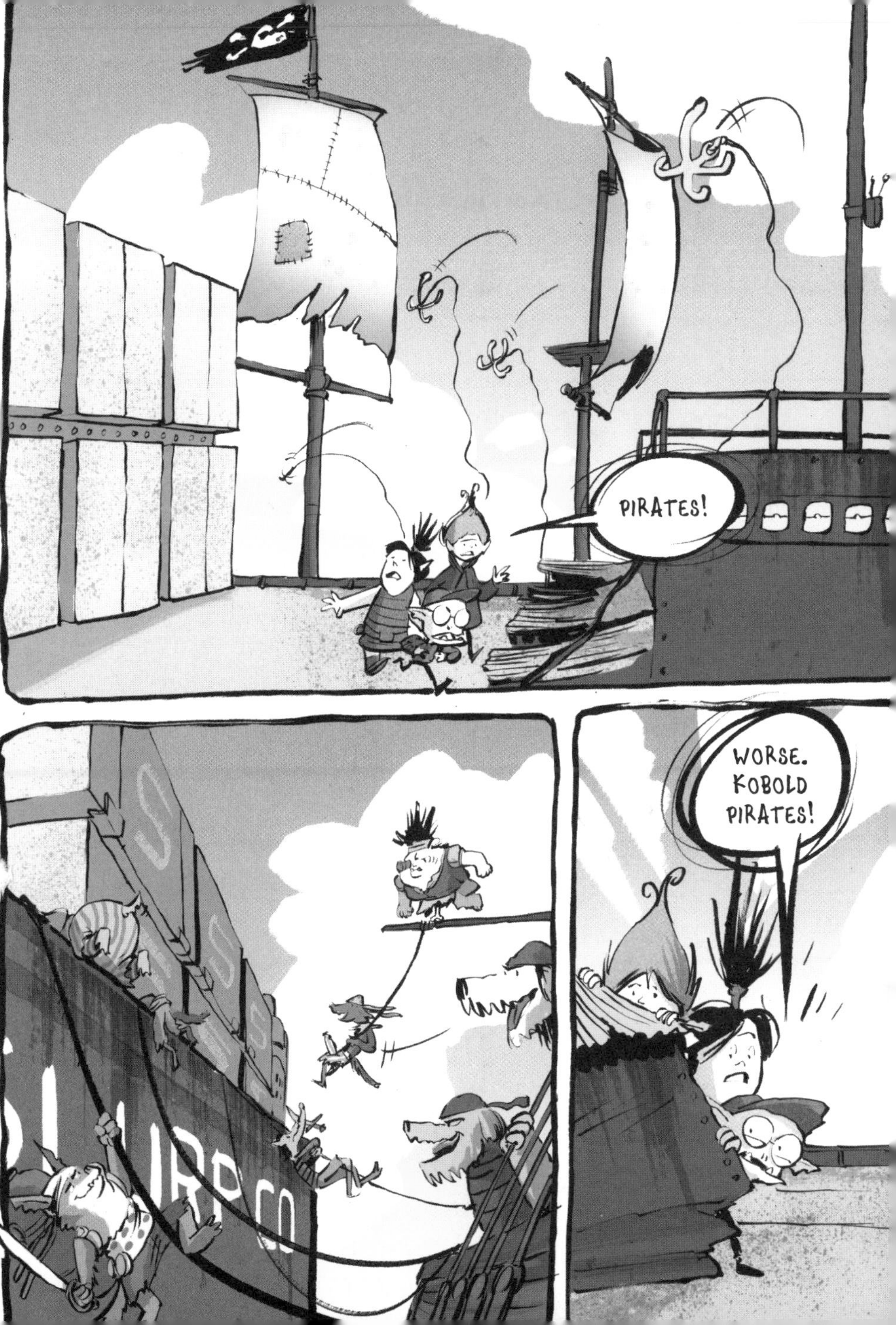
PIRATES!
WORSE. KOBOLD PIRATES!

Kobolds are dog-faced bullies on the best of days. They have splotchy orange fur, stink-eye stares and fangs sharp enough to chew through the bones of a grizzled rockboar. And those are the nice kobolds who live in Slick City. The kobolds scrambling onto the *Wave Dancer* wouldn't be allowed within a dragon's breath of the city limits. They had sinister scars in their fur, gold rings in their snouts and vicious-looking swords in their paws. One by one, the kobold pirates scurried along the ropes and stepped onto the deck of the *Wave Dancer*.

My scales had turned to ice. We were lost, far from home and about to become chew toys for a bunch of marauding muttheads.

CHAPTER SIX
Pirate Surprise

We ran to hide on the opposite side of the ship.
Behind us the kobolds clambered aboard.
They yapped with glee and raced to the far end of the
Wave Dancer, where the massive shipping containers
sat loaded with SlurpCo products. We watched from
a distance as the pirates hacked at the containers'
locks with their sharp blades.

"They're not after us," Tank whispered.

"They're more interested in what's inside those
containers," I said. "Let's hope it stays that way."

"It won't," Aleetha muttered. "They'll search the
ship for any remaining crew. We need to find a place
to hide until they're gone."

The kobold pirates ran around the deck barking and snarling. So far they'd been too busy breaking into the cargo containers to notice us. But Aleetha was right. It wouldn't be long before that changed.

Tank rushed over to a jumble of twisted metal that had been ripped loose when the giant tentacle thingy grabbed the ship.

"Under here!" Tank hissed. "They won't be interested in a bunch of broken ship parts."

"Good thinking!" Aleetha shimmied into the small opening created by the fallen debris.

I squeezed in beside her, and we made room for Tank. Our hiding spot was cramped but safe—for now. It also turned out to be well located. A hole in one of the pieces of sheet metal gave us a clear view of the containers the kobolds were so interested in.

A cheer erupted from the pirates as the first lock was broken. The doors to the container swung open. The kobolds leaped on the boxes inside like a first-grader on a dropped candy bar.

"Leave that loot alone, you tick-infested mongrels!"

Fur froze at the barked command. The pirates stopped their looting and cowered before the large kobold marching toward them. The new arrival stood a head taller than the biggest pirate. He wore a weathered red coat with tarnished brass buttons and a three-cornered hat that looked like it'd been run over by a school bus.

A pirate with a crooked snout stepped forward. "Apologies, Captain Stitch." The kobold dropped his gaze to the ship's deck. "The fellas got a little excited with the new haul."

"Don't let it happen again, Deekin, or you'll be swimming with the eight-armed beast," Captain Stitch snarled. A badly stitched scar ran from the tip of his snout to his forehead. Whatever had cut him had taken one of his eyes with it, leaving behind an empty socket that had been hastily sewn closed. Stitch turned his one eye on the crew of kobolds. "That goes for all of you mutts. Keep your sticky paws off my loot, unless you want to go swimming with the beast."

The kobolds fell back at the threat. They scrambled off the boxes and watched their captain warily.

"That's better," Stitch growled. "Now get the density-inverters in place, so we can get these off of this rust bucket."

A pair of kobolds came forward and placed a wooden chest on the ship's deck. They opened the lid to reveal a pile of metal discs the size of my head. On each disc, little lights flashed like twinkling glow-shrooms. The kobolds rushed to the chest, snatched up several discs and scurried back to the containers.

Beside me, Tank pushed in closer and peered through our spyhole with hungry eyes.

"Look at that tech!" she whispered. "Where did these mutts get their paws on density-inverters? I wonder what they're using them for?"

"Whatever it is, it can't be good." I said in a quiet voice. "These pirates must be the monsters stealing the ships."

"These guys are just the cleanup crew," Aleetha said. "It's the big monster with tentacles that's doing the stealing."

Tank sat back from the hole. "What does a sea monster want with the cargo of a SlurpCo ship? It's just a bunch of cheap appliances."

"Good question," Aleetha whispered.

"I've got a better question," I said. "Who is *that*?"

Another monster approached the containers and stood beside Stitch. The creature was as tall as Stitch, but too thin to be a kobold, and it wore a long cloak the color of the ocean. The hood of the cloak covered the new arrival's face, but a blue-tinged hand poked out from the sleeve and gripped a staff encrusted with seashells.

"A wave mage!" Aleetha gasped

"How long will this take, Captain Stitch?" The wave mage's words gurgled like it was speaking underwater.

Stitch bowed quickly to the stranger before speaking. "Not long, Hilsa. Once the density-inverters are attached, you will be able to work your magic."

Hilsa scanned the deck of the *Wave Dancer* with his bulbous eyes. "I sense others on this ship. Have you searched everywhere?"

"I have a team searching belowdecks," Stitch replied. "If there are any stowaways, those mutts will let me know."

"Those fools are looking in the wrong place," Hilsa said.

The wave mage turned to our hiding spot, and my heart stopped.

THE STOWAWAYS ARE MUCH CLOSER.

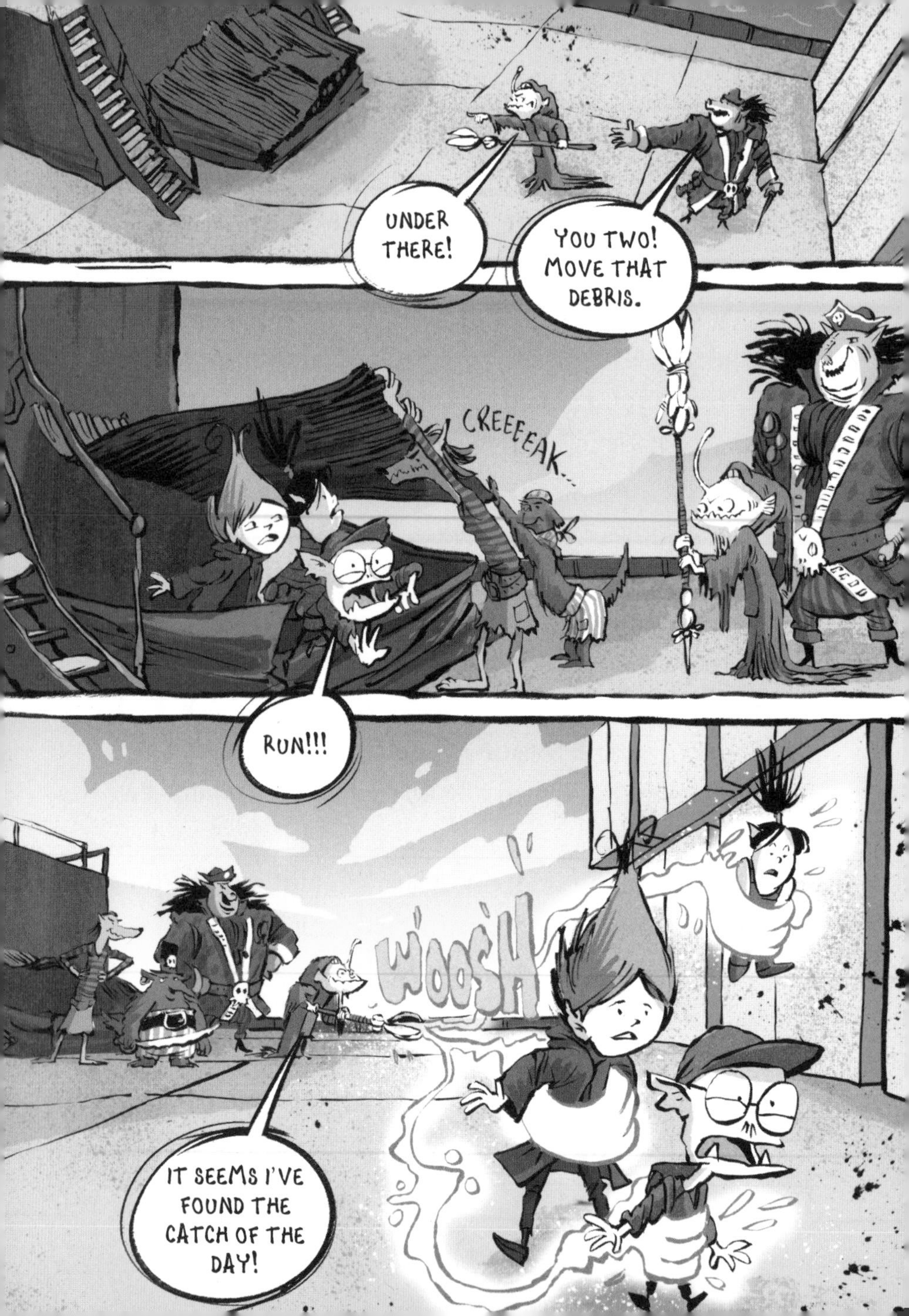
UNDER THERE!
YOU TWO! MOVE THAT DEBRIS.
CREEEEAK...
RUN!!!
WOOSH
IT SEEMS I'VE FOUND THE CATCH OF THE DAY!

I wriggled, squirmed and kicked, but Hilsa's spell held me tight in its grip. Who knew water could be as hard as stone? Next to me, Tank and Aleetha weren't having any luck breaking free either.

"Save your strength, young monsters," the wave mage said.

"Yeah, you'll need it for the swim back home!" Stitch growled. "Throw them overboard. We don't have time to babysit stowaways."

"Not so fast, Stitch. Let's see who we caught."

Hilsa's water fists held us in place, allowing him to get a closer look. He stopped in front of me and peered out from under his robe's deep hood. His green-blue eyes bulged, and his skin had a watery sheen. I spotted gills on his neck, the telltale sign of a stream elf. Hilsa smirked and moved over to stand in front of Aleetha.

"Curious," he said. "Why are a goblin, a troll and a lava elf hiding on a SlurpCo cargo ship?"

Stitch let out a frustrated bark. "What does it matter? Get rid of them. We're behind schedule. You know I don't like delays."

"And I don't like mysteries," Hilsa snapped. "That's exactly what these three are. A mystery to be solved."

Hilsa turned his bulging eyes to me. "And you know all about solving mysteries, don't you, little goblin?"

My claws curled. The watery gaze of the stream elf seeped under my scales. It was like he could see straight into my mind and read every thought.

Deekin ran up to Stitch.

"All the density-inverters are in place, Captain!"

"About time," Stitch said. "Get everyone back to the *Hound's Revenge*. We leave as soon as this is done."

Deekin ran back to his shipmates, barking Stitch's order as he went.

I struggled against Hilsa's spell and managed to turn my head enough to see the shipping containers. Each one of the massive crates was dotted with several of the flashing density-inverters. Hilsa faced the containers. Even with his back to us, his spell held the three of us in place. The wave mage called to a pair of kobolds standing on either side of smaller figure completely covered in a black cloak.

"Bring the conduit to me!" Hilsa commanded.

The kobolds dragged the cloaked figure to Hilsa. He placed a webbed hand on the figure's shoulder. The monster under the cloak flinched at Hilsa's touch but remained standing. With his other hand, the wave mage raised his shell-encrusted staff over his head.

Stitch stepped away from the wave mage and grinned at us. "Ready for a show, little monsters?" The pirate captain chuckled.

"Close your eyes!" Aleetha said to Tank and me as she struggled uselessly against her watery bindings. "He's going to cast a spell."

But I couldn't close my eyes. I couldn't look away. The words of magic spilling from Hilsa's mouth held me entranced.

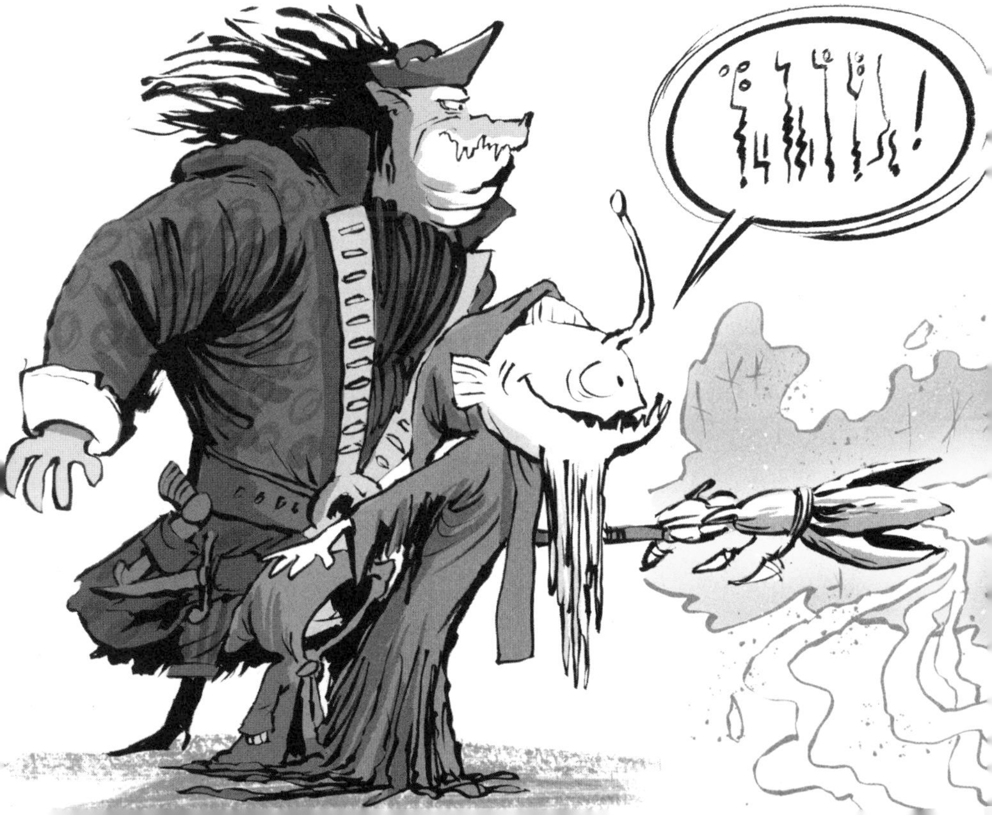

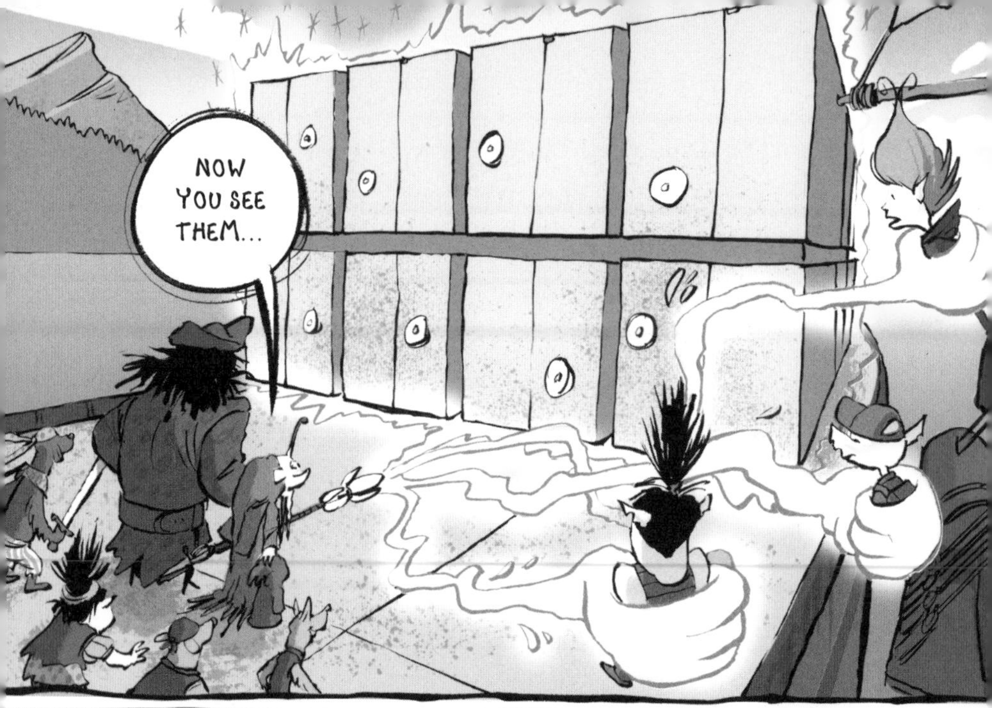
NOW YOU SEE THEM...

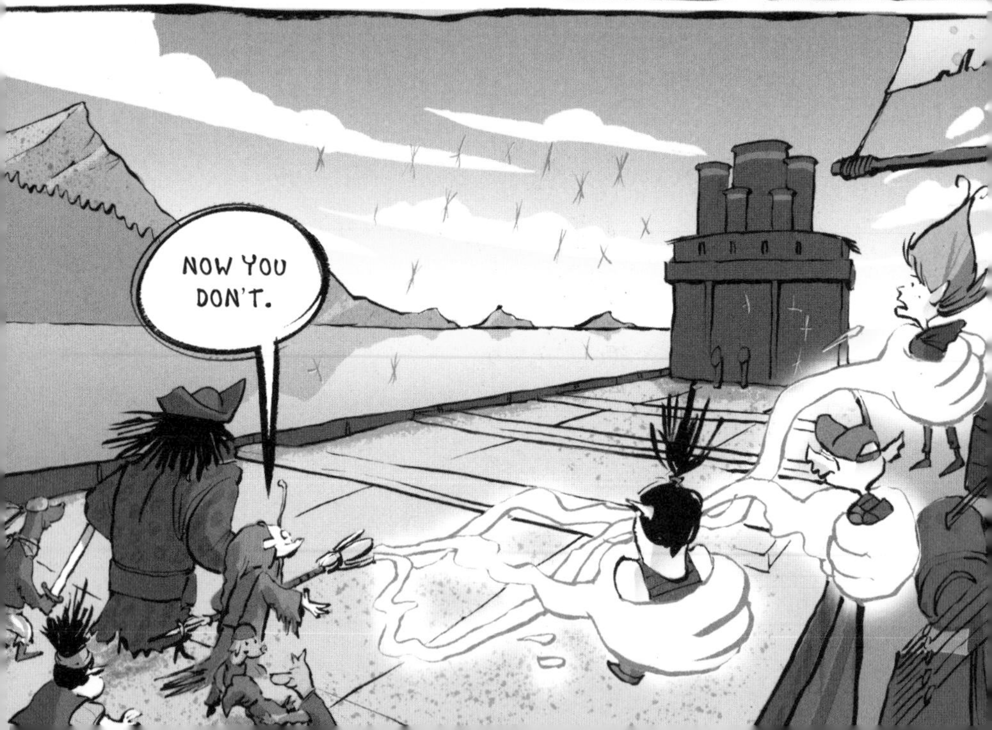
NOW YOU DON'T.

My brain hurt from trying to understand what I'd just seen. More than a dozen shipping containers had just vanished right in front of my scales. Beside me, Aleetha and Tank looked on, wide-eyed and speechless.

Hilsa leaned on his staff, looking exhausted but satisfied. If casting the spell had tired Hilsa, it had completely knocked out the mysterious monster under the black cloak. As the pair of kobolds dragged the figure away, a thin tail not unlike my own poked out from under the cloak. I looked quickly to see if Tank had noticed, but she was still too busy trying to wrap her brain around the vanishing containers.

"You just used magic and technology together!" my friend gasped.

"That's impossible!" Aleetha said.

"Not impossible, little wizard." Hilsa's words came slowly, like he was trying to catch his breath. "It just requires a little creative thinking." The wave mage looked at Stitch. "You were correct about our stowaways, Captain. They are of little interest to our mission."

Captain Stitch glared at us with his one good eye. "Then get rid of them."

"Very good." Hilsa nodded to the pirate captain.

The wave mage waved his free hand, and the watery shackles around my waist lifted me into the air. Tank and Aleetha were also raised off the deck of the ship.

"What's happening?" Tank squirmed against her bonds.

The water carried us over the edge of ship and held us high above the choppy waters below. The kobold pirates gathered along the ship's sides and yapped with excitement at what was to come. Captain Stitch stepped forward and waved a mottled paw at us.

"I don't know how you got on this ship," the kobold said, "but I know how you're getting off it. Goodbye, little monsters. Enjoy your swim."

With a command from Hilsa the fist of water holding us turned to vapor, and we fell.

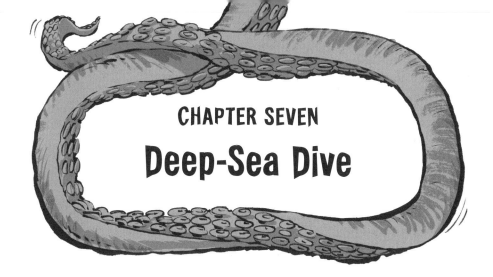

CHAPTER SEVEN
Deep-Sea Dive

The world became a murky green blur.

Frigid liquid gushed up my snout and under my scales as I crashed into the icy water around the *Wave Dancer*. I tumbled head over tail and spotted the blurry shapes of my friends. Tank paddled like she was crawling up a mountain. Aleetha fought to free herself from the tangle of her wizard's cloak, which billowed around her and threatened to drag her deeper down into the water. I began to swim toward her and then froze.

A thick tentacle emerged from the swirling bubbles. It stretched back as far as I could see, disappearing in the murky water. Along the tentacle were dozens of density-inverters. Tiny lights flashed on the discs. The tentacle sliced through the foul water but stopped directly in front of us. The lights on the discs grew brighter and seemed to join together as one. In an instant the light leapt toward me.

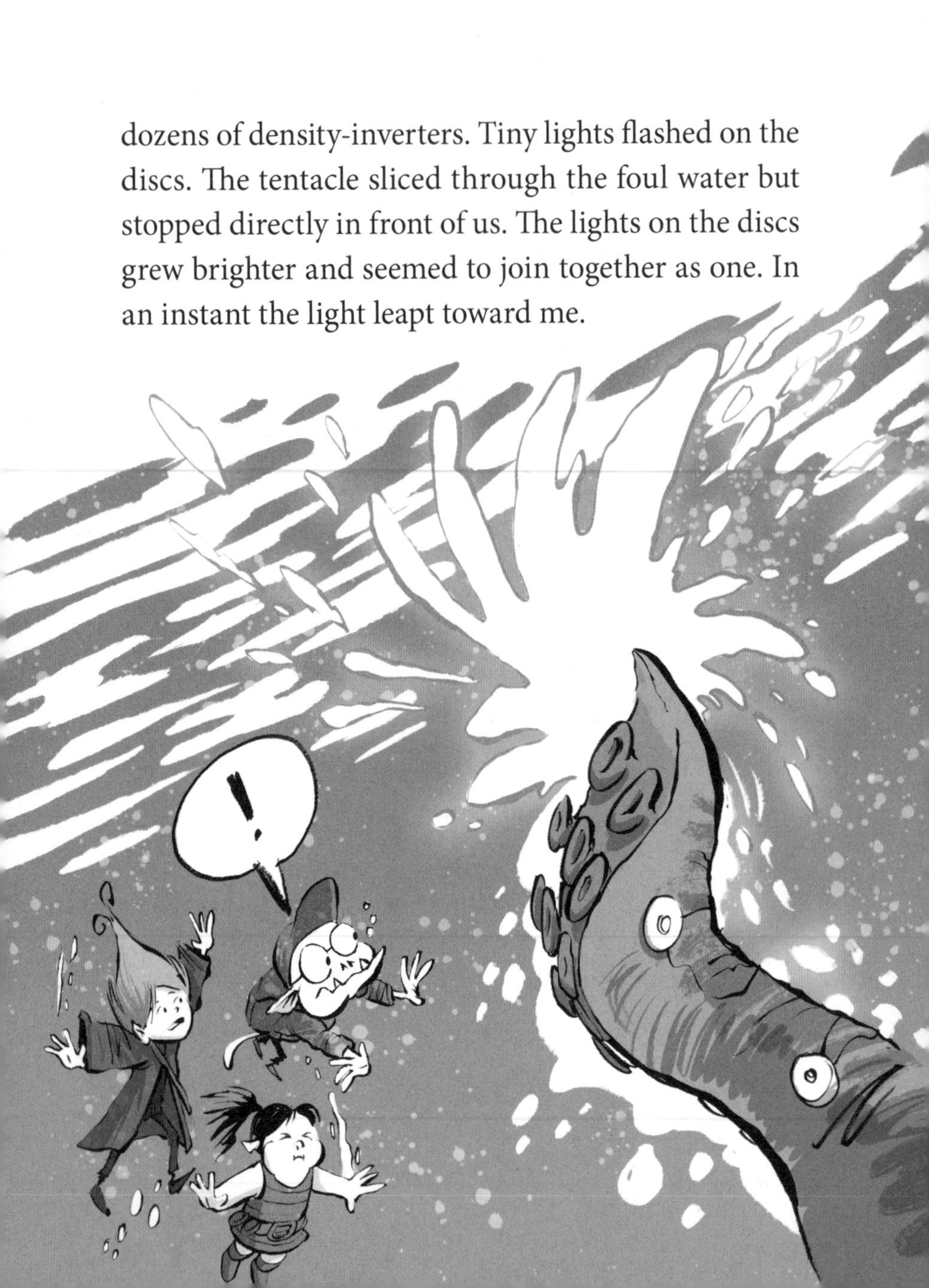
!

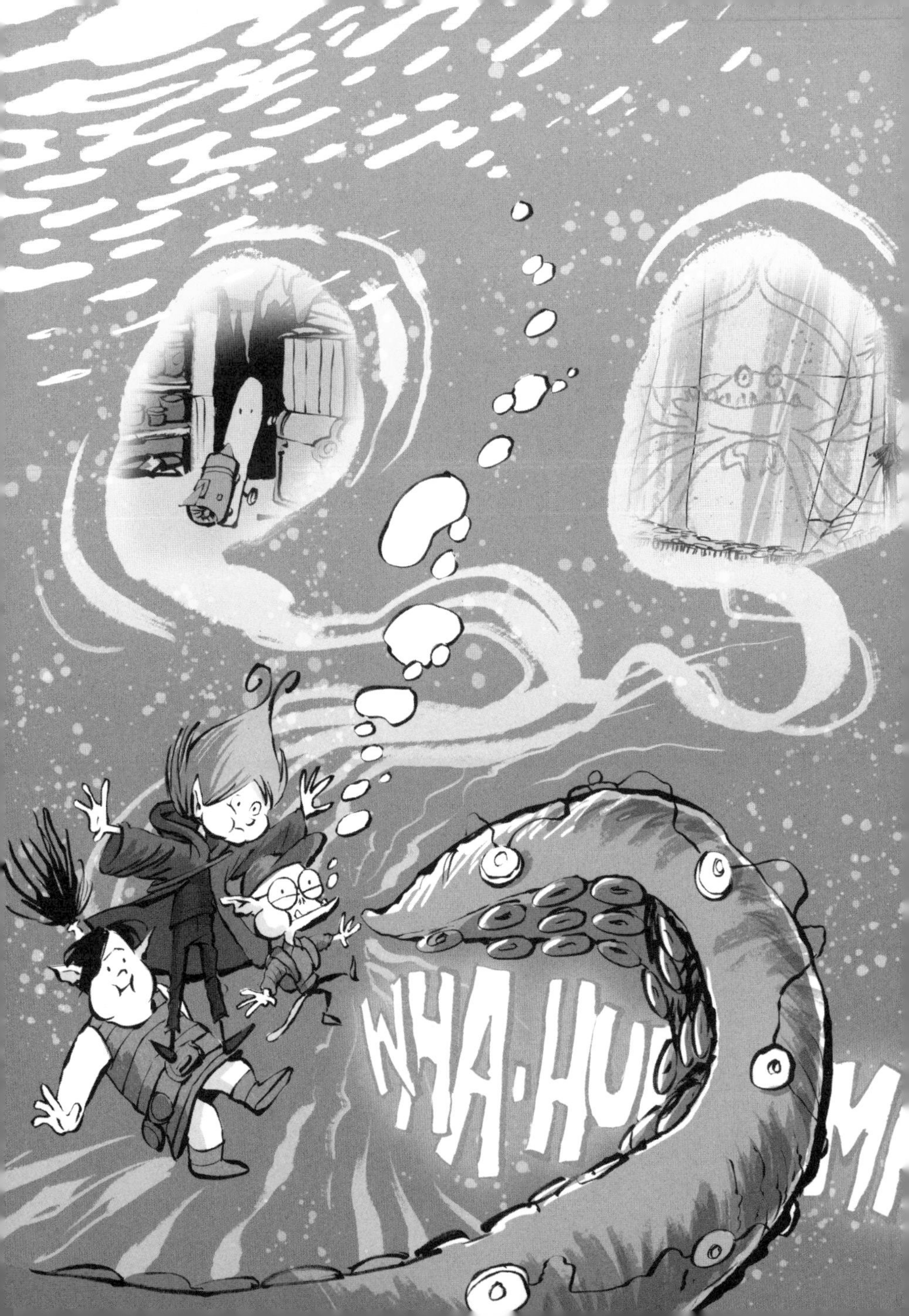
WHA-HU
M

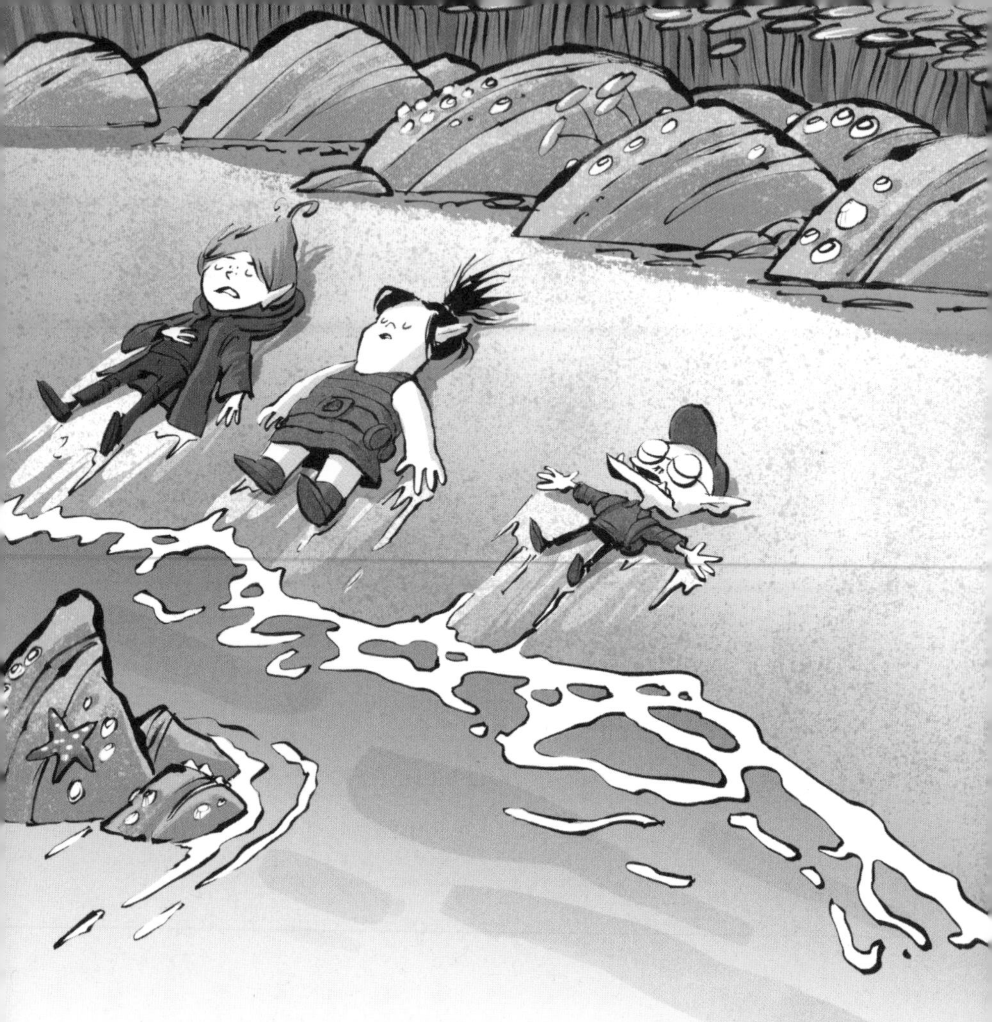

I woke with a snoutful of sand.

Cold water rushed across my scales, jolting me to my feet. Next to me, Tank and Aleetha groaned and slowly stood up.

"What happened?" Tank shook sand from her ponytail.

Aleetha wrung water from her cloak. "And where are we?"

Above us, the sun shone and puffy, white clouds drifted across the blue sky.

"We're still outside the mountain," I said.

We had washed up on a wide beach with warm sand the color of a vanilla slugshake. Beyond the beach stood a tangled forest of green. Trees, vines and plants covered the ground and reached toward the sun above. I'd never seen plants like this before. In the darkness of Rockfall Mountain, only slimes and fungi grew. Here, under the sun, flowers of all colors and sizes flourished alongside fat green leaves and thick branches of dark brown. The forest and the beach ran uninterrupted in both directions before curving out of view.

Aleetha shielded her eyes from the sun and looked out at the water. "There's something way out there."

Tank pulled her zoomers over her eyes. She turned the dials on the goggles and studied the water. She pulled them off and opened the pockets on her tool belt one by one.

"All my tech is wet," she growled. "It will need to dry out before anything will work again."

She turned her back to the water and continued inspecting the pockets of her tool belt.

Aleetha kept her focus on the dot floating on the water in the distance.

"I bet that speck is the *Wave Dancer*," she said. "And we must be on the island we saw earlier when we were standing on the ship's deck."

"Okay, but how did we get *here*?" I asked. "And what was that arm that zapped us under the water?"

"It wasn't an arm," Aleetha said. "I think it was a tentacle."

"Do you think it was the same creature we saw grab the *Wave Dancer* from Fang Harbor?"

"There's more to that monster than tentacles." Tank brushed sand out of the pockets of her tool belt. "Did you see the discs running along the tentacle? They were the same density-inverters those pirates put on the containers. They're used to make things lighter and easier to move."

Visions of the discs washed into my mind. The light from those discs had reached out and swallowed us whole. And that wasn't all.

"Those discs did more than just transport us." My scales burned at the memory. "It's like they reached into my brain."

"I felt that too!" Tank's ears stood at attention. "They sent some kind of energy into us."

"I remember that." Aleetha nodded. "I felt like the creature was trying to tell me something."

"I felt that too!" Tank's ears stood taller. "But all I saw was a drawing of a monster's eyes."

My claws dug into the sand. "I saw that too. And a rocketboard, I think."

"I saw a rocketboard too," Aleetha said.

"A SlurpCo rocketboard," Tank added.

"We all saw the same things?" I gulped.

Aleetha's brow furrowed. "It sounds like a shared vision of some kind. I've read about creatures who can project thoughts into the minds of others."

"You think that's what the owner of the tentacle did?" Tank asked.

"I don't know what to think." Aleetha sighed. "Somehow the three of us saw the exact same things, and now we're stranded alone on this beach."

The plants behind us shook back and forth. A low growl came from within the greenery.

"Stranded, yes. Alone, no." Tank gulped.

Farther down the beach, the source of the noise stepped out of the trees.

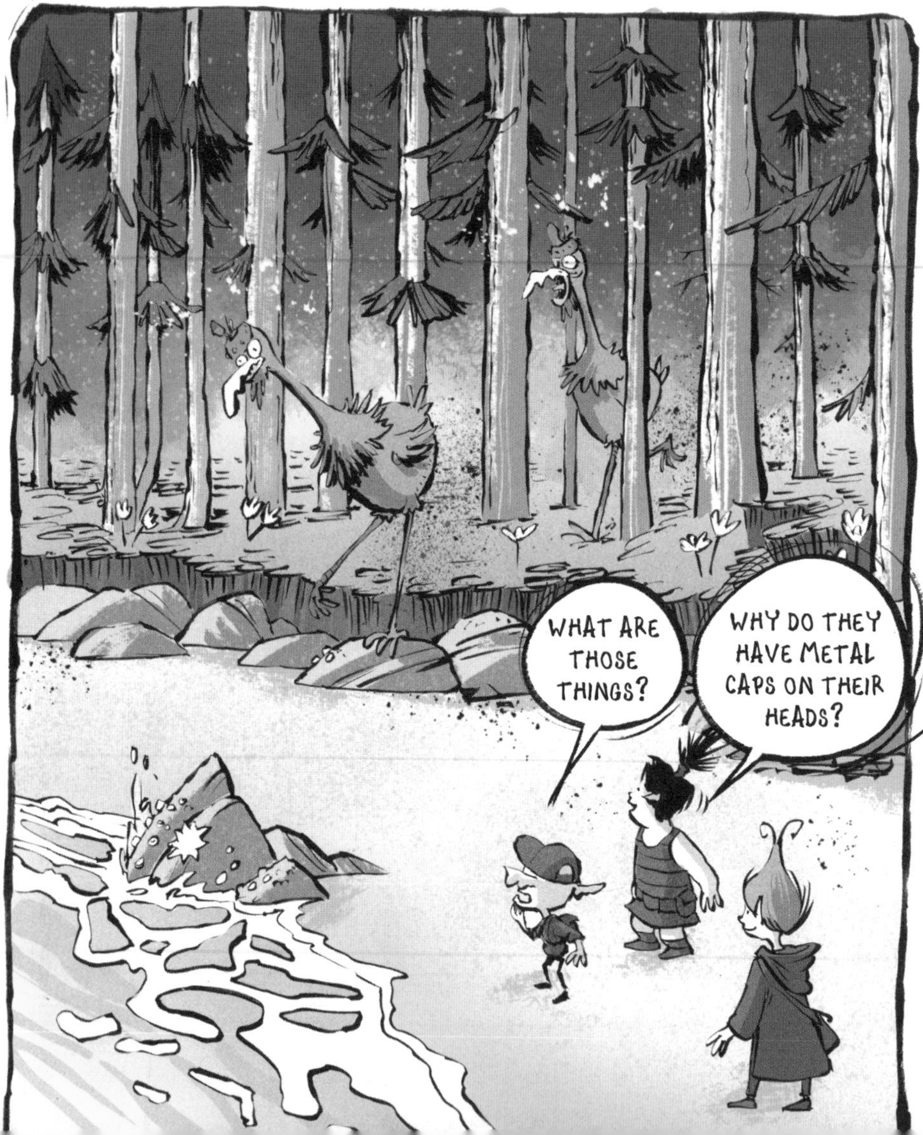
WHAT ARE THOSE THINGS?
WHY DO THEY HAVE METAL CAPS ON THEIR HEADS?

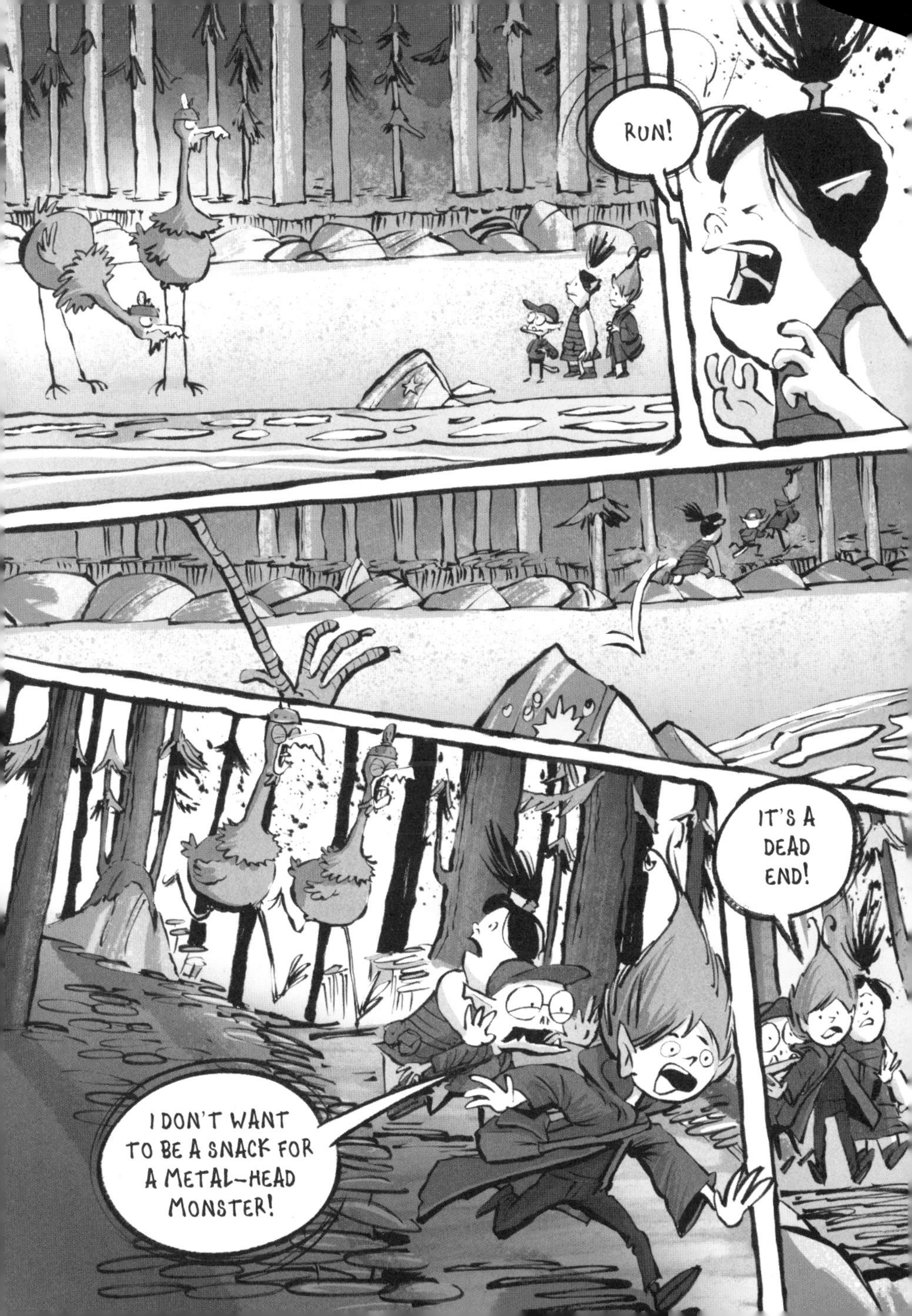
RUN!
IT'S A DEAD END!
I DON'T WANT TO BE A SNACK FOR A METAL-HEAD MONSTER!

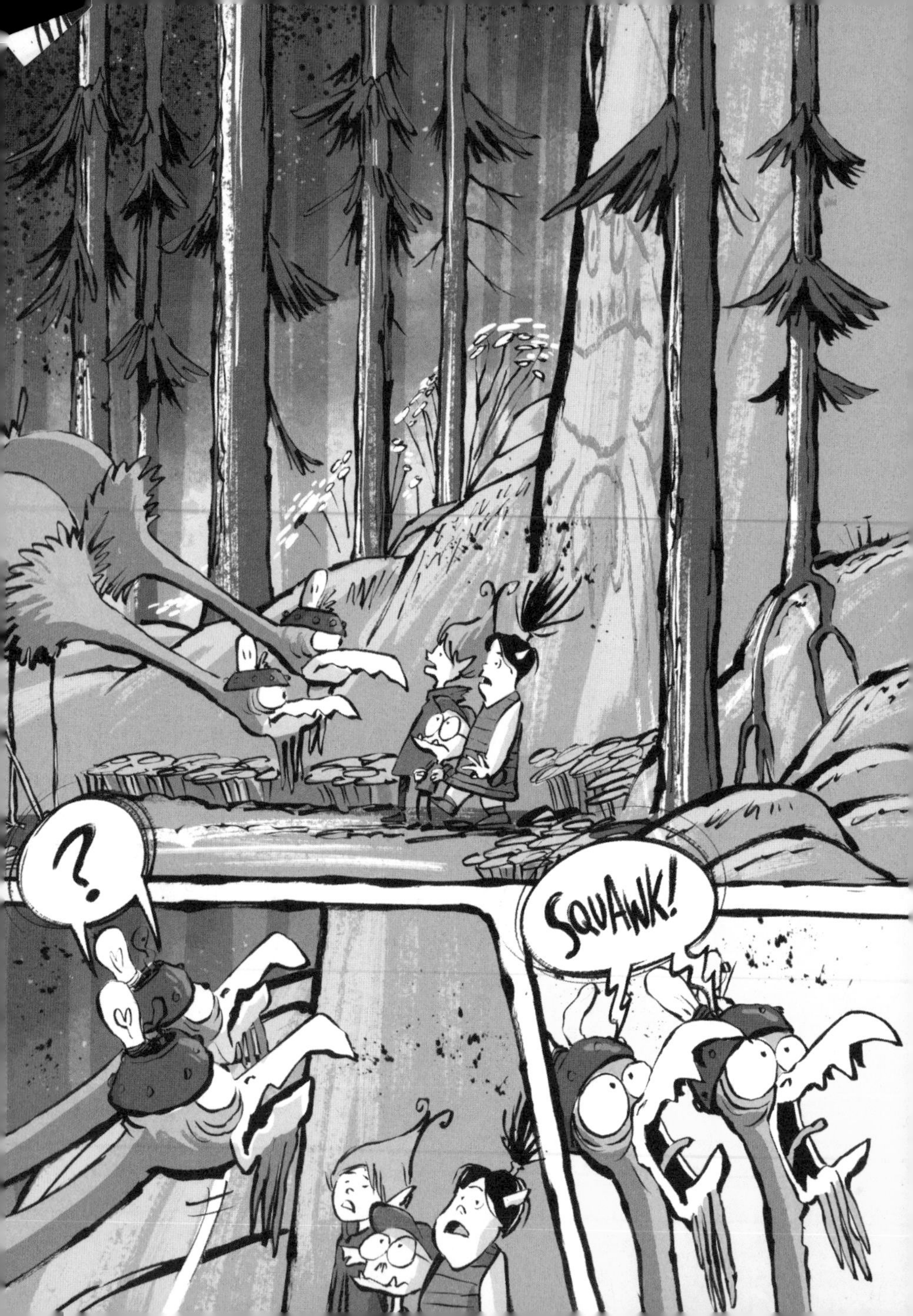
?
SQUAWK!

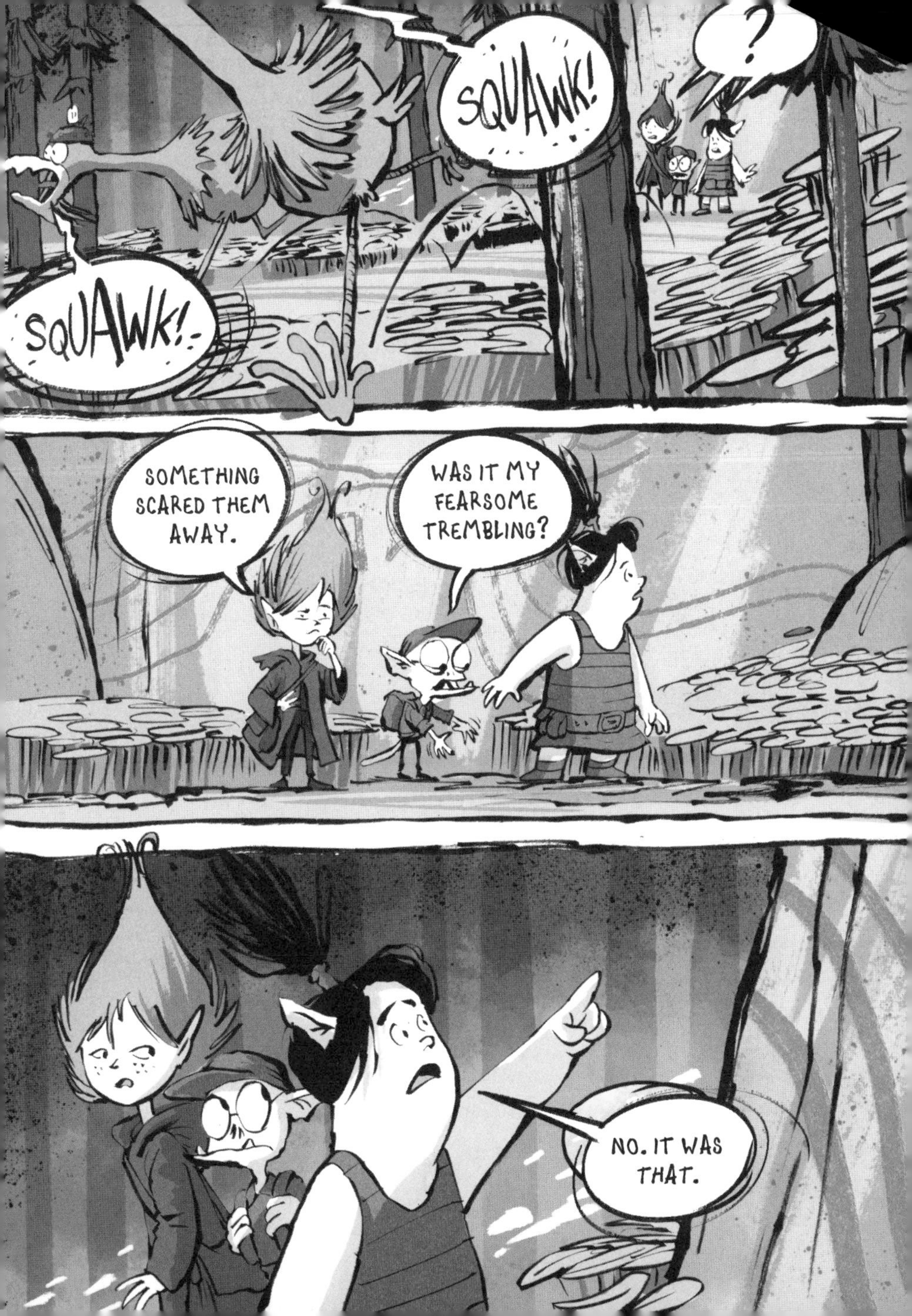
SQUAWK!
SQUAWK!
?
SOMETHING SCARED THEM AWAY.
WAS IT MY FEARSOME TREMBLING?
NO. IT WAS THAT.

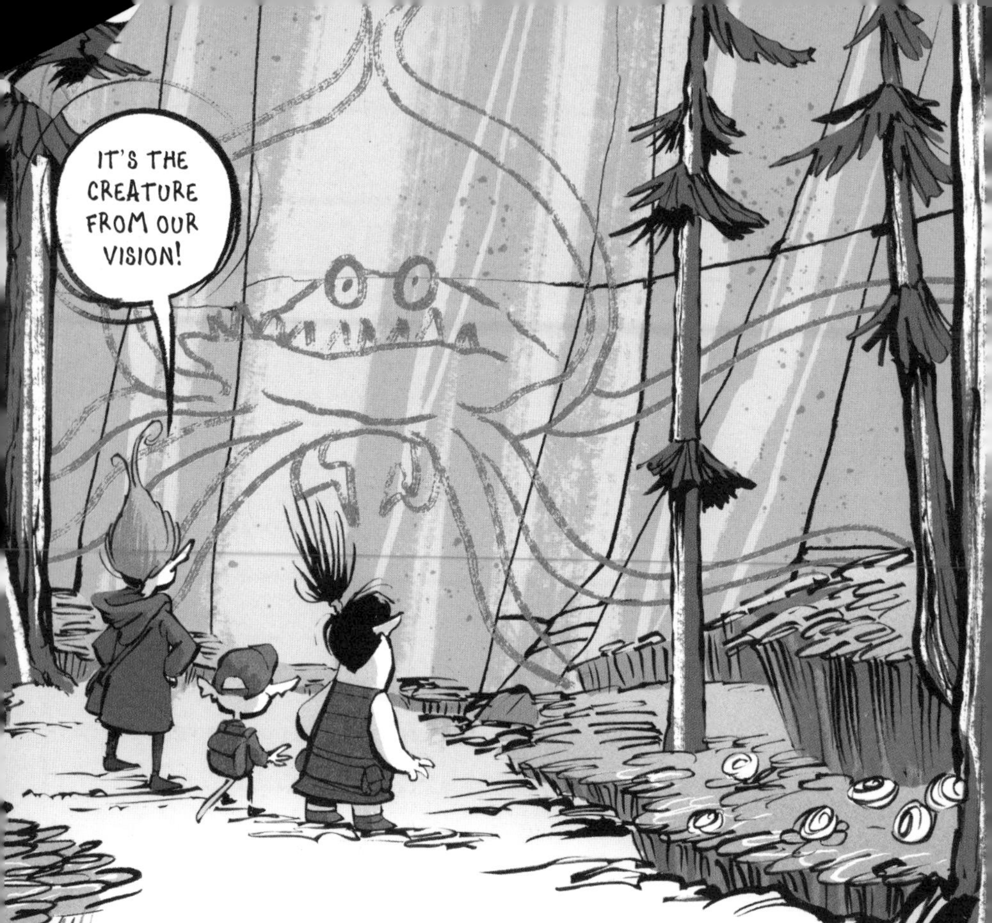
IT'S THE CREATURE FROM OUR VISION!

Now *I* wanted to run away. Staring down at us from the face of the cliff were the eyes from our shared underwater vision. Smart detectives don't use visions to solve mysteries, but seeing this painting had to be more than mere coincidence. I was lost and clueless, but clearly someone knew why we were here. And the tingling in my tail told me that someone had tentacles.

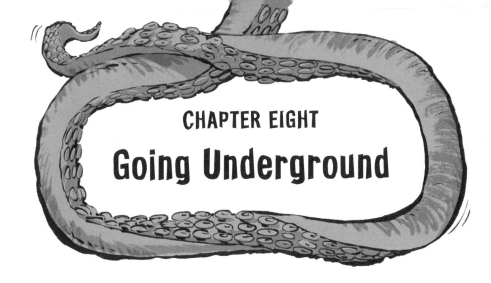

CHAPTER EIGHT
Going Underground

Tank found the entrance to the cave by accident.

"I was looking for something to dry the receptors on my sonic hatchdriver, and look what I found." She pushed some leaves aside to reveal a hole in the cliff face.

Aleetha peered into the darkness beyond the opening. "There's a path leading deeper underground."

I scratched the back of my neck. My scales were hot. "Underground sounds good to me. I've had enough baking in the sun like a slinkworm pie."

"Me too." Tank wiped sweat from her forehead. "I don't want to be around here if those beak-brains come back."

"Maybe getting us underground was the plan all along." Aleetha stepped back from the opening. Her eyes drifted up to the drawing on the cliff face. "Back in the water, that tentacle zapped us and we all had a vision of this painting."

"And now we're here," I said. "You think the tentacle was trying to tell us to come here?"

"But we were chased here by those birds," Tank said. "We found this place by pure luck."

Aleetha shrugged. "Maybe it wasn't luck at all."

"I don't buy it." Tank shook her head. "It's just a coincidence. There must be a scientific reason for us seeing the same thing. And we ended up here by chance."

"Whatever the reason, let's see where the cave leads. Standing around here won't help us find a way back home." Aleetha tugged at the collar of her cloak. "You're right, Fizz—it's getting hot out here."

Tank grinned. "You're a flame mage! You're supposed to like the heat."

"What can I say?" Aleetha chuckled. "I like my heat from pools of lava, not from big balls of fire in the sky."

My scales relaxed the moment I stepped through the opening and into the cave. Cool darkness wrapped around me like a hug.

"That's much better," Tank said, stepping through the opening. "How is anyone able to live outside with that sun shining down on them?"

The path in the cave led us steadily downward. Each step took us away from the surface and its burning sun and deeper into the coolness of the underground. The path was wide and smooth, and the dusty ground was covered with traces of footprints. Wherever we were, this was once a busy route. Questions bounced around my brain as we walked. Where did this path lead? Who had built it? Would they help us get home?

My stomach ached at that thought. I'd been so busy trying not to drown or get eaten that I hadn't realized how much I wanted to be back home, snacking on a pile of choco-slug cookies with my mom bugging me to finish my homework. She was probably freaking out right now. This was all my fault. If I hadn't been so eager to solve a big-time mystery, we wouldn't have snuck into the stakeout. We wouldn't have gotten too close to the SlurpCo cargo ship and been picked up by that giant tentacle. And we wouldn't be here in a strange land, lost and alone.

"Fizz, hurry up! You have to see this."

Tank's words echoed down the tunnel. Lost in my thoughts, I had fallen behind. I ran to catch up with my friends.

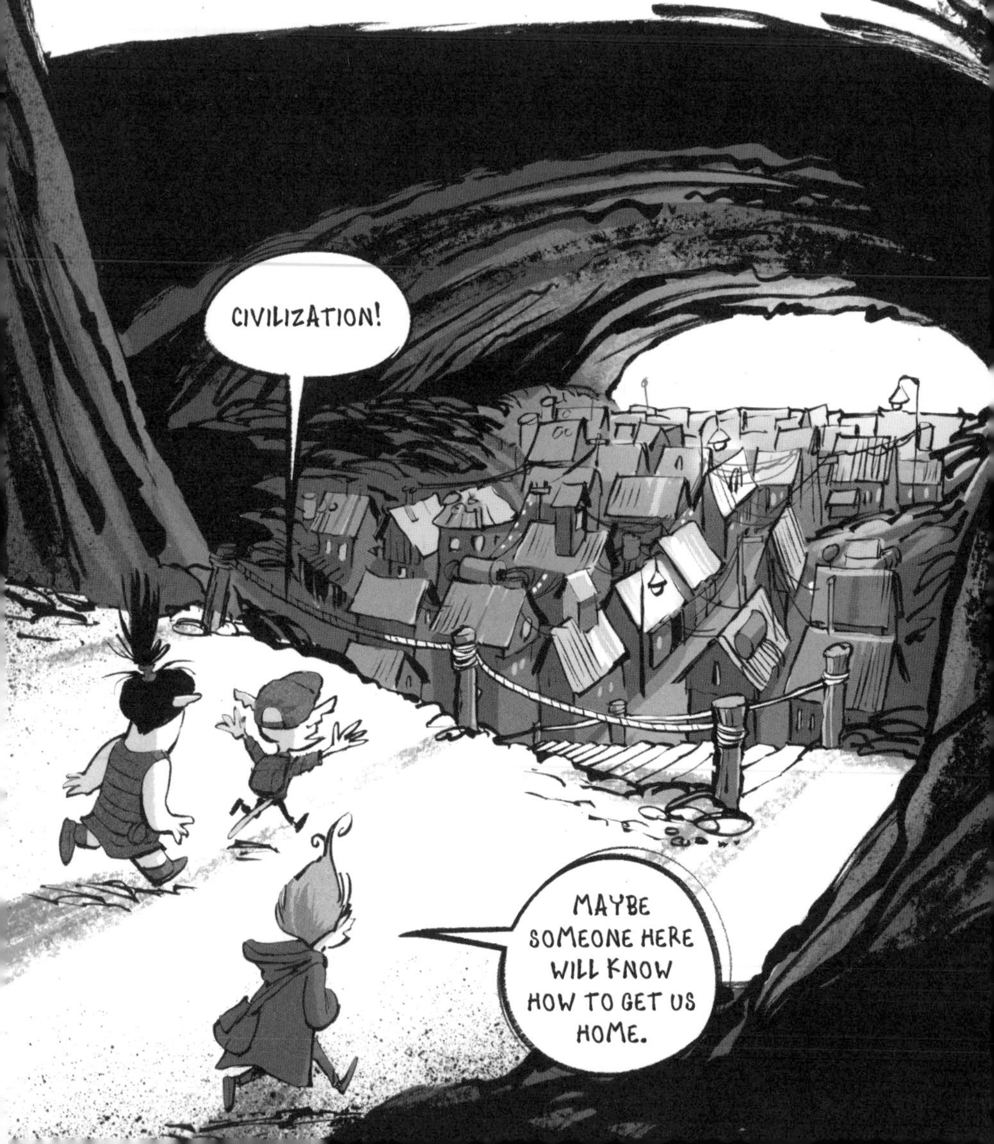
CIVILIZATION!
MAYBE SOMEONE HERE WILL KNOW HOW TO GET US HOME.

We followed a set of winding stairs down to the cavern floor. The dirt path turned into a cobblestone road wide enough for three ogres to walk side by side.

"Let's find someone and see." Tank slapped me on the back and walked quickly along the cobblestones.

Finding someone turned out to be hard. The streets on the outskirts of the village were deserted. The houses were empty, and the yards were free of any children playing and parents watching them. At many of the homes the front door hung open, but there wasn't a monster in sight. We walked a couple of blocks in silence, watching and waiting for someone to show their face.

"Where is everybody?" Tank asked.

Aleetha pulled her cloak tightly around herself. "It's definitely odd that it's so quiet."

After walking for a few minutes we arrived at a plaza. Shops with brightly colored awnings lined the edges of the open area. Many had their doors open but looked deserted. In the middle of the plaza sat an empty fountain carved of dark stone. A statue of a big-eyed creature with tentacles rose from the fountain and loomed over the square. The stone tentacles stretched out in all directions, as if it were climbing off its pedestal. It was the same creature we'd seen painted on the cliff face.

Aleetha moved slowly through the square, keeping one eye on the fountain. "They really like that creepy creature around here."

Tank walked through the doorway of a shop that looked like it sold tools. A few seconds later she emerged holding a long pipe with wires poking out at either end. "This store is amazing," she announced. "Check out this multisocket ionizer. For a place in the middle of nowhere, they've got a good selection of tech."

Aleetha ran her hands along a rack of shirts standing outside a clothing shop next door. "And it's all just been left out in the open, but no one is around. Weird."

"Maybe this town was abandoned," I said.

Aleetha frowned. "Why wouldn't they take their things with them?"

"They had to leave in a hurry?" I suggested.

"It makes no sense." Aleetha peered through the clothing shop's window. "Why would monsters abandon a perfectly good town?"

"I've got a better question," Tank said. "Why is there smoke coming from that fountain?"

Black smoke silently poured from the statue's tentacles. The smoke rolled along the ground and began to wrap around my legs. My head started to swim.

"It's like the smoke from when the *Wave Dancer* was taken!"

My words were thick on my tongue. My head felt as heavy as a boulder. Black smoke filled my vision. Through the billowing clouds I saw Tank stumble and drop her multisocket whatever-it-was. I also saw something coming toward us.

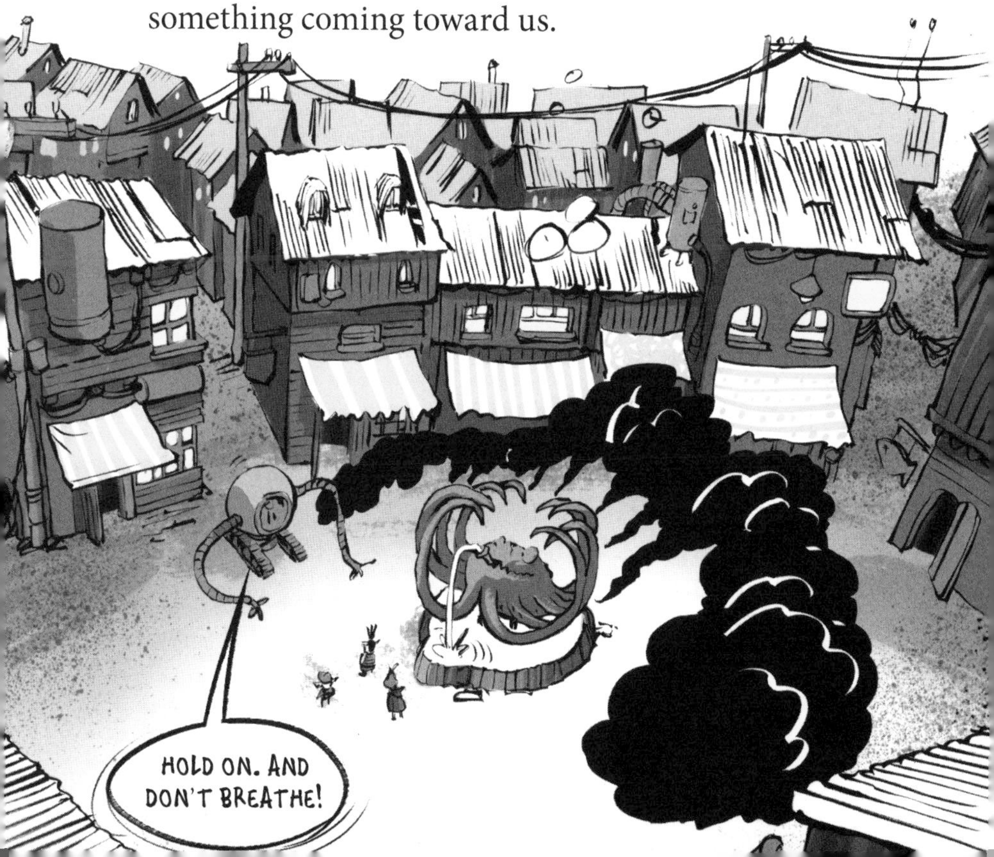
HOLD ON. AND DON'T BREATHE!

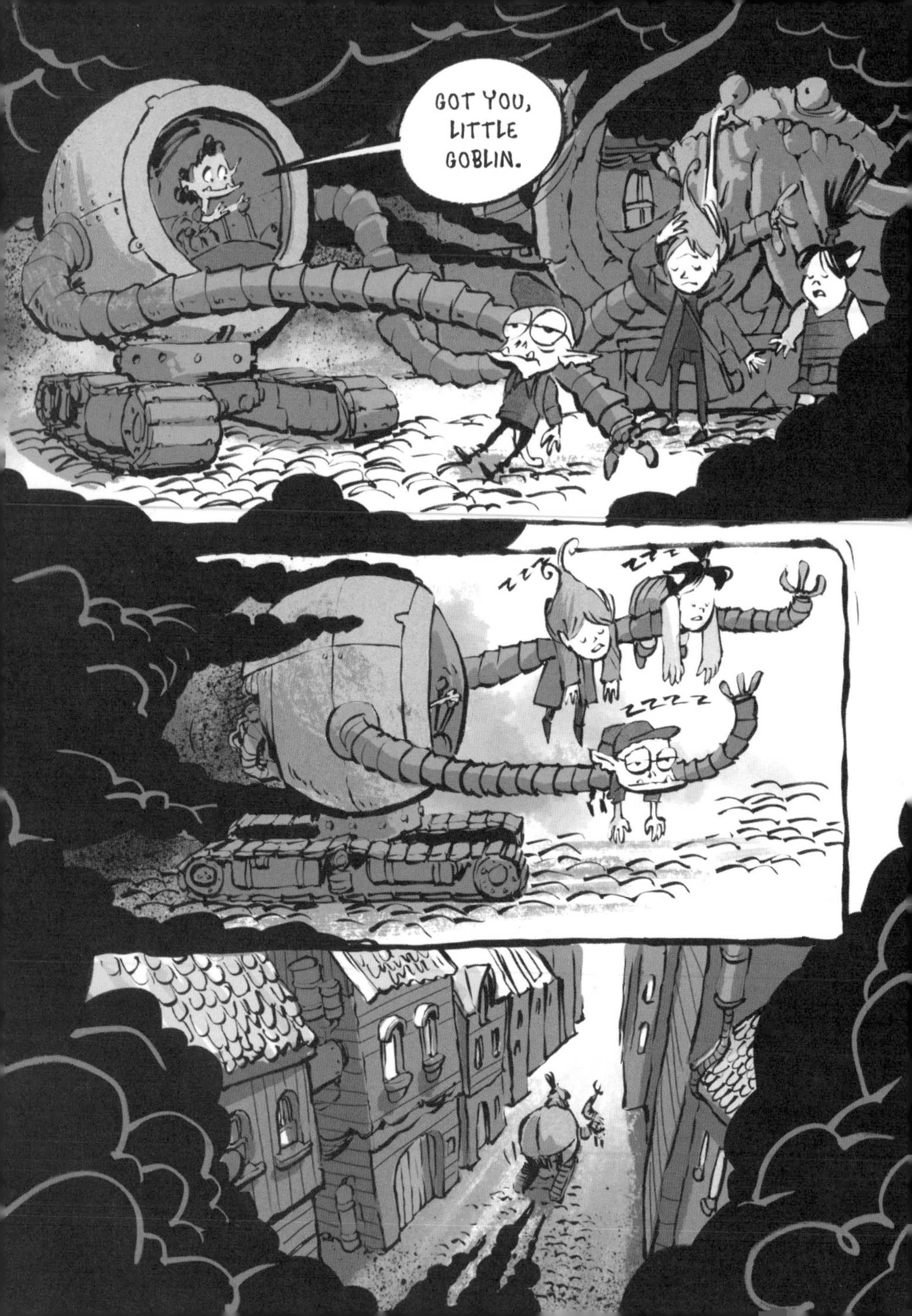
GOT YOU, LITTLE GOBLIN.
Z Z Z
Z Z Z
Z Z Z Z Z

CHAPTER NINE

Breakfast on the Beach

I woke to the smell of cooking.

My stomach growled. I hadn't eaten since before the stakeout at Fang Harbor. I slowly sat up. Everything was a blur of dim yellow lights. I blinked and rubbed my eyes.

"It will take a minute for your mind to clear." The voice came from somewhere above me. It was steady and calm.

A mug of steaming liquid appeared under my snout.

"Take a sip," the voice said. "Slowly."

My stomach rumbled again. I took the cup and sipped. Hot green liquid soothed my sore throat. I found my voice.

"Where—?" It was all I could manage.

"You're safe." The blur in front of me took shape. A green face with a stubby snout and wide eyes.

"Y-you're a goblin?" I croaked.

"And so are you." The stranger smiled. "I'm Gwena. The smoke's grip is slipping from you. Drink more tea. It will help."

The tea sent warmth through my body and cleared my head. I was in a dimly lit cave. In front of me, gentle waves of water splashed onto a rocky beach. A sturdy-looking pier ran out from the beach to half a dozen small fishing boats anchored nearby. Beyond the boats, sunlight spilled in from a cave mouth that reminded me of Fang Cove. A row of low wooden huts ran along the length of the beach. Fishing nets were hung to dry on racks next to the huts. Tank and Aleetha lay on either side of me, eyes closed.

Gwena saw me looking at my friends. "They'll be all right," she said. "Your goblin blood must make you more resistant to the effects of the smoke."

"I didn't know there were goblins outside Rockfall Mountain." I held the mug of tea under my snout and enjoyed its warmth. "That's where we're from. And where we'd like to get back to."

"I know Rockfall Mountain, but I've never a met a goblin from there." Gwena stirred something steaming in a pot that rested over the flames of small stove. "What are you doing so far from home?"

Between sips of tea I explained our whole mess to Gwena. She listened and laid out four bowls as I spoke. Tank and Aleetha began to stir. By the time I had finished explaining, both of my friends were awake and had been introduced to my new goblin friend.

Gwena used a long spoon to scoop something hot and steaming from the pot. She poured a portion into each of the four bowls and handed them to us. It was some sort of stew with vegetables I didn't recognize, but it tasted better than anything I'd eaten before.

Tank breathed in deeply over her bowl. "Smells delicious!"

"You can't beat dulce and yarrot stew," Gwena said.

We ate in silence for a minute. Gwena chewed slowly before speaking again. "It seems our problems have the same root cause."

Aleetha's brow furrowed. "What do you mean *our* problems?"

"We share a dilemma," she said. "Your hometown is losing ships. My hometown lost its population and more. And they were all taken by the same monsters—Captain Stitch and his band of pirates."

"Captain Stitch?" I said. "The ugly kobold with one eye?"

"That's him." Gwena nodded. "Stitch controls Howler's Bay, on the other side of the island. His band of pirates has been there since before I was born. He usually leaves us alone here."

"Where exactly is *here*?" I asked. "What is this place?"

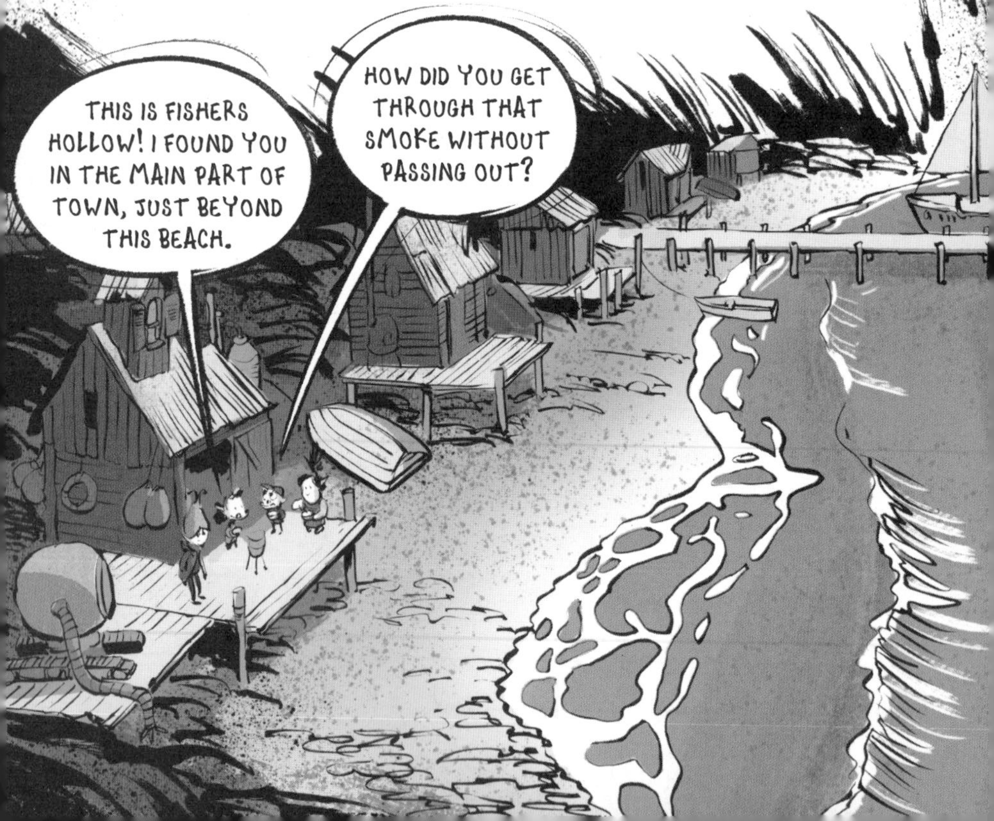
THIS IS FISHERS HOLLOW! I FOUND YOU IN THE MAIN PART OF TOWN, JUST BEYOND THIS BEACH.
HOW DID YOU GET THROUGH THAT SMOKE WITHOUT PASSING OUT?

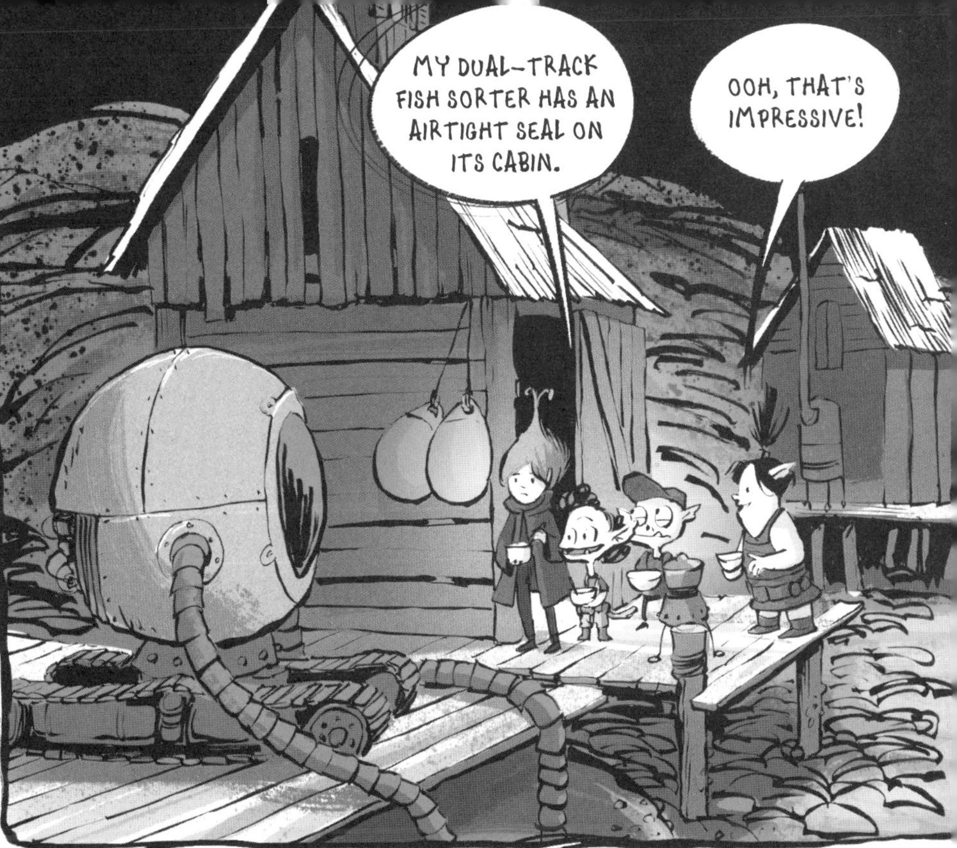
MY DUAL-TRACK FISH SORTER HAS AN AIRTIGHT SEAL ON ITS CABIN.
OOH, THAT'S IMPRESSIVE!

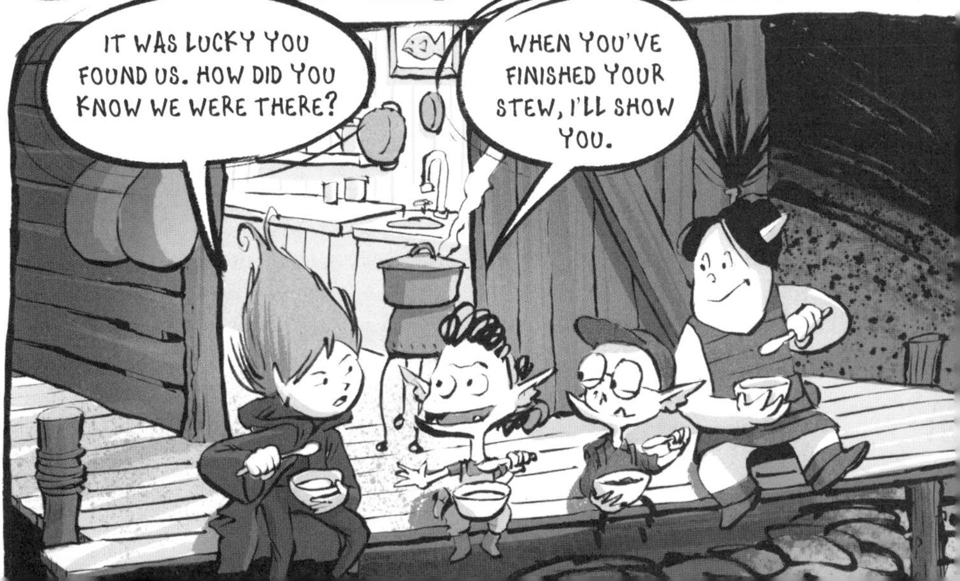
IT WAS LUCKY YOU FOUND US. HOW DID YOU KNOW WE WERE THERE?
WHEN YOU'VE FINISHED YOUR STEW, I'LL SHOW YOU.

"Fishers Hollow is my home," Gwena said. "We're simple fisher-goblins, catching fish from the coastal waters." She gestured with her spoon to a point farther down the beach. "We live all through the caves that run under the island. We sell our fish to vendors who come to us in their ships. There are no other settlements on the island except for Stitch and his pirates."

"And they don't bother you?" Aleetha asked.

"They leave us alone. For a price." Gwena pushed her spoon around her bowl. "Stitch and his pirates don't bother us if we give them a portion of the fish we catch. Last year Stitch demanded that one goblin from our village live with his pirates." Gwena wiped something from her eye. "The goblin he chose was my father. They took him away, and I haven't seen him since."

"That's awful," I said. "Why did they choose him?"

Gwena set down her bowl. "I don't know. But just last week the smoke came, and Stitch returned. The clouds appeared around the outskirts of town. It swept through the streets and put to sleep anyone caught in its path. When it had cleared, everyone was gone. I think Stitch and his gang took them to Howler's Bay."

I scratched my scales. "Why would a pirate take your dad and then come back a year later and take the rest of your village?"

"That's what I've been asking myself all week." Gwena sighed. "I've been hiding here, hoping some of the goblins would find a way back. So far, no one has returned."

Aleetha cocked her head to one side. "Why weren't you taken by the smoke?"

The goblin's gaze dropped. "I ran away. I should have been there to help my family, but I was too scared."

Gwena grew quiet. No one else spoke. The sounds of eating were the only noises in our little hideout. Eventually Tank broke the silence.

"That smoke sounds like the mist that covered the cargo ships in Fang Harbor."

"That smoke shimmered with magic." Aleetha swallowed the last bite of her stew and put her bowl onto the sand. "The smoke from the statue must also have been magical."

"That is the work of Hilsa, the wave mage," Gwena said.

"The stream elf who dumped us in the water!" My words echoed across the water.

"He only appeared about a year ago," Gwena said. "We kept a close eye on Stitch and his crew when we gave them their monthly portion of fish. Last year we noticed someone new at Howler's Bay. A stream elf with a wagonload of magical equipment. We learned his name was Hilsa, but we don't know where he comes from. We do know he likes to do experiments. Shortly after he arrived, strange creatures appeared on the island. Part monster, part machine."

I nearly dropped my spoon. "Like the creatures that chased us! They had metal caps on their heads."

"Those are hookbeaks," Gwena said. "They used to bother us, but they aren't very smart. We were able to scare them away."

"That's why they fled when we got to the cave leading to your village," I said.

Tank looked at Aleetha. "How can a wizard like Hilsa use technology? First it was the the density-inverters on the shipping containers and now the caps on the hookbeaks. I thought technology messed with their spells."

"I've been wondering about that too." The lava elf tugged at the hem of her cloak. "Hilsa must have discovered a way to combine magic and technology so they work together. I have no idea how. Mixing magic and technology can mess with ionic field stability or even rip the temporal fabric that surrounds everything."

"I have no idea what that means," I said. "But it doesn't sound good."

"It's not," Aleetha said. "Combining magic and tech is also banned because it can be used to control other living creatures. There are magic spells that can make a monster obey you, although only for a short time. But with the right mix of magic and technology, a mage can create devices that dominate the creature's mind for life. Unfortunately, the process makes the creature so ill that its life isn't long."

My tail curled at the thought of being controlled like that.

"It's never really been a problem," Aleetha continued, "because it's very rare to find a mage who is able to control both magic and technology. Most, like me, simply don't have the ability to do it."

"But Hilsa can," I said.

"So it would seem." Aleetha's gaze fell on the water lapping against the pier. "The mages at the Shadow Tower would be very interested in talking to him about his abilities."

Gwena stood suddenly. "Ready to find out how I knew you were in the town square?" She collected our bowls and piled them near her cooking stove. "You're going to love the view!"

Our new friend was definitely a good cook and no friend of Captain Stitch and Hilsa. But as I watched her wipe the bowls clean, I couldn't shake the feeling that we hadn't heard the full story.

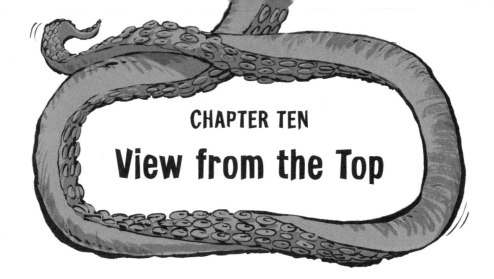

CHAPTER TEN
View from the Top

Gwena led us to the top of the world.

We followed her to the end of the beach. A tunnel ran into the darkness and led back to the heart of Fishers Hollow and the town square. Next to the tunnel, a spiral staircase rose from the sand and into an opening in the cavern's ceiling. We climbed the spiral staircase all the way through the opening and emerged in the center of a round building on the surface of the island. A door in the curved wall led outside. Sunlight streamed through a few small windows. The staircase continued to spiral upward, ending at another floor at the very top.

“Welcome to our lighthouse!” Gwena climbed the remaining steps and walked onto the top floor. “You’re going to love the view from up here.”

I scrambled up the steps after her.

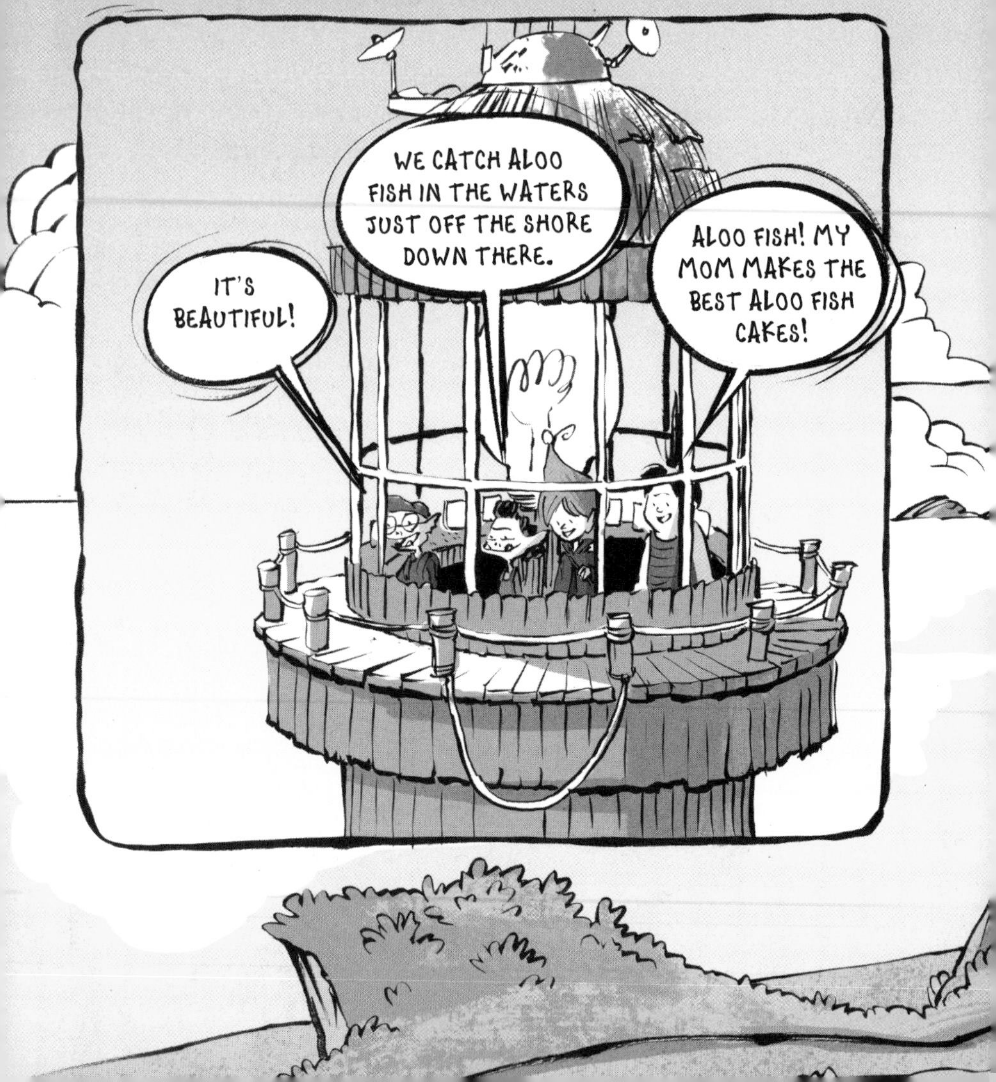
WE CATCH ALOO FISH IN THE WATERS JUST OFF THE SHORE DOWN THERE.
IT'S BEAUTIFUL!
ALOO FISH! MY MOM MAKES THE BEST ALOO FISH CAKES!

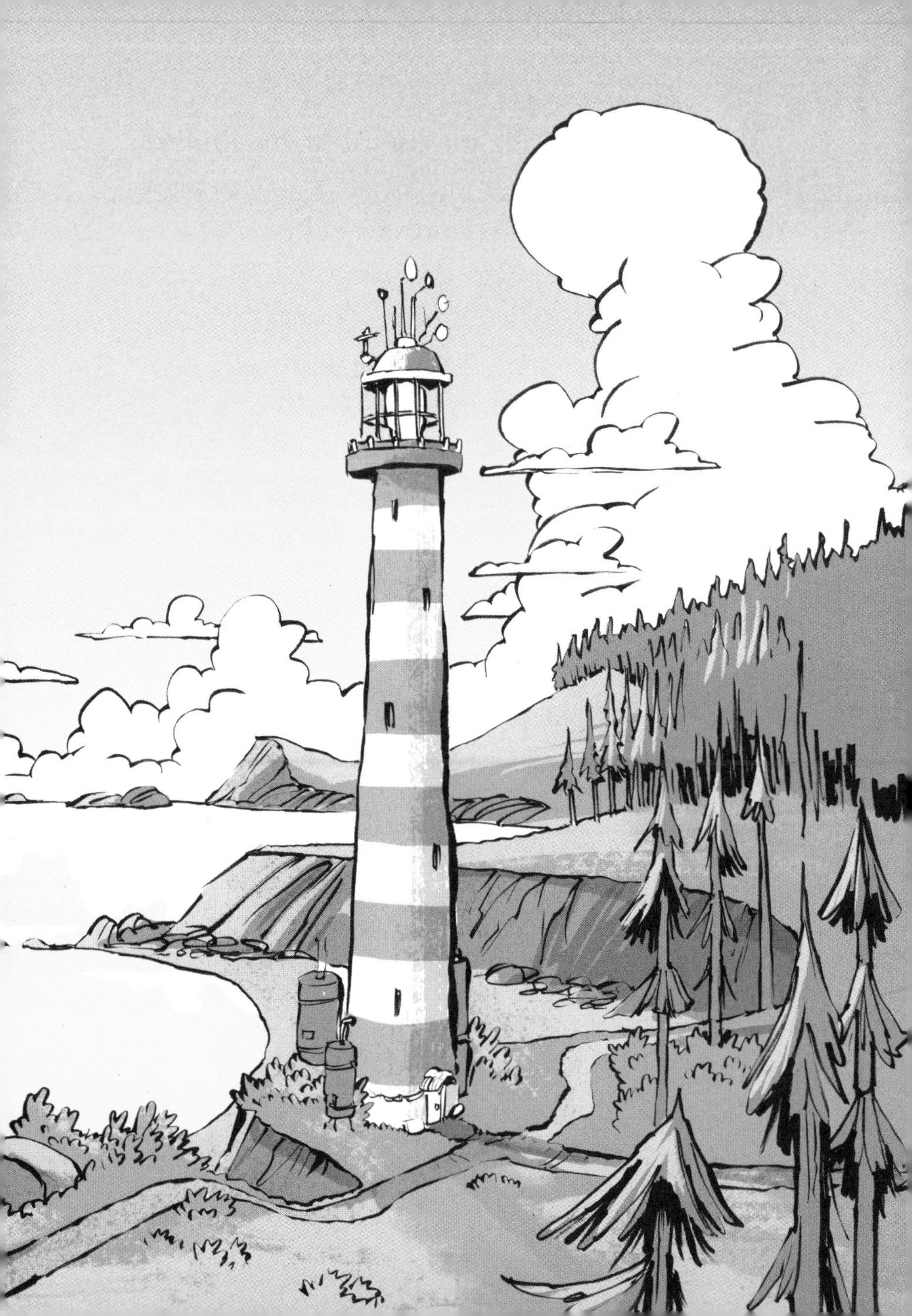

The lighthouse stood on the edge of a high cliff overlooking the open water. It was nearly as tall as the Shadow Tower back home but had a much better view. On one side, blue water stretched as far as I could see. On the other, green hills rolled into the distance. Forests of trees stood alongside open spaces of green, covered with something Gwena called grass. High above, the sun hung in the sky, sending down its light and warmth. Aleetha stared out at the scene below.

"I never realized there was this much space outside the mountain."

"And this is only a tiny part of it all. We're on Hook Island, far from the mainland and Rockfall Mountain." Gwena pointed to a line of low hills on the far side of the island. "Howler's Bay is on the other side of the island, beyond the forest."

The view was pretty spectacular, but I was more captivated by a simple framed drawing sitting on top of one of the many machines in the lighthouse. A creature with familiar eyes and many tentacles stared out from the frame.

"That's the drawing from the cliff!" I said.

Gwena picked up the drawing and smiled. "That's

Pequod! Without her help, we couldn't catch the aloo fish."

"How does an octopus help a bunch of goblins fish?" I asked.

"Pequod is not an octopus. She's a meglohydra, and a very old one at that," Gwena said. "Meglohydras are intelligent creatures who come from deep in the ocean. Pequod likes to swim along the coast. She uses her massive tentacles to herd the aloo fish into large groups that are easy for us to scoop up with our nets. Pequod and the aloo both eat the same types of smaller fish."

"So when you catch the aloo, that means more smaller fish for Pequod to eat," Aleetha said. "Sounds like a good arrangement."

"It was Pequod's idea." Gwena looked sadly at the drawing in her hands. "Like all meglohydras, Pequod can put words into your mind as if she is talking to you."

"Can she put pictures into your mind too?" Aleetha asked.

Gwena nodded. "That's how she tells the fishing goblins where to find the groups of fish."

"That explains the images we saw when we were in

the water," I said. "Pequod put them into our minds so we would find you."

"Some of the fisher folk say my family has a special bond with Pequod," Gwena said. "She always placed visions of the fish in my father's head, before he was taken by Stitch. Then she sent images to my brother, Attan, but that stopped shortly before Stitch took him and the rest of the village away. From what you've told me, it's clear that Pequod has been captured by Captain Stitch and Hilsa."

"And now she's helping them steal cargo ships." My scales went cold at the memory of seeing Pequod's massive tentacles wrap around the *Wave Dancer.*

"I can't understand why she is doing that." Gwena put the picture back on top of the computer. "Pequod is a gentle giant. She has never attacked ships before."

A row of monitors whirred to life on the other side of the lighthouse. Tank looked up, her ears wiggling.

"I found the On switch!" She grinned. "I hope that's okay."

Gwena laughed. "It's more than okay."

Clearly, my friend had been more interested in the lighthouse's technology than the view. While we'd been talking about Pequod and the island, Tank had been poking around at the screens, dials and computers that lined the walls of the lighthouse.

"What's it all for?" I asked. "Seems like a lot of tech just to warn ships to stay clear of the island."

"It does a lot more than that." Gwena sat in a chair in front of a set of important-looking buttons. She pressed the controls with expertise. "This tower is also a communication and surveillance center. From here we can monitor what's happening along the coast and in our village. Watch this."

Gwena pressed some buttons on her control panel. The screens in front of her flashed. Suddenly images of the goblin village appeared on them. One screen showed the long staircase leading down from the cave entrance. Another showed the town square. The smoke had cleared from the plaza, and the empty shops could be seen clearly.

"Why do you have cameras all over your town?" I asked. "I'd be freaked out knowing I was being watched all the time."

"I agree." Gwena sighed. "But we goblins love technology, and once someone suggested the cameras, everyone thought it was a great idea."

Aleetha narrowed her eyes at Tank. "I thought nobody loved technology more than trolls?"

"So did I." Tank shrugged. "I guess things are different outside Rockfall Mountain."

"Speaking of your home, the antennas on top of the lighthouse can receive signals from Rockfall Mountain." Gwena bounced the same way Tank did when she got a new gadget.

"Can you send a message to Slick City?" I said.

Tank's eyes lit up. "We can let our parents know we're all right and tell Officer Hordish who is stealing the cargo ships."

"I wish we could," Gwena said. "But there is something in the stone of the mountain that blocks our outgoing signals, so there is no way to send a message."

"I've heard that before." Tank nodded. "The veins of ballardium crystal that run through the rock can play havoc with communication devices."

"It doesn't affect signals coming out from the mountain," Gwena said. "We're able to get most of your TV channels, which is nice. We can even keep up on the latest news."

Gwena typed some commands into the computer. Tank looked on with appreciation. I was more interested in the view outside the lighthouse window. Then an image appeared on screen that grabbed me by the scales, and I couldn't look away.

"That's my mom!" Tank gasped.

Mrs. Wrenchlin's face stared out at us from the top right of the screen. Her picture floated over the shoulder of the host of the *Slick City News*. Gwena turned up the volume, and the voice of the news anchor, Trina Trallastar, filled the lighthouse.

"*Our top story today: Mayor Grimlock has removed Janaka Wrenchlin from her position as harbor master at Fang Harbor. The decision comes only a day after the mysterious disappearance of the* Wave Dancer, *the third SlurpCo cargo ship to vanish from the harbor.*"

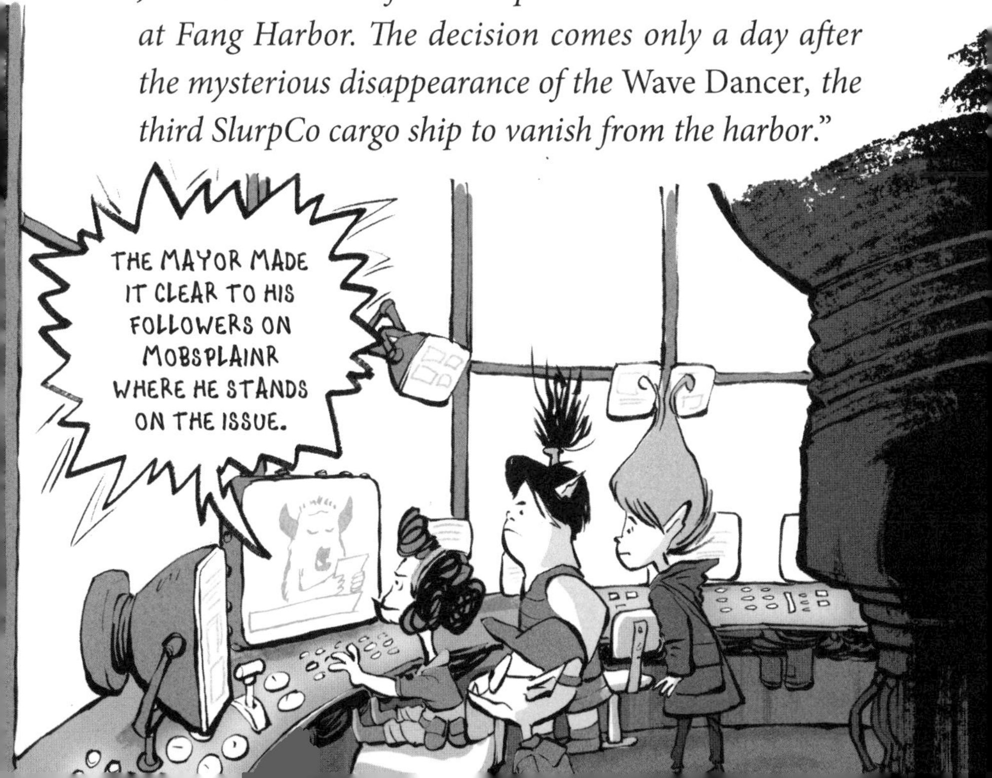
THE MAYOR MADE IT CLEAR TO HIS FOLLOWERS ON MOBSPLAINR WHERE HE STANDS ON THE ISSUE.

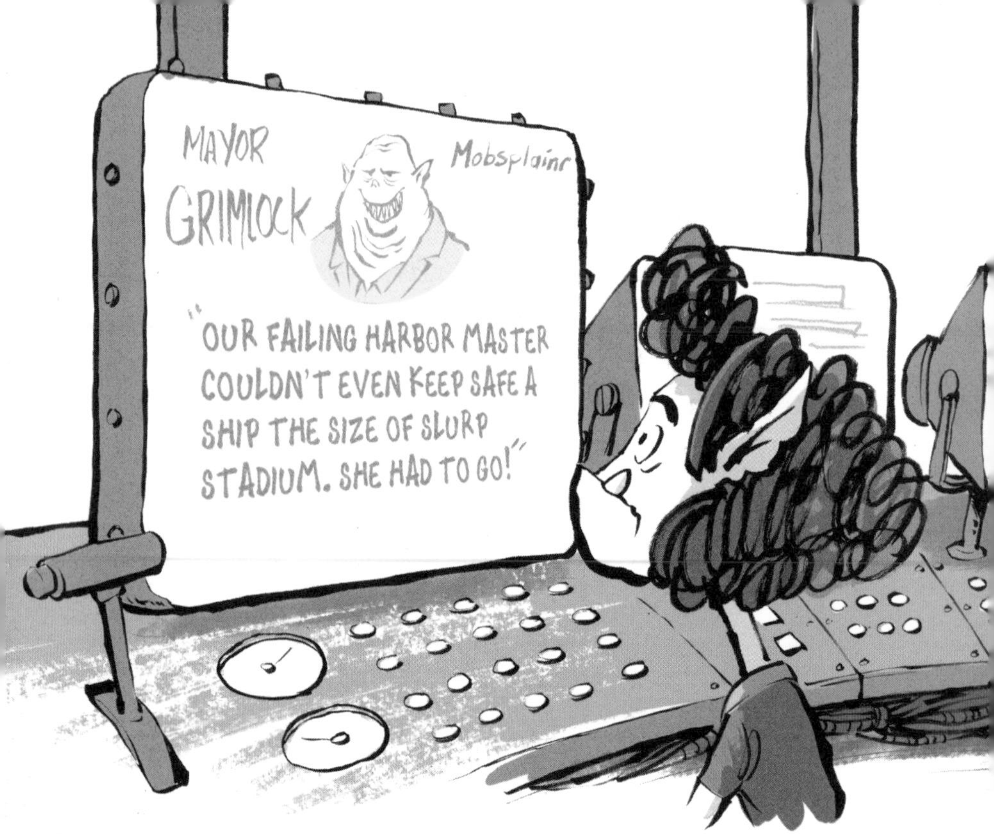
MAYOR GRIMLOCK
Mobsplainr
"OUR FAILING HARBOR MASTER COULDN'T EVEN KEEP SAFE A SHIP THE SIZE OF SLURP STADIUM. SHE HAD TO GO!"

Tank stared at the screen and sniffed. "My mom lost her job?"

"Don't worry, Tank," I said. "We'll get back home and prove she isn't involved. Then, we'll make Grimlock give back her job."

Tank spun to face me. Her lips quivered and her ears sagged. "How are we going to do that? We're more lost than we've ever been before and have no idea how to get back home."

"I agree it doesn't look good," I said.

A light on the control panel flashed red. An alarm buzzed from the panel's speakers.

Gwena pushed her chair along beside the control panel and pressed buttons frantically. "I'm afraid it's looking even worse now."

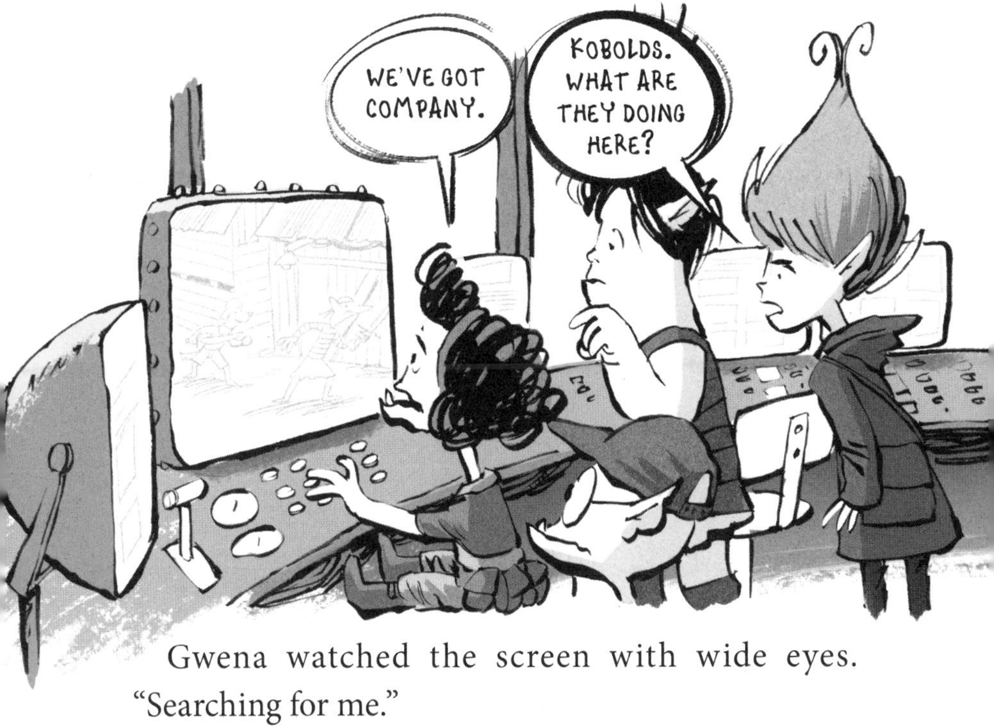
WE'VE GOT COMPANY.
KOBOLDS. WHAT ARE THEY DOING HERE?

Gwena watched the screen with wide eyes. "Searching for me."

"Stitch has everyone from your whole village," I said. "Why does he want you too?"

"I don't know." Gwena pressed the controls on the computer. "I think Hilsa cast a spell on the statue so it spews his knockout smoke when someone enters the town square. I triggered it once before but got away before falling asleep. Once the smoke had cleared, a group of kobolds came searching. They searched the whole town before giving up and going away."

We watched on the control panel's screens as the kobold pirates moved through Fishers Hollow. They searched through the town square, moving in and out of shops. They sniffed their way along alleyways and down side streets, barking to each other as they went.

"How far will they search this time?" I asked. "Will they find us here?"

Below us, the door on the ground floor creaked open. Furry bodies moved past the camera at the base of the tower's stairs.

"That'd be a yes," Aleetha said.

The walls of the tower closed in around me. Outside, a whole world stretched as far as I could see, but in a few seconds my world was going to be nothing but kobold claws and fur.

CHAPTER ELEVEN
Return of the Mutts

Footsteps sounded on the steps below.

Gwena rushed to the top of the spiral stairs.

"This is the only way down. If we get to my dad's fishing boat, we might be able to hide out until Stitch's kobolds are gone. But that means getting past those furballs on the stairs."

"And how are we going to do that?" I said.

"We're not. You are." Tank rummaged through her tool belt. Her hands stopped on something in her pocket, and she smiled. "Hopefully, this has dried out. Fizz, stand at the top of the stairs."

The stairs were the last place I wanted to stand. The pounding of kobold footsteps echoed up them.

They'd be swarming this room in a matter of seconds. Tank dragged me to the edge of the staircase.

"No time to argue, little buddy." In her hand she held a badge of some kind. It was the size of her fist, and she stuck it to my chest. She pushed the badge, and everything around me turned green.

"What happened to my eyes?" I cried.

"Nothing." Tank chuckled. "You're inside a snorp-orb. It's a heliozodic shield that will stop anything from touching you. I designed it as protection for food fights in the school cafeteria."

"Very smart," I said. "You were always an easy target during those battles."

"Yeah, well, now you're the target," Tank said. "Sorry."

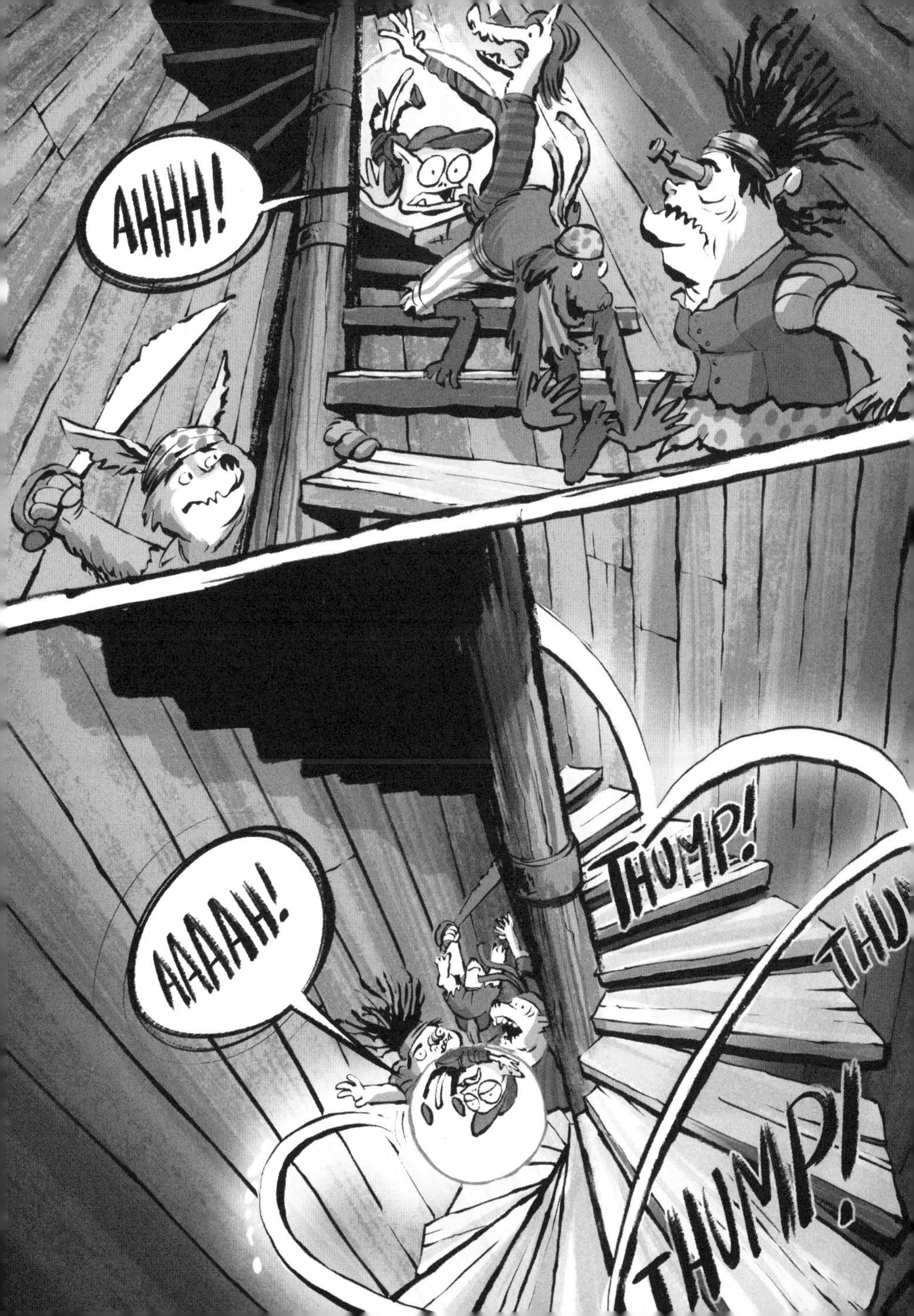
AHHH!
AAAAH!
THUMP!
THU
THUMP!

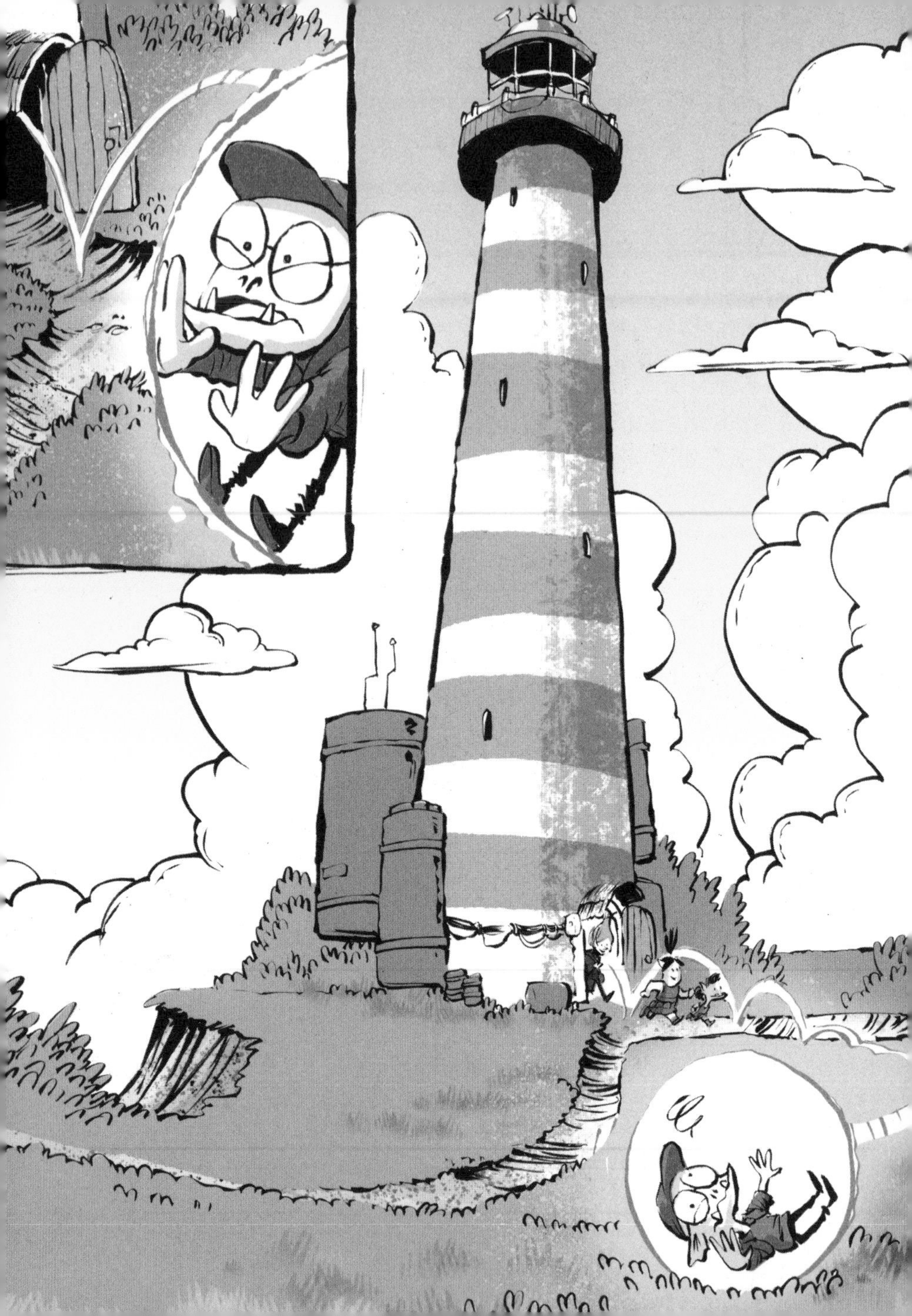

The world around me stopped spinning. The green leaves of the island forest came into focus, and the rattling in my brain slowed to a dull thud. I was out of the lighthouse and alive—barely. With fumbling claws I pressed the little badge, and the shield vanished.

Tank rushed from the lighthouse and helped me to my feet.

"That was awesome!" she gushed. "You knocked out all the kobolds. A perfect score."

"Well done, Fizz," Aleetha said.

"You totally saved us," Gwena added.

"Thanks. I think." I wobbled on my feet. When my brain had stopped shaking, I spun to face Tank. "You could have warned me that you were going to toss me down the stairs!"

My friend grinned. "You wouldn't have let me, and we'd still be trapped up there. This way was better. Trust me."

The sound of barking came through the trees and silenced any argument I could muster.

"We need to move. This way." Gwena set off along the edge of the cliff that overlooked the water.

We followed her to a break in the cliff face. The steep drop became a sandy slope that led to the water's edge.

Gwena descended the slope in wide leaps. Another group of pirates emerged from the woods near the lighthouse. The kobolds sniffed the air and immediately looked in our direction. They charged at us, barking like their fur was on fire.

"Time to go!" I jumped down the sandy slope after Gwena.

When we reached the bottom, Gwena was already farther along the beach. She waved to us from the mouth of a cave. Aleetha led the way as we ran through the sand. Once inside the cave, I recognized the beach and huts where Gwena had fed us stew. The goblin crouched just inside the mouth of the cave.

"Wait here," she whispered. "There will be more kobolds on the beach."

Gwena slipped into the water without making a splash. We watched as she silently swam to the nearest fishing boat. She scrambled onboard and disappeared from view.

"What is she doing?" Tank asked as loudly as she dared.

An engine on the fishing boat roared to life. Water churned behind the vessel as it moved toward us.

"I think she just found us a ride," Aleetha said.

Barks erupted on the beach. Angry kobolds ran along the shore, yapping and waving their swords at the escaping boat. A couple of keen pirates ran into the water and splashed after Gwena. But there was little they could do. Gwena had already maneuvered the boat far from the beach and expertly steered it through the water.

Gwena sat at the back of the vessel, guiding the sputtering motor with one hand. The words *Misty Marple* were painted on the side of the boat in bright red letters.

"Get in!" she called when she pulled up alongside us. "I know a spot we can hide out until Stitch's kobolds get tired of looking for us."

We piled into the little boat. Gwena gunned the engine, sending us racing out into the open water. We zoomed past kobolds scrambling down the sandy slope. They howled from the beach as we cut through the water and away from the shore.

"See you later, suckers!" Tank waved goodbye to the frustrated kobolds.

Water splashed up from the front of the boat as it pushed through the waves. Gwena squinted against the spray and steered us into deeper water.

"We'll circle around to the far side of the island," she shouted over the engine. "There's a sheltered cove that should keep us hidden for a little while."

Aleetha peered through the mist and frowned. "I think it's too late for hiding."

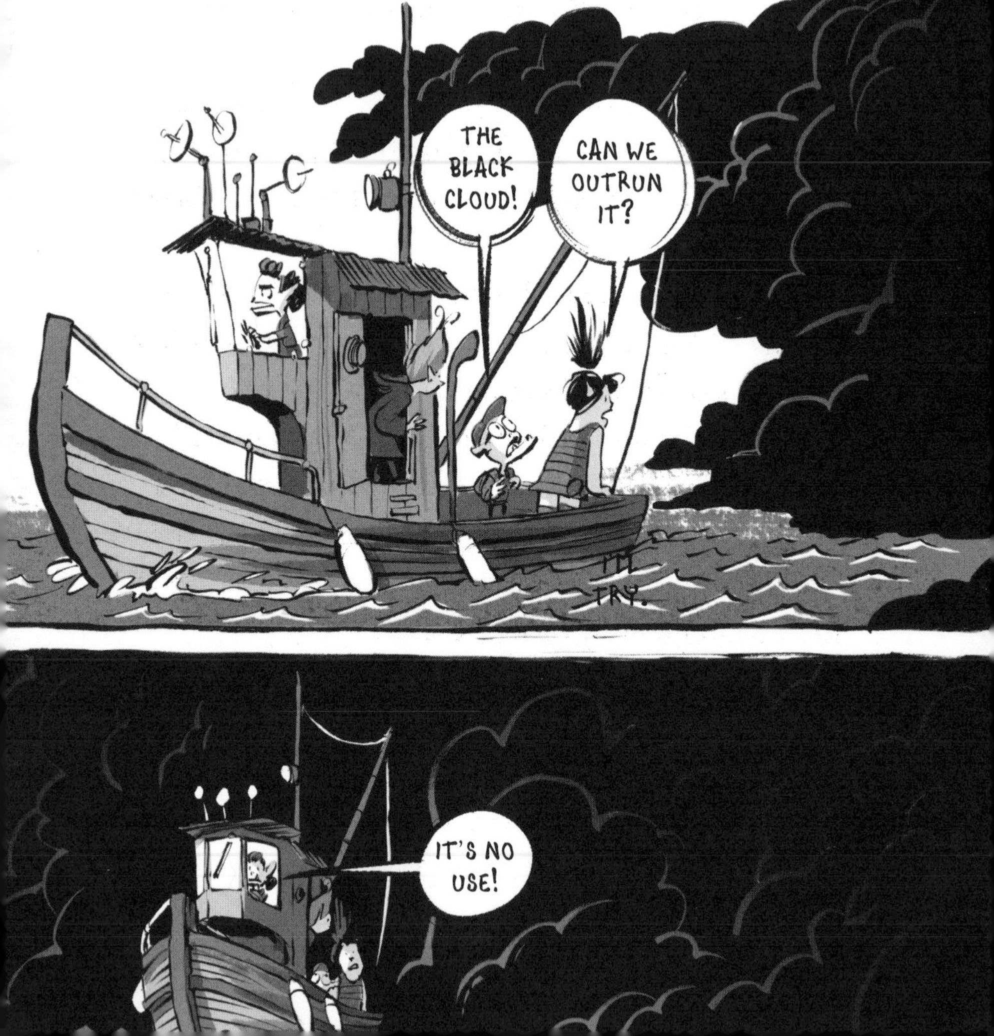
THE BLACK CLOUD!
CAN WE OUTRUN IT?
I'LL TRY.
IT'S NO USE!

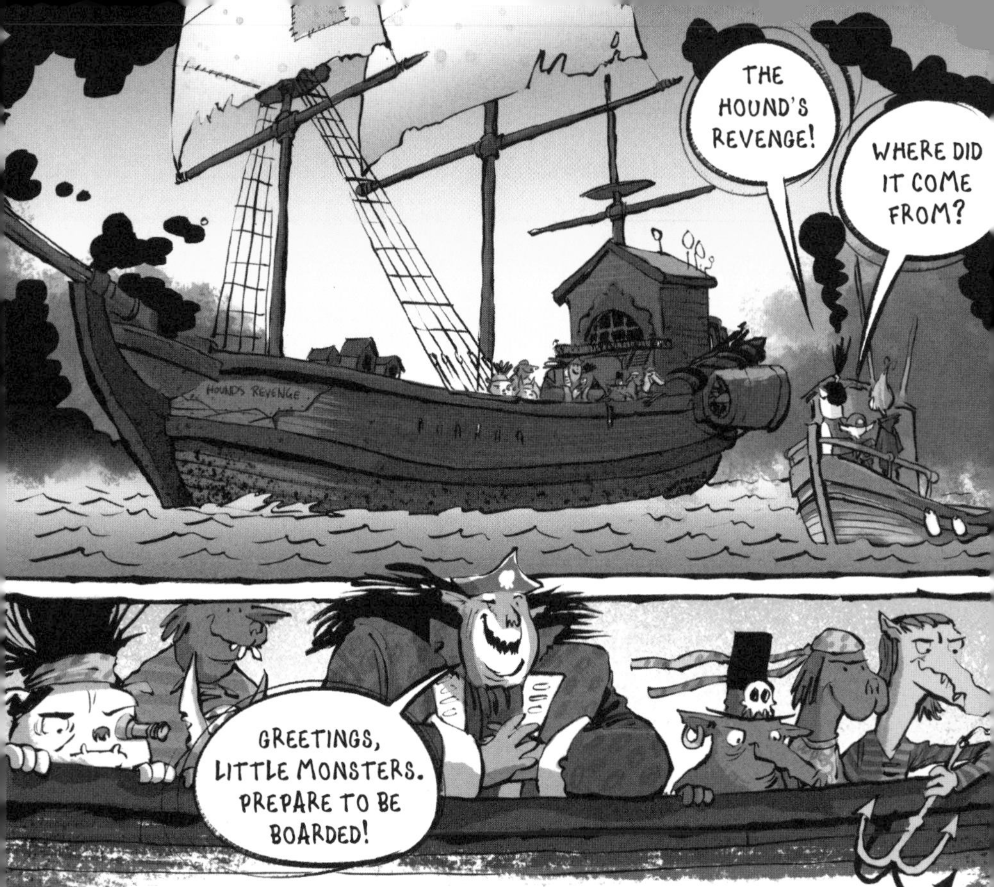
THE HOUND'S REVENGE!
WHERE DID IT COME FROM?
GREETINGS, LITTLE MONSTERS. PREPARE TO BE BOARDED!

A rusty grappling hook tied to a rope flew from the deck of the *Hound's Revenge* and bit into our fishing boat. The rope was pulled tight, and the sharp tines of the hook locked into our boat.

Captain Stitch stood on the deck of the *Revenge*, looking down at us with his one eye.

"The chase is over, little monsters. You're Stitch's prisoners now."

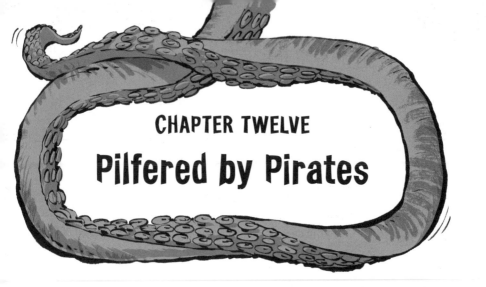

CHAPTER TWELVE

Pilfered by Pirates

Kobold claws pulled me onto the *Hound's Revenge*. The moment I reached the top of the rope ladder, furry paws grabbed my scales and dumped me alongside my friends at the feet of Captain Stitch.

"The pests from Rockfall Mountain have returned," Stitch growled. "I see you survived your little dip in the ocean. You are either all accomplished swimmers or extremely lucky."

I wasn't sure if being zapped by a giant tentacle could be considered lucky, but I kept my mouth shut and let Stitch continue his rant. If the kobold captain was surprised to see us again, he was overjoyed to get his hands on Gwena.

"Finally, we catch the elusive last goblin from Fishers Hollow. Your brother will be very happy to see you, Gwena. And now perhaps he'll be a bit more cooperative."

Those words sent Gwena lunging at Stitch. Kobold paws pulled her back before she'd even taken a step.

"You are a feisty one. No wonder we had such a hard time catching you." The captain waved a dismissive paw at us and walked away. "Secure the prisoners in the brig and set sail for Howler's Bay."

A cheer erupted from the kobolds on the deck at this announcement. Rough paws grabbed at my scales and hauled me to my feet. Aleetha and Tank were treated the same way. A kobold tore off Tank's tool belt and tossed it aside. It landed on the deck of the ship with a thud before three snarling pirates descended on it and rummaged through the pockets.

Tank's eyes welled up with tears. "My belt!"

We were led down a set of narrow stairs into the bowels of the ship and pushed into a tiny, damp room that smelled of wet rats. Gwena slumped to the ground with her head in her hands. Aleetha sat next to the goblin.

"It will be okay," she whispered. "We'll figure a way out of this mess. Somehow."

"It's not that." Gwena sniffed. "I haven't been entirely truthful with you all. I know why Captain Stitch is searching for me. It's my family."

"What about them?" Tank paced the musty room like a trapped dragon.

Gwena's eyes had glazed over with exhaustion. "I only know fragments. The night before Stitch took my father away, he explained it to us. My brother and mother listened, but I was too upset that he was leaving to really pay attention. All I remember is it had to do with my dad's side of the family and magic. We were special, he said. We had gifts other goblins did not have."

"Like how only your family could receive the messages from Pequod about the aloo fish?" Aleetha asked.

Gwena nodded. "Our talents were the reason Stitch chose to take my father away from all the villagers. And then last week Stitch came looking us. He didn't want my mother, just me and my brother. My brother was caught, but my mother helped me escape before the smoke knocked her out. When Stitch couldn't find me, he had his pirates take away the rest of the villagers."

"It doesn't make sense," I said. "Why would Stitch want your family just because you can hear messages from a brainy meglohydra?"

"I think there's more to it, Fizz." A weary smile spread across Gwena's snout. "We can do other things too."

Aleetha's fiery gaze locked onto Gwena. "What sort of things?"

Before she could answer, the door flew open and hit the wall with a sound like thunder. Two kobolds with mottled fur sauntered in. The first, keys jangling, looked us over. The second kobold watched the door to the brig nervously. They both stepped aside to let a third monster into the room.

He was taller than the others and carrying a shell-encrusted staff. It was Hilsa, the wave mage. He moved silently toward us, glancing briefly at us before fixing his bulbous eyes on Gwena. She stood to attention under his gaze.

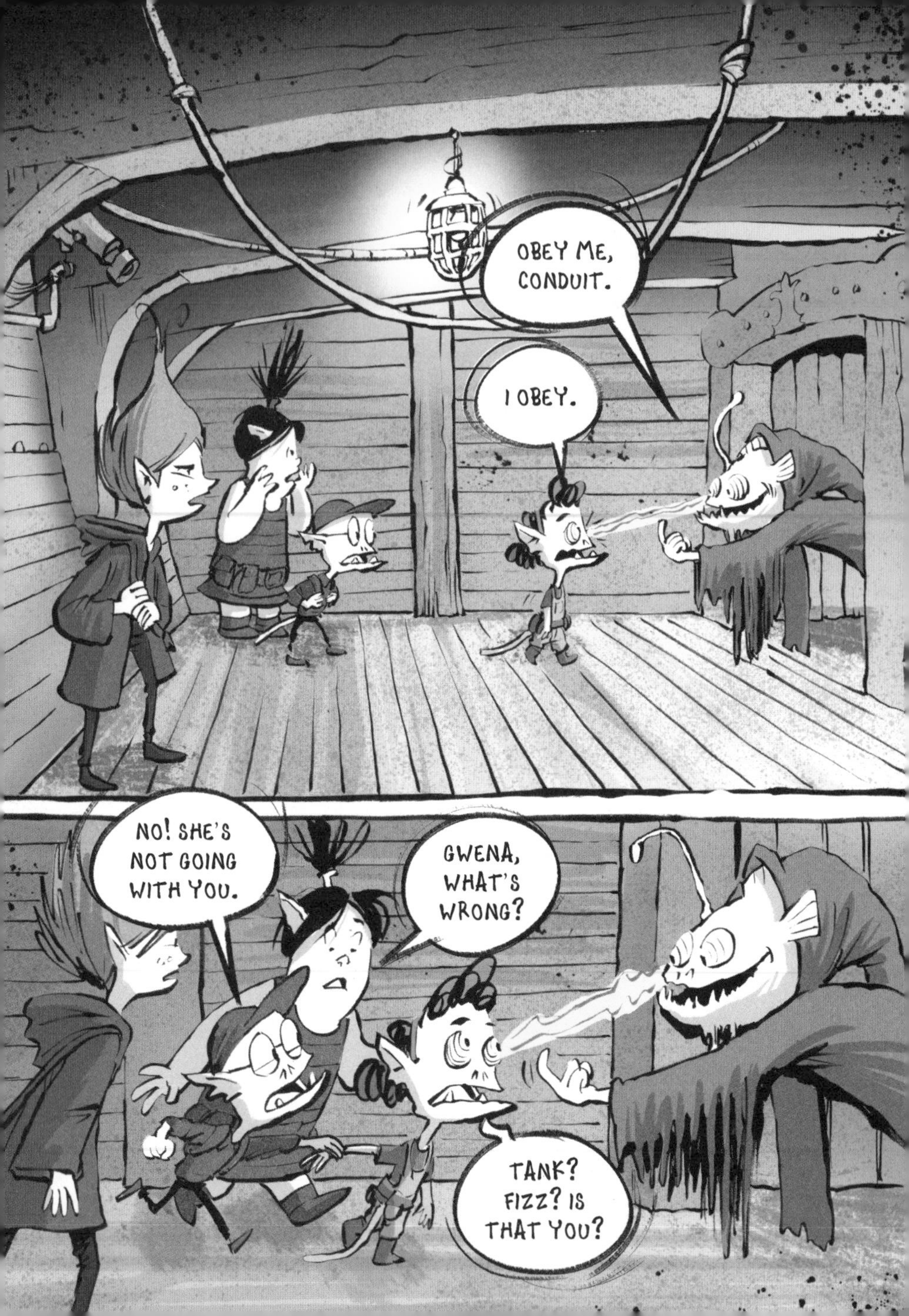
OBEY ME, CONDUIT.
I OBEY.
NO! SHE'S NOT GOING WITH YOU.
GWENA, WHAT'S WRONG?
TANK? FIZZ? IS THAT YOU?

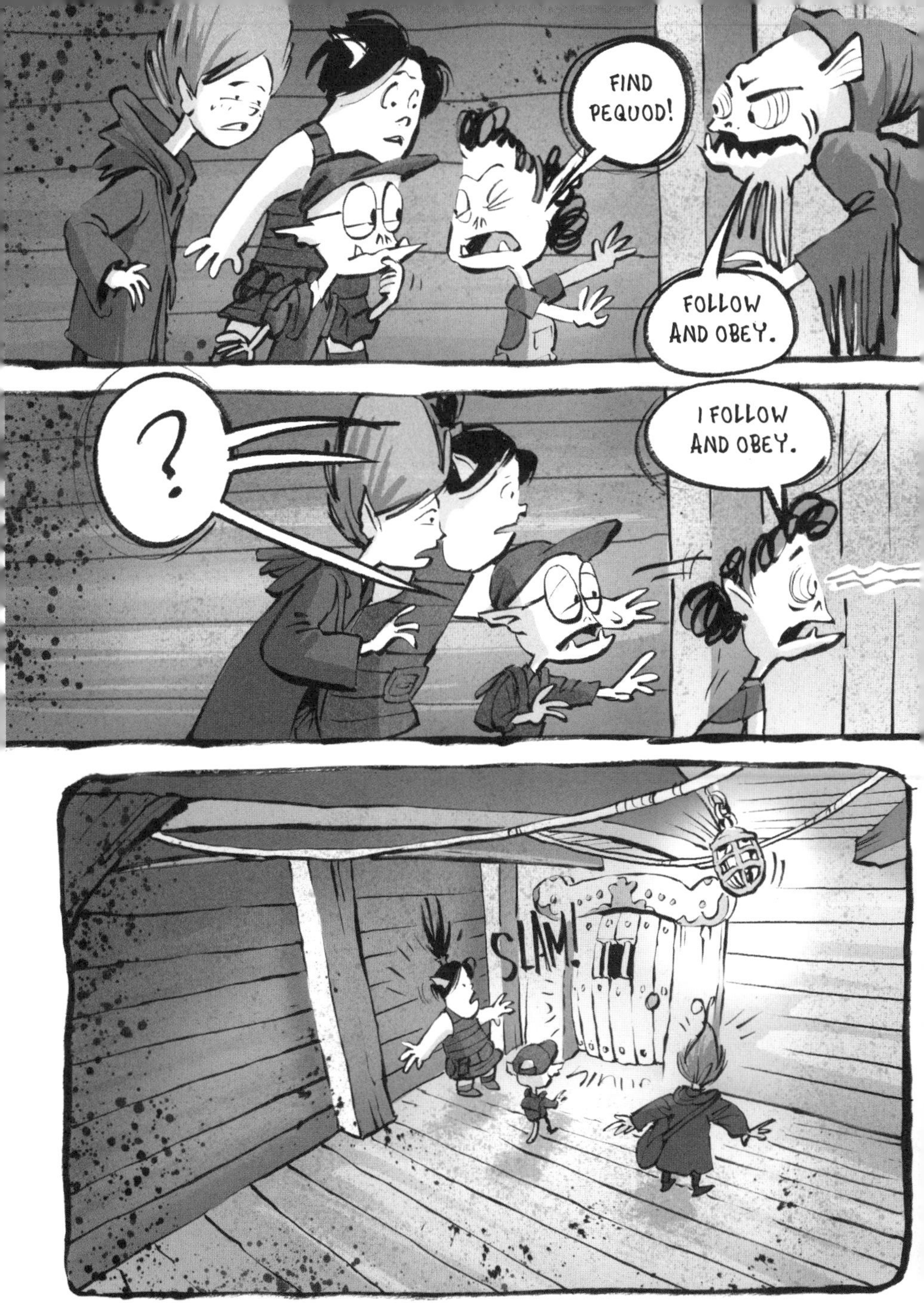
FIND PEQUOD!
FOLLOW AND OBEY.
?
I FOLLOW AND OBEY.
SLAM!

The door slammed shut and the kobold guard locked us in again. Tank rattled the door, but it would not budge.

"Why did she leave with that creep?" the troll growled. "She just walked out of here like they were going for ice cream!"

"Hilsa had her under some kind of command spell," Aleetha said. "He's a powerful wizard to be able to cast a spell like that so effortlessly."

"We need to get her back." Now I began to pace the room. "What did she mean, *find Pequod*? How do you find a meglohydra? And what do you say when you've found it?"

"Before we can worry about that, we need to get out of here." Tank's hands went to her waist but stopped when she realized she had no pockets to search. "And we have to get my tool belt back!"

"One thing at a time," Aleetha said. "Even if we do escape this room, then what? We're on a ship crawling with pirates. There's nowhere to go while we're on board. Unless you want to go swimming again."

"No way," I said. "I'd like to keep my scales dry from now on."

Aleetha pulled her cloak closer around her. "Then

let's bide our time with these pirates and wait for our chance to escape."

The ship lurched to one side, making the thick wooden walls creak in protest. Seconds later it tilted in the other direction.

"I think we're on the move." Tank placed a hand on the wall to steady herself.

The ship continued to slowly rock back and forth, making my pacing wobbly. I moved to the corner of the room, where the floor was somewhat dry, and sat down. The others sat in silence, lost in their own thoughts.

My mind drifted back to the first time we had met Stitch and Hilsa, on the deck of the *Wave Dancer*. They had seemed more interested in the cargo containers than in the actual ship. Hilsa had used the density-inverters and magic to make them disappear. I sat up straight. There was something else. Another monster had helped with the spell.

"Conduit!" I said loud enough to make Tank and Aleetha open their eyes.

Aleetha rubbed her eyes. "That's what Hilsa called Gwena before he took her away."

"Exactly." I was on my feet pacing again. "What is a conduit? Is it some magic word wizards use?"

"If it is, I haven't heard of it," Aleetha said.

"I have." Tank stretched her arms over her head like she was trying to touch the ceiling. "And so have you, Fizz. You'd remember if you ever listened in science class."

"I do listen!" I grumbled. "Sometimes."

Tank chuckled. "Then you'd remember that a conduit is a pathway that allows stuff to travel through it. Like a pipe that lets water flow through it. Anything able to carry or transmit something can be a conduit. I use them all the time when I'm building stuff."

"Okay, but why call Gwena that?" I said. "Hilsa also called that monster in the black cloak his conduit when he made the steel containers disappear."

"I forgot about that monster," Tank said. "The poor thing didn't look happy. Not that I could see its face under that robe. But still, it can't be much fun getting dragged around by a fish-head like Hilsa."

"I saw the monster's tail," I said. "After Hilsa cast his spell, the monster collapsed, and its tail poked out of the robe. It looked like mine."

"You think it was a goblin?" Aleetha asked.

The door slammed open again, making us all jump.

The kobold with the jangling keys and mangy fur sauntered in.

"On your feet, you lazy layabouts!" he barked. "Captain wants you on deck."

We marched out of the room and down the ship's cramped corridor. As we approached the steep stairs leading to the deck, Aleetha leaned in close to me and whispered, "Remember, just go along with things until we figure a way out of here."

Behind us our kobold jailer snarled. "Stop yapping, you two, and get up them stairs!"

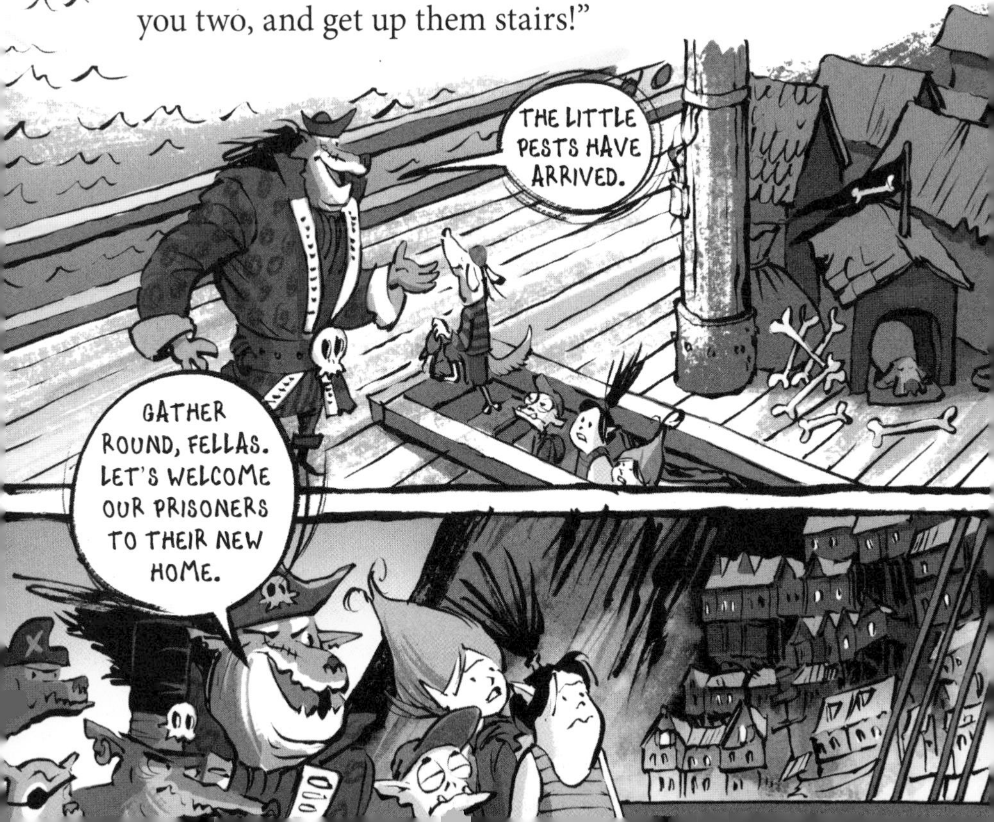
THE LITTLE PESTS HAVE ARRIVED.
GATHER ROUND, FELLAS. LET'S WELCOME OUR PRISONERS TO THEIR NEW HOME.

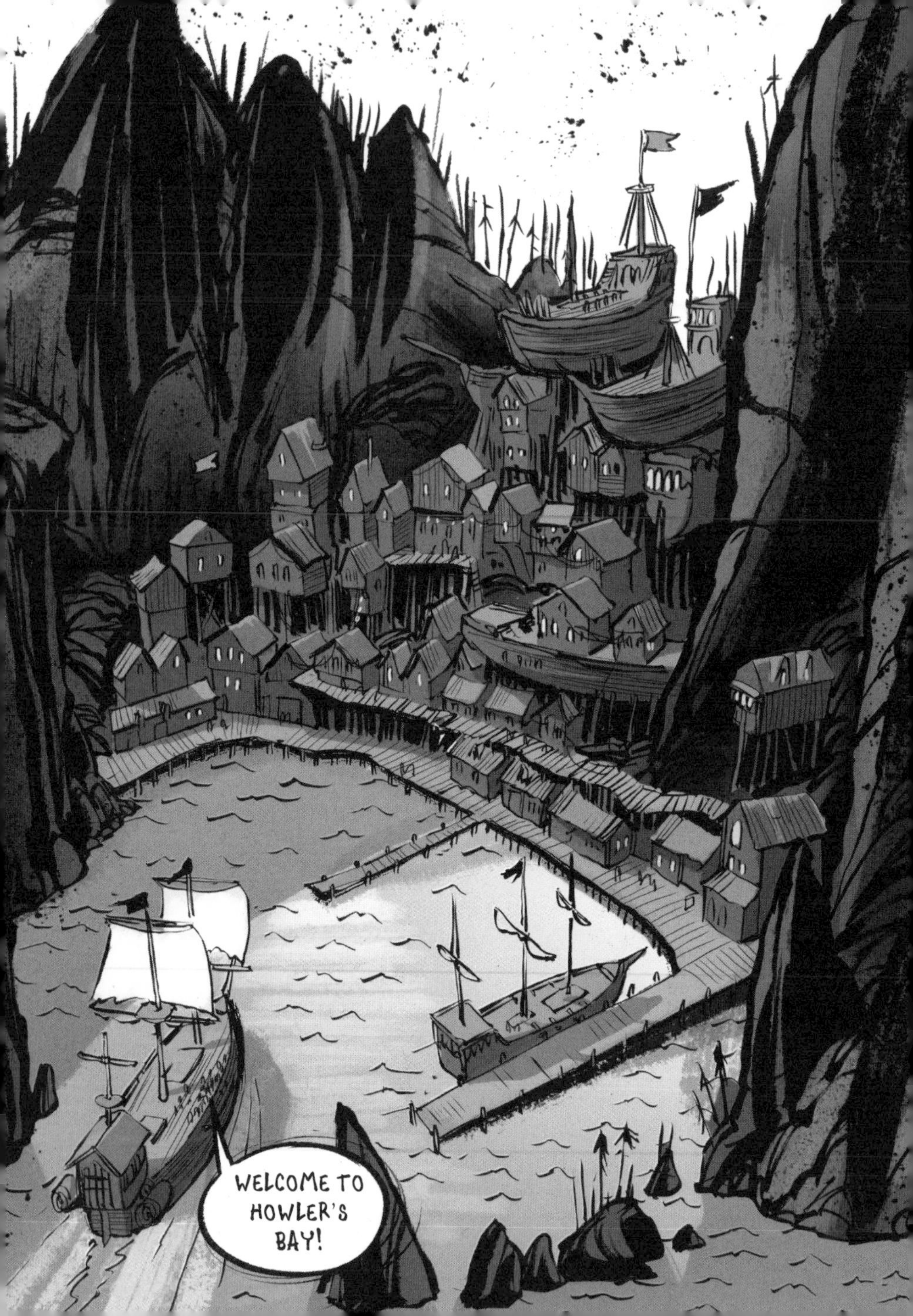
WELCOME TO HOWLER'S BAY!

The crew of the *Hound's Revenge* cheered at Stitch's words as we anchored in the harbor.

"I gave you critters a chance to swim away, but you came back," the pirate captain growled. "Now you'll never leave."

It felt like a boulder had landed in my gut. Beside me, Tank gulped. Aleetha blinked away tears. The plan was to bide our time and wait for a chance to escape. But as we were led off the ship and into the den of pirates, I doubted that time would ever come.

Like it or not, Stitch was right. Howler's Bay was our new home.

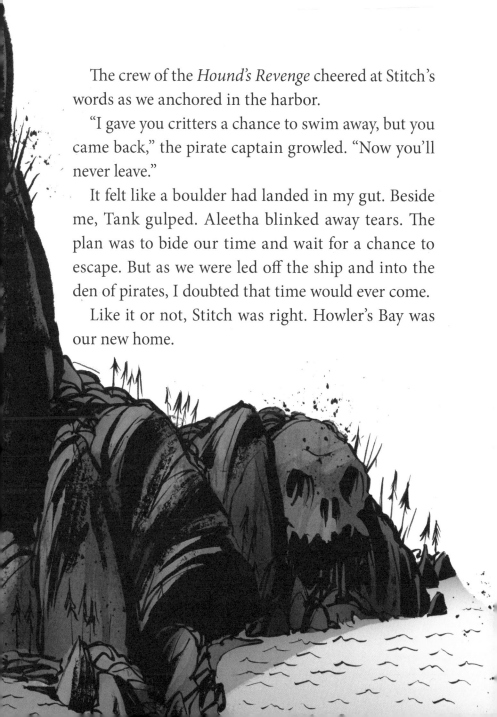

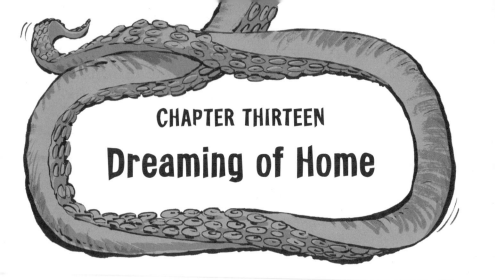

CHAPTER THIRTEEN
Dreaming of Home

Howler's Bay smelled like wet fur.

Our new home was a collection of tumble-down shacks poorly built from pieces of old ships and stolen loot. Kobolds barked from rooftops and howled from windows on that first day we were led from the *Hound's Revenge* to Stitch's mansion overlooking the bay. Calling it a mansion was a stretch. It was really just an old ship that had been dragged to the top of the hill. Stitch called it his mansion, and so the other pirates did as well. In Howler's Bay, Stitch's word was law.

Inside the mansion, the ship's hull had been hacked open to reveal a series of tunnels dug deep into the hill.

When we first arrived, we were led down these tunnels to a large cave crowded with dejected-looking goblins, trolls and even an aging ogre. They didn't speak much, but we learned they were all travelers who had made the mistake of getting captured at sea by Stitch and his crew. None of the goblins were from Fishers Hollow, and no one knew where the missing villagers might be. Most worrying of all, there was no sign of Gwena.

Each day we were all led from the cave and put to work. In the evenings we came back, dirty, sore and exhausted. On our third day of captivity, my dreams got seriously weird.

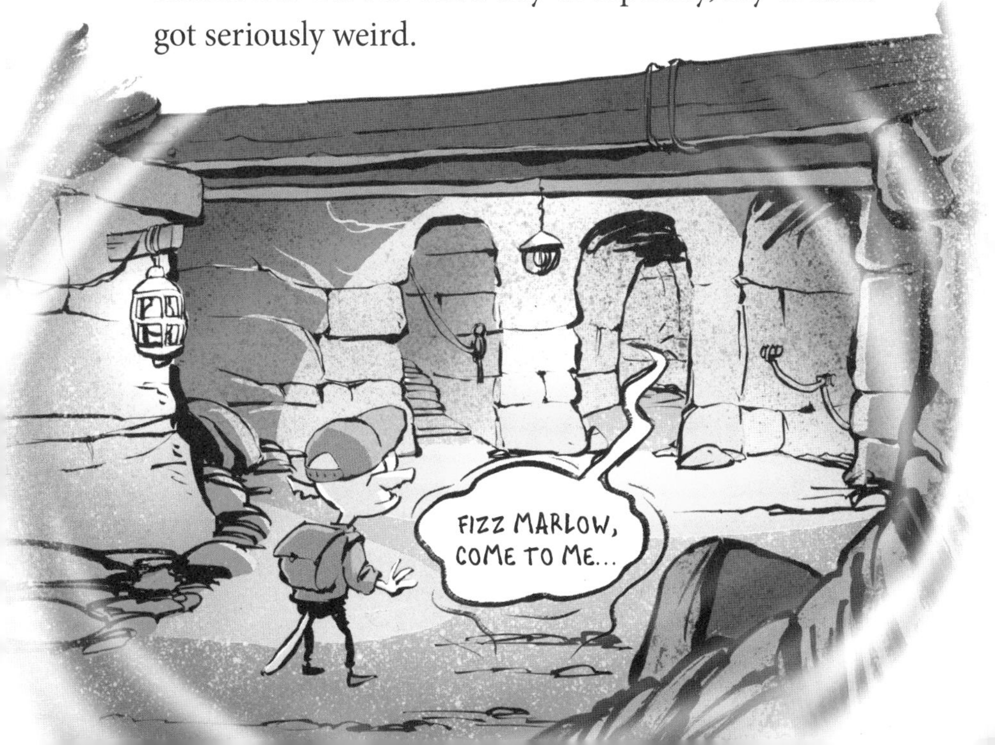
FIZZ MARLOW, COME TO ME...

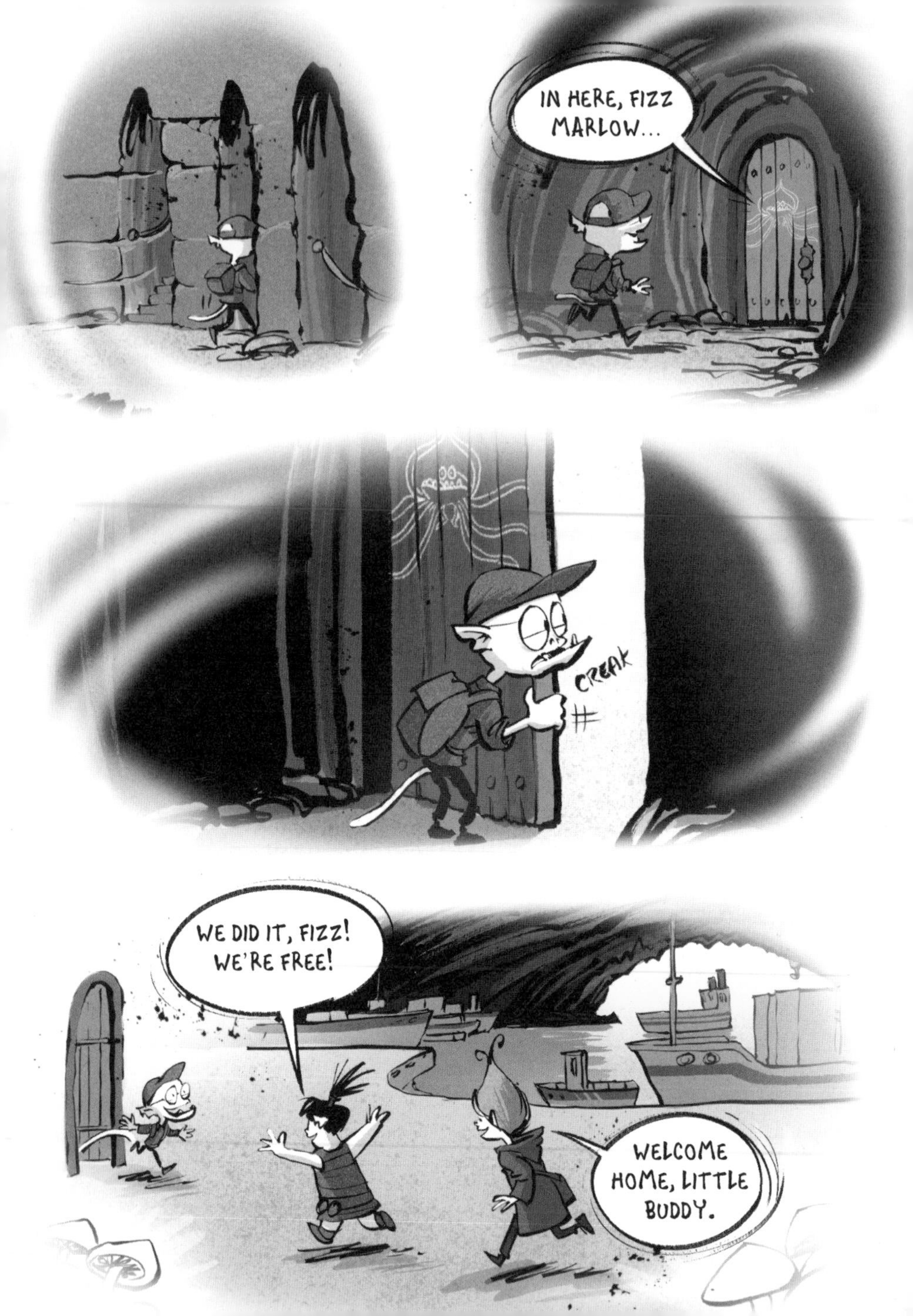
IN HERE, FIZZ MARLOW...
CREAK
WE DID IT, FIZZ! WE'RE FREE!
WELCOME HOME, LITTLE BUDDY.

A wave of cold air gripped my scales. I sat up, half awake. Tank stared down at me. In her hand was my blanket.

"Sorry, but snatching this was the only way I could wake you up." She tossed the blanket back to me. "Don't go back to sleep. Deekin will be prowling through here soon, ready to kick anyone who's not up and ready to work."

"Do I have to? I was having such a nice dream." I pushed away the dirty blanket and reluctantly got to my feet. "I found my way back home to Fang Harbor."

"I dreamed the same thing," Aleetha said, chuckling. The lava elf rolled up her blanket and pushed it into a corner for safekeeping. "Wishful thinking, I guess."

Tank's eyes narrowed. "Wait a minute. You *both* had a dream about being in Fang Harbor?"

Aleetha nodded. "I was wandering the tunnels in here and heard a voice."

A chill ran down my scales. "Was it calling you to come?" I asked.

"Yes," Aleetha said. "And then I found a door."

I gulped. "Did the door have the drawing of Pequod on it?"

"Yes," Aleetha said slowly. "And when I stepped through the door, I was in Fang Harbor. You guys were there waiting for me."

"That sounds exactly like my dream," I said.

Tank chewed nervously on her fingers. "And mine."

Aleetha's gaze darted between the two of us. "Did we all have the same dream?"

"I think we did," I said. "And I think I know who's responsible."

We discussed it over our meager breakfast of stale bread and cold soup.

Aleetha picked something that could have been fur from her bowl. "You think Pequod, the meglohydra, made us all have the same dream?"

"How else can you explain it?" I said. "Gwena said he was the one who put the image of the cave drawing into our minds. And that drawing was on the door in each of our dreams."

"Okay, but in the dream that door led me right to Fang Harbor," Tank said. "You think there's a door around here that will take us back home?"

"Who knows?" I said. "So far we've been teleported by a mind-reading tentacled beast, captured by kobold pirates and nearly eaten by birds with metal hats. Is a magic door any weirder than that stuff?"

Tank smiled. "You make a good point."

"It's settled." Aleetha pushed her bowl away from her. "We'll search for this door with the meglohydra on it and see what lies beyond."

"We can do it later today," I said. "Stitch is having a big feast for some special guests tonight. Most of his muttheads will be too busy gorging themselves to worry about us wandering around."

Aleetha got to her feet. "Let's get to our jobs before some fur-face barks at us for being late."

As we left, not even the nasty gruel sloshing in my gut could take the spring from my step. We might be lost, trapped and alone, but for the first time since arriving in Howler's Bay, we had a plan.

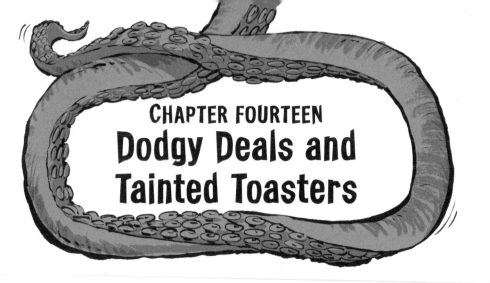

CHAPTER FOURTEEN
Dodgy Deals and Tainted Toasters

The smell of baked beetle guts filled my snout.

Around me, the monsters in Stitch's kitchen were busy preparing for the pirate captain's big feast in honor of his special guest. If they knew who his guests were, they didn't tell a pot-scrubber like me. And it didn't really matter. Dishwashers weren't invited to the feast. I'd be called in to clean up after the kobolds had made their mess. While they were stuffing their furry faces, however, I'd be searching for a way home. I was scrubbing the encrusted beetle guts from a dented cooking pot when Chef Gunzik barked at me.

"You!" The crusty kobold pointed a sharp knife at me. "Go to the storage room and get me a sack of bargle berries. Now!"

I left the kitchen and walked down the corridor to the storage room. I'd never been sent to fetch anything before, so in a way this was a promotion. My mom would have been proud.

When I entered the dark storage room, the first thing that hit me was the smell of fresh fruit. My mouth watered at all the food Stitch and his crew had managed to plunder. I found a bag of bargle berries near the back of the room. I found something else too.

A ROCKETBOARD!

The image of a rocketboard had been burned into my mind since Pequod's tentacle zapped me onto that beach. And now here it was in a storage room, staring me right in the snout. The bag of bargle berries fell to the floor. Why was the rocketboard in a food-storage room? Was it loot from one of Stitch's earlier voyages?

I picked up the rocketboard and inspected it closely. It was old, covered in dust and seriously in need of a tune-up. I put it on the ground and gave it a push. It barely moved. The wheels were seized. It was useless. Why had Pequod put an image of it in my head?

A cool wind blew against my ankles. I looked down and saw a goblin-sized hole in the bottom part of the wall. The rocketboard had been blocking the hole. Suddenly I knew why I'd seen the board in Pequod's visions.

I tossed the board aside, dropped to my knees and crawled through the hole. On the other side was a full-sized tunnel, tall enough for an ogre. A set of wooden steps in front of me led deeper under-ground. Looking behind me, I saw that the hole I had just crawled through was actually in a bricked-over doorway. Someone didn't want anybody to come this way. But Pequod definitely did, and that was good enough for me. Hoping Guznik would forget about the bargle berries, I made my way down the stairs.

They led me deep under the foundation of Stitch's mansion. The walls became bedrock, hacked away to form a tunnel. I crept slowly along the tunnel, hoping it would lead me to more than just the pirate king's secret wine cellar. When I heard voices, I froze. They were coming from farther down the tunnel.

"This ends now, Captain Stitch."

It was a woman's voice. It sounded familiar, but I couldn't place it.

"You're wrong about that." The second person laughed. It was Stitch, no doubt about it. "It's only the beginning. If you tell your guards to stand down, I'll show you."

Guards? My mind raced. Was Stitch being arrested? Were we too late to bust the mutthead? I moved as quickly as I dared toward the voices. Farther along, the tunnel opened onto a large cavern. Another set of stairs led to the cavern floor. I didn't take them. Instead, I scurried into a shallow crevice to watch the two monsters at the foot of the stairs.

Stitch stood with his back to the steps, speaking to someone I could not see. What I could see was the row of SlurpCo security guards on the far side of the cavern. I nearly fell off the ledge. What was SlurpCo doing here? Who had led them here, so far from Rockfall Mountain? Stitch stepped aside, and I had my answer. Mirella Ballaworth's tiny eyes burned into Stitch.

"My guards will not stand down," the SlurpCo executive said. "We tracked you all the way here to get what is ours."

"Tracked me?" Stitch chuckled. "My dear Mirella, we've been expecting you. Why do you think you made it all the way to Hilsa's laboratory without a struggle? We're even preparing a big feast in your honor."

"I'm not here to feast with you, Stitch," Mirella snapped. "I'm here to arrest you, by the authority of Mayor Grimlock himself."

"Can he even do that?" Stitch chuckled. "We're a bit out of his jurisdiction, aren't we?"

Mirella buzzed right up to Stitch's furry face. "Never underestimate what Mayor Grimlock can do."

Stitch stumbled back, his paws raised in mock defense. "No need to get upset."

"I'm not upset." Mirella's words oozed sweetness that quickly turned sour. "I'm livid! You have stolen from SlurpCo Industries. No one does that and keeps their tail."

"You should be thanking me, Mirella." Stitch prowled around the little blaze fairy. "Because of me, your precious cargo destined for department stores will now let you control Slick City and the rest of that pathetic mountain you call home." The kobold grinned, showing sharp teeth from ear to ear. "And you'll make SlurpCo Industries a dragon's hoard of money in the process."

Mirella buzzed to a stop. "Did you say money?"

"Lots of money."

"Now I'm intrigued." Mirella resumed her route. "Continue."

Stitch's tail wagged like it was trying to escape his butt. I'd never seen the pirate king so happy. Not even when he was stuffing his face with grilled slabberjacks after a long nap.

"Hilsa!" Stitch called toward somewhere deeper in the cave. "It's showtime!"

The far wall of the cavern slid to one side.

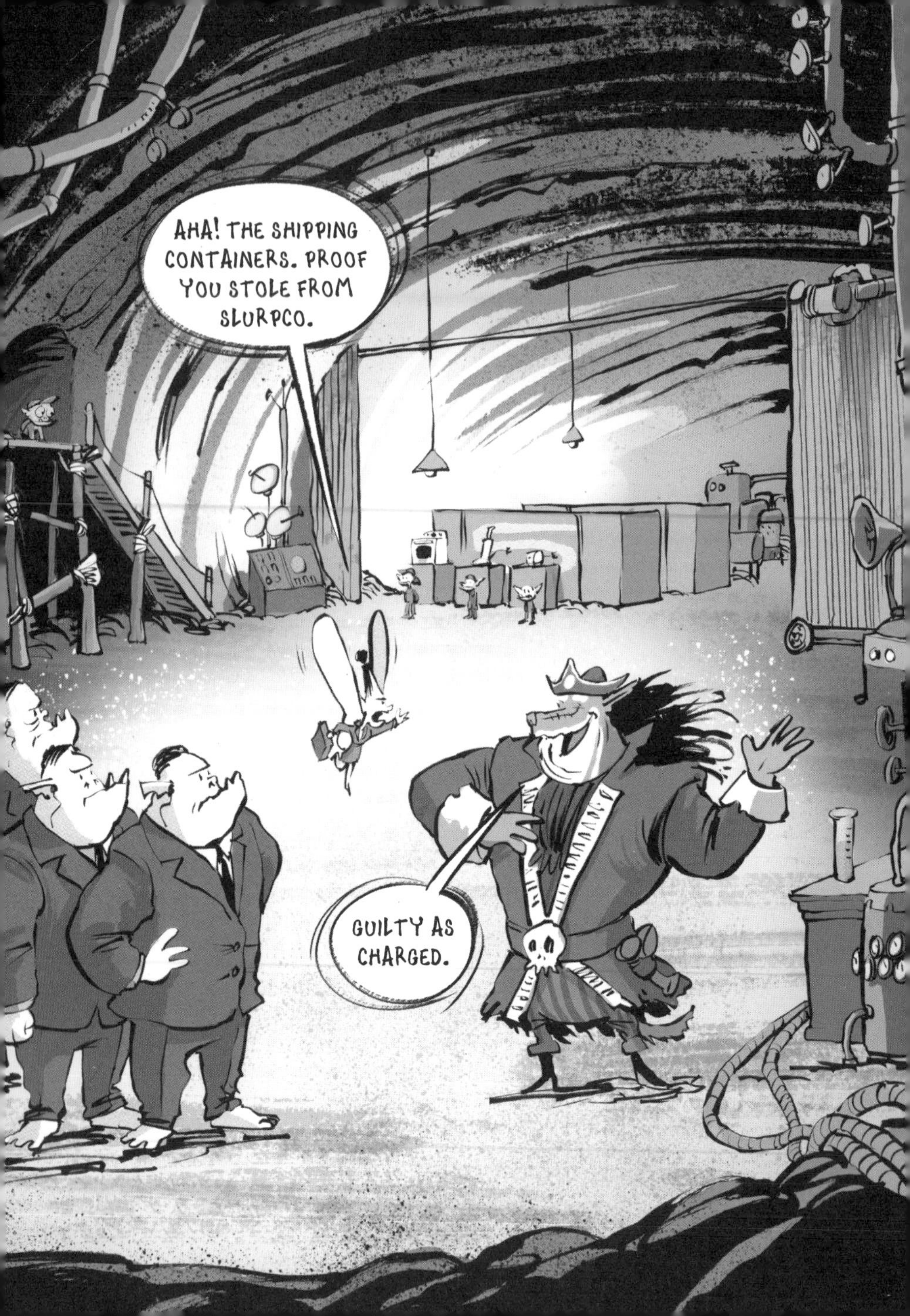
AHA! THE SHIPPING CONTAINERS. PROOF YOU STOLE FROM SLURPCO.
GUILTY AS CHARGED.

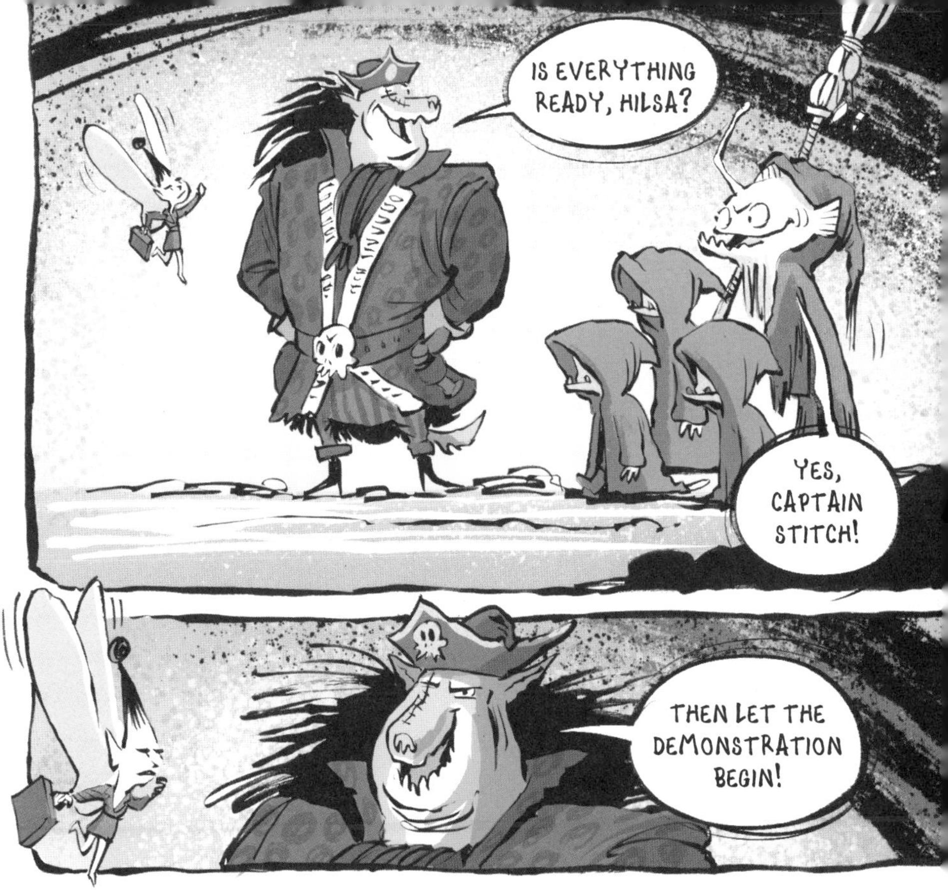
IS EVERYTHING READY, HILSA?
YES, CAPTAIN STITCH!
THEN LET THE DEMONSTRATION BEGIN!

My claws dug into the rocky ledge. My brain struggled to take in what I was seeing. Sitting in front of me were the shipping containers from the deck of the *Wave Dancer*. This was where they had ended up after Hilsa made them vanish. The appliances sitting on the pedestals must have been the contents of the containers. And I'd bet a month's supply of choco-slug cookies that the goblins standing next to the pedestals were from Fishers Hollow. But what really gripped my scales were the three cloaked figures next to Hilsa. Was one of them Gwena? Were the other two her father and brother?

Captain Stitch grinned like a game-show host. "Before you, Ms. Ballaworth, is a selection of SlurpCo Industries' finest products for the home." Stitch held up a tiny, dark square no bigger than a coin. "Inside each of these products we have installed one of these amazing computer chips. Designed by my chief wizard, Hilsa, this little chip promises to unlock a world of wealth and power for your company."

Mirella eyed the captain with skepticism. "This I'd like to see."

"You will." Stitch passed the computer chip to Hilsa.

Hilsa placed the chip on the pedestal in front of the three cloaked monsters.

"Right now that is an ordinary computer chip," the wizard said. "A piece of simple technology found in everyday devices like your appliances. But when you combine this tech with magic, you can turn those devices into money-making machines for SlurpCo."

"Impossible," Mirella scoffed. "Our labs have worked on combining magic and technology for years.

The results were nothing but explosions and disaster. In fact, we very nearly blew up all of Rockfall Mountain before we shut down all the research."

"Yes, but the brilliant Hilsa has found a way," Stitch said. "Watch."

Hilsa raised his staff over his head and uttered words of magic. Light streamed from the wizard's staff, engulfed the cloaked monsters in front of him and flowed into the chip on the pedestal. The chip briefly glowed before the magic light faded. Hilsa lowered his staff. The three cloaked monsters collapsed to the ground.

"The process is quite a drain on the conduits," Hilsa said. "What is important, however, is the end result."

"As you can see, the chip has been transformed." Stitch held up the chip for Mirella to see. It now sparkled with the purple light that could only mean one thing.

"Magic!" Mirella gasped. "You successfully mixed technology with magic?"

"We did." Stitch beamed. "We call it MagTech! One of these magically enhanced chips has been installed into each of these household devices."

"Why?" Mirella asked. "Whatever for?"

"Officially, it will make the devices more energy efficient. Unofficially, it does something much better. Watch and see." Stitch turned to face the goblins standing next to the appliances. "Get to work, you layabouts!"

The goblins began using the devices. The poor monsters were clearly too terrified to disobey the pirate captain. One goblin turned on the vacuum cleaner and began pushing it back and forth on the cavern floor. Another popped slices of bread into the toaster and began making toast. Mirella watched them all with growing confusion.

"This is your plan to make SlurpCo money?"

"No. This is." Stitch held in his hands a small metal box the size of a TV remote. The box had a short antenna and a microphone. The pirate captain spoke into the microphone. "Stop."

Immediately the goblins froze in place. They stood as still as statues.

"Turn and face me," Stitch said.

The goblins spun to face him.

"Raise your right arm over your head," he commanded.

The goblins obeyed.

"Is this meant to impress me?" Mirella scowled. "Your mage has them under a spell. Simple wizardry."

"It *is* wizardry, but it is not simple." Stitch waved a paw toward the SlurpCo guards lining the wall. "See for yourself."

A second group of goblins with more appliances stood near the guards. I'd been too focused on Hilsa and Stitch to see them arrive. The goblins stood with their right arms raised. And they weren't alone. The SlurpCo guards also stood motionless, right arms raised over their heads.

"Put your arms down!" Mirella buzzed furiously. The guards didn't move. The blaze fairy turned on Stitch. "What have you done to them?"

"We've turned them into obedient consumers of SlurpCo products," Stitch said. "Inside each appliance is a MagTech chip loaded with a command spell." The pirate captain held up the box with the microphone. "With this little controller, you can activate that spell and control the actions of anyone within range of a SlurpCo device containing a MagTech chip. Launching a new gizmo and want to ensure it's a hit? Simply use this box to command your customers to buy it, whether they need it or not. They will dutifully obey and make your sales soar."

Mirella looked down her tiny nose at Stitch. "And what happens when the spell wears off and they return their unwanted products?"

"They won't," Hilsa answered. "I've designed the command spell to ensure there is no buyer's remorse. Customers will remain convinced they need your product and simply not bother to return it."

"You'll never have a failed product launch again, Mirella," Stitch said. "Every new SlurpCo toaster, TV or washing machine will be a smash hit! Just tell your customers to go out and buy, buy, buy, and watch SlurpCo's profits grow, grow, grow."

"It'll never work." Mirella shook her tiny head. "Combining magic and technology is illegal. We would never be able to sell our appliances if monsters knew what was inside. And if we didn't tell folks about the chips, it wouldn't be long before some tinkering troll found one in their toaster and started asking questions. There's no way your plan will work while combining magic and technology is against the law."

"Then change the law." Stitch grinned. "If a SlurpCo blender can tell a customer what to buy, it can tell a citizen who to vote for. The perfect gift for the politician in your pocket, er, life."

Mirella buzzed around in a tight circle, thinking. "Mayor Grimlock could use this to help him win the next election."

"All he'd have to do is change the law." Stitch stepped closer to the blaze fairy, looking like a dragon ready to pounce. "And, as you said, never underestimate what Mayor Grimlock can do."

"Why do this for SlurpCo, Captain Stitch?" Mirella asked. "I thought pirates only looked out for themselves."

"We do, Mirella," Stitch said. "Our original plan was to do all this without telling SlurpCo. My crew would have made millions by commanding those fools in Slick City to hand over their life savings. By the time the MagTech chips were discovered, we would have been long gone. But since you found our little operation so quickly, I decided to cut you in on the action. Take the appliances and use the MagTech chips to make SlurpCo's sales soar. You'll get all the credit. Who knows? You could be promoted and running the company within a few years." The pirate captain licked his snout. "In return, you drop the charges of theft against us and give us a slice of the profits."

The blaze fairy buzzed around the cavern, inspecting the appliances closely. After a minute she stopped in front of Stitch.

"Very well." Mirella's eyes burned into Stitch. "But if you breathe a word of this to anyone, you and your crew of furballs will take the blame for it all."

"We have a deal!" Stitch clapped his paws in delight. "This calls for a celebratory feast!"

I was numb from snout to tail. Stitch had just confessed to stealing the ships, yet he was going to get away with it. Not only that, but he had just made a deal worth a lot of money with the monsters he'd stolen from! Mirella might be willing to let Stitch go for piles of cash, but I definitely wasn't. My heart pounded at the injustice of it all. My friend Gwena and the rest of the villagers were still held captive. And back home, Tank's mom was still out of her job as harbor master. Stitch and SlurpCo might think the case was closed, but for this detective, it was still wide open.

CHAPTER FIFTEEN
Dream Walking

The rest of the day was a blur.

After Chef Gunzik nearly pulled my scales off for taking so long with the bargle berries, I scrubbed dishes and mopped floors until the evening shift took over. The whole time, my mind ran in circles trying to figure out a way to stop Stitch and Mirella and free Gwena and the other goblins. At the end of the day, I was still a detective without a plan. I filled in Tank and Aleetha as I forced down another bowl of watery gruel.

"So when SlurpCo found out Stitch's plan, he cut them in on the action and invited Mirella to be the guest of honor at tonight's feast," Tank said when I had finished bringing them up to speed. "He's a quick thinker. I'll give the mutthead that much."

"Mirella will be sitting with Stitch and Hilsa in the rooftop dining room." I had overheard the dinner details from Gunzik in the kitchen. "Apparently, it provides an excellent view of the bay."

Aleetha rolled her eyes. "That's good to know."

Tank dunked a chunk of rock-hard bread into her lukewarm soup. "Why don't we find Mirella and tell her how Stitch is holding us all prisoner? She'll remember us from the harbor master's office."

"Mirella doesn't care about any of that," I said. "She's only interested in making more money for SlurpCo. Even if it means lying, cheating and breaking the law."

"That's the only way you become an executive in a company like that," Aleetha said. "Besides, if Mirella did see us, she definitely wouldn't want us returning to Slick City to expose their plan to secretly put MagTech chips in new SlurpCo products."

Tank swallowed her bread. "So we stick to our original plan and search for the door we saw in our dreams?"

"And hope it leads us back to Fang Harbor," I said. "It's a long shot, but it's the only shot we have."

After dinner Aleetha led us through the tunnels under Stitch's mansion. The big feast was just getting started, so the tunnels were empty. All the kobolds were up top with their captain. The only kobolds we saw were ones late for the party, and they were too focused on getting up to the roof in time to stuff their snouts to bother us. After a short while Aleetha stopped at a spot where tunnels branched off in three directions.

"I passed this way earlier today," she said. "Look familiar?"

One tunnel climbed upward, and another sloped downward. Between them a third tunnel stayed level and continued straight ahead.

"This is where my dream began," I said. "I was facing three tunnels just like this."

Aleetha's eyes brightened. "That's what I was hoping you'd say. My dream started here too."

"And mine," Tank said. "I walked down the middle tunnel."

"So did I," I said.

"That makes three of us." The lava elf marched down the middle passage. "Let's go find this door!"

I hurried after her with a spring in my step. But by the time we'd passed the tenth door without a match from our shared dream, my steps had become pretty much free of any bounce, and I had lost hope.

"This is crazy," I said. "I don't remember walking this far in my dream."

"It was a dream, Fizz." Tank sighed. "I don't think it's going to be an exact match. But I agree, we have walked a long way."

Just a little farther.

I moaned. "Okay, Aleetha, whatever you say. I'll go a little farther."

Aleetha's eyes narrowed. "I didn't say that. I thought you did."

"I heard that too," Tank said. "But it was in my head."

A little farther. Hurry.

"There it is again!" I said.

The words echoed in my mind, but each of us heard it as if the speaker were next to us.

"It's the voice from the dream." Aleetha looked down the tunnel. "We must be getting close."

Aleetha ran ahead, Tank close on her heels. My friends clearly didn't think it was strange we'd all heard a voice in our heads—at the same time! My tail twinged with doubt. Who was behind the voice?

Was it a message from home, like the news reports we'd watched in the lighthouse? Was it one of Hilsa's tricks? Before I could voice my doubts, Aleetha's voice rang out from around the corner.

"We found it!"

I rushed to catch up with my friends, letting my doubts fall away.

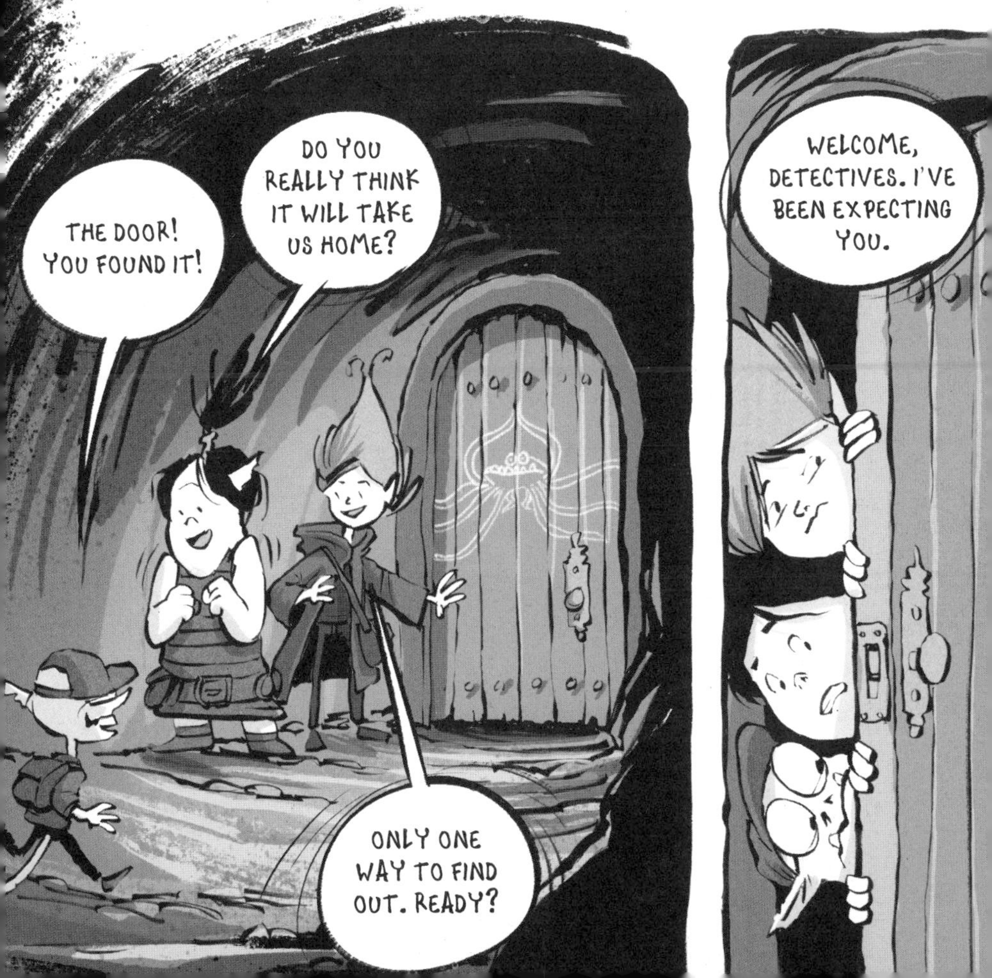
THE DOOR! YOU FOUND IT!
DO YOU REALLY THINK IT WILL TAKE US HOME?
ONLY ONE WAY TO FIND OUT. READY?
WELCOME, DETECTIVES. I'VE BEEN EXPECTING YOU.

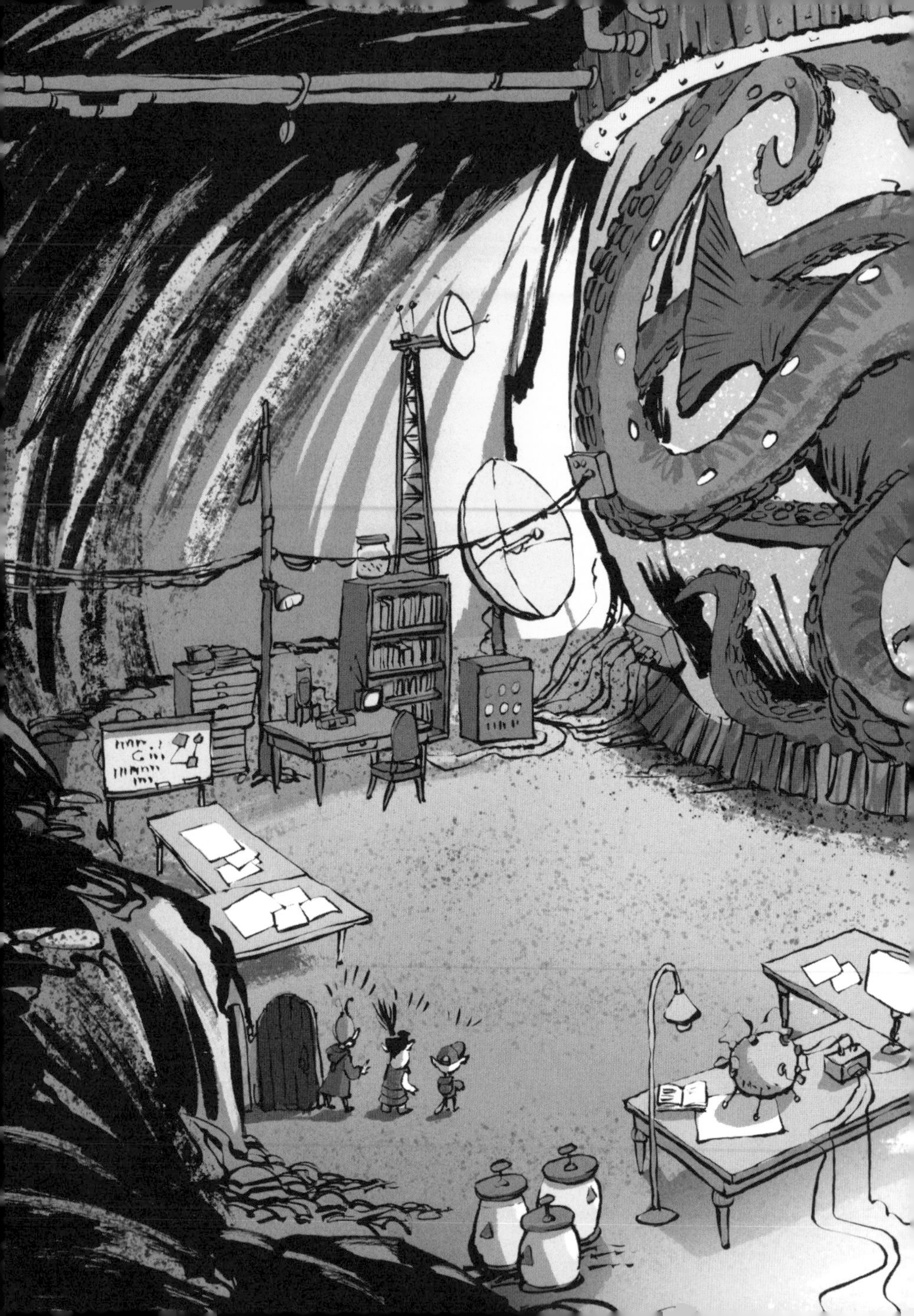

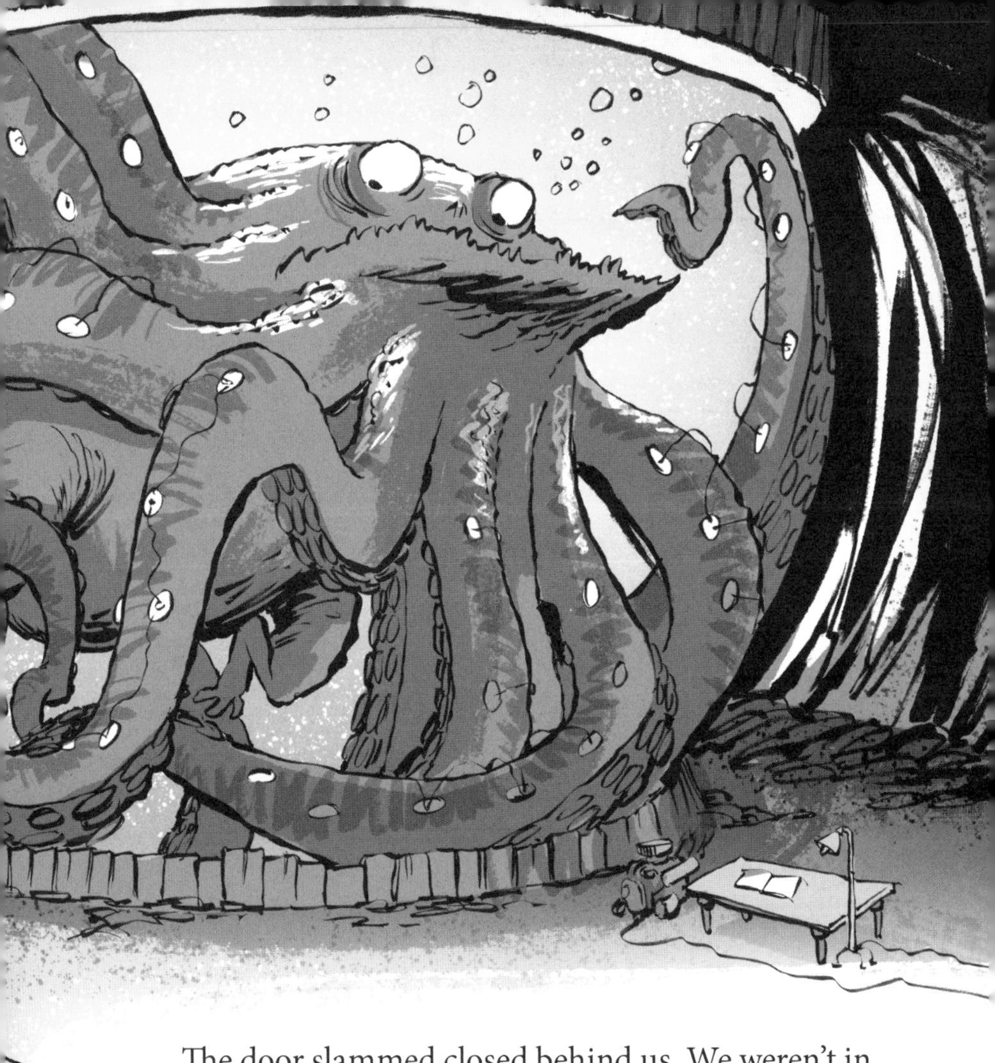

The door slammed closed behind us. We weren't in Fang Harbor. We were still in Howler's Bay and still in big trouble.

Another large cavern opened around us. Rough stone walls on either side stretched off into darkness.

The cavern ceiling was high overhead. There was enough room in here for a dragon to land. Tables, some covered in thick books, tools and sharp blades, dotted the room. The place looked like another one of Hilsa's demented workshops. Looming in front of us was the subject of the wizard's experiments, the source of all our strife and the reason we weren't in Slick City anymore.

The giant ship-stealing meglohydra Gwena called Pequod floated in a glass tank the size of city hall. A pair of monstrous eyes stared out from behind the glass. The creature's gaze didn't fill me with terror as I had expected. There was something else in those eyes.

"It looks sad," Aleetha said.

"Or hungry." Tank worked the handle of the door without luck. "And the door is locked."

"Of course it is," I moaned. "We shouldn't have come here."

But I am very glad you did.

Pequod's words filled my head as if they were my own thoughts. The others heard them too. It was the voice from our dreams, and the one that had led us to this door.

Do not be afraid. The door is locked to prevent the

guards from returning. I sent them away to join Stitch's feast, so that you could come to me.

"You sent the guards away?" Aleetha moved slowly toward the water tank. She looked at Pequod like she was trying to solve a tricky math problem. "How did you do that?"

The same way I brought you here. The creature's words filled my mind. *I convinced them to leave, just as I convinced you to come.*

"Through our dreams and thoughts." Aleetha nodded. "That's why there are no kobolds around here."

I do not wish to harm you. I need your help.

"Our help?!" I growled. "You're the one stealing ships for Captain Fur-Face and his goons. You nearly killed us with your thrashing and smashing tentacles. Why should we help you?"

Because I can take you home.

That got my attention.

And if you help me, you will be able to rescue Gwena and stop Stitch's plan to flood Slick City with MagTech appliances.

"You're in a tank of water!" I said. "How do you know about that stuff?"

A deep gurgling sound came from the tank. Pequod's tentacles swirled in the water, creating large bubbles. It took me a second to realize the meglohydra was laughing.

I know all that happens on this island. I've watched the three of you, Fizz Marlow, Tatanka Wrenchlin and Aleetha Cinderwisp, since you fell onto the deck of the Wave Dancer.

"You picked us up and dumped us on that ship!" I said. "That was your fault."

"Fizz!" Aleetha growled.

Pequod didn't seem bothered by my pointing out the truth. The meglohydra's calm voice filled my mind again.

It was an accident, but now I see it might have been destiny. That is why I led you to Gwena.

"You put the image of the cave drawing in our minds!" Tank said. "And the rocketboard that led Fizz to overhear Mirella and Stitch's plan."

"And you sent the dream that led us here," I said. "How?"

I will explain. We do not have much time. You must act quickly, if we are to succeed.

Aleetha pulled out two chairs from a nearby table and slid one next to me.

"Sit down, Fizz," she hissed. "And try not to argue with the meglohydra that could fry our brains."

I sat down and kept my snout shut. Pequod's long tentacles drifted slowly through the water as his words flowed into our minds.

Hilsa captured me many months ago. He has found a way to combine magic with technology to control my mind and my actions. He forced me to steal those ships from your harbor.

"How can he do that?" Tank asked. "You're so big, you could crush him with one tentacle."

Don't think I haven't tried. He is able to take over my neural network and control my mind through these discs on my body.

"The density-inverters?" Tank pointed to the flashing discs dotting the meglohydra's body. "They decrease your mass and make it easier for Hilsa to teleport you. Like he did with the shipping containers on the *Wave Dancer*. But the discs aren't designed for mind control."

"They could be if Hilsa put MagTech chips in them," I said. "Just like the toasters and vacuum cleaners."

Exactly, Fizz. The chips inside the discs force me to follow Hilsa's commands. The density-inverters allow Hilsa to teleport me in and out of your harbor. In order to do this, however, the wave mage also needs his staff and the ones he calls conduits.

"Gwena and her family!" I said.

They are the ones who can combine magic and technology. Hilsa merely controls them with his staff of shells. Without the staff, his power falls away. Even with three conduits, Hilsa struggles to control me. Not only am I large, but I am also very smart. Hilsa is able to take control of my mind and bend my actions to his will. But I soon break free. When he is not forcing me to steal ships, he locks me in this tank. But my mind is able to wander free.

"Free to sneak into monsters' dreams," I said.

And into the minds of Stitch and his band of kobolds. I controlled the minds of my guards to clear a path to this room so you could find me. I will do the same to the kobolds at Stitch's feast. You should be able to sneak by them unnoticed and put my plan into action.

"What exactly is your plan?" Aleetha asked.

First, you are going to set me free...

We listened as Pequod laid out his plan. To be honest, I didn't hear much beyond the words *set me free*. This meglohydra had smothered giant ships and nearly crushed my friends and me. Who knew what he would do if we released him? What if he snatched us in his tentacles for a light snack before swimming away from Hook Island? Maybe he was controlling our minds right now and tricking us into setting him free.

My claws curled at the thought of all that could go wrong. But if we wanted a chance to return home and stop Stitch and Mirella, we'd have to trust the tentacles.

CHAPTER SIXTEEN
Crashing the Pirate Party

I t was time to say goodbye.

We had made our way from Pequod's room back through the tunnels and into the ship that served as Stitch's home.

The three of us huddled in the shadows at the tunnel opening, watching for kobolds. So far we had seen very few pirates. The ones we did see had let us walk right by without so much as a growl. Pequod was true to his word. Somehow he was able to control the minds of the kobolds so they didn't look twice at us.

And for our part, we kept our promise and set the meglohydra free from his tank. The whole cavern was actually under the water of the bay, not far from where Stitch's ships were anchored. There was no time to remove the density-inverters covering Pequod's massive body, but we were able to flip the switch that opened the top of his tank and watch him swim away.

Wait for my signal.

Those were his last words before disappearing into the waters of Howler's Bay. I had my doubts we'd ever see the big ball of tentacles again but Aleetha, was convinced we could trust the meglohydra. Only time and tentacles would tell.

"Okay, this is where we split up." Aleetha turned to Tank. "Think you can remember the way to where the Fishers Hollow goblins are being held?"

Tank tapped the side of her head with a finger. "Pequod planted the route right in here."

"Good. Bring them down to the docks," Aleetha said. "After that, you know what to do."

"Are we certain the SlurpCo containers are down there?" I asked.

"According to Pequod," Tank said, "the kobolds just finished filling them with MagTech appliances. And now the containers are just sitting there, ready for Hilsa to zap them back onto the *Wave Dancer* after the feast."

"Tentacle-Face better be telling the truth," I grumbled. "How do we know he didn't just swim away and leave us here for good?"

"We don't," Aleetha said. "But if he really just wanted to escape, he could have used his mind tricks to get some kobolds to open his tank. Following his plan is our best chance of rescuing Gwena and her family, getting back home and exposing SlurpCo for being jerks. And that, hopefully, will be enough to get Tank's mom's job back."

A cheer erupted on the deck of the ship. Stitch's feast was in full swing above us.

"Time to go." Tank punched my shoulder playfully. "See you later, buddy. And don't worry—Pequod will come through."

My friend hurried back down the tunnel and disappeared into the shadows. Aleetha stuck her head around the corner.

"The way is clear."

The lava elf slipped out of the tunnel and into the ship without another word. I followed her to the bottom of the steps leading up to the deck. From here the sounds of shouting, barking and general chaos were louder. Ice gripped my scales. We were walking into a kobold party, and the only things keeping us safe were our own wits and a promise from a talking meglohydra.

"Once we get up top, we'll need to find a spot to hide and then look for Gwena and her brother and father," Aleetha said. "We need to get them away from Hilsa."

I nodded. "Hopefully Pequod's distraction will be big enough to keep Stitch and his pirates busy while we separate Hilsa from his precious conduits."

"I don't think that meglohydra does anything that isn't big." Aleetha stepped aside and nodded at me. "After you, detective."

With me in the lead, we walked up the final set of steps.

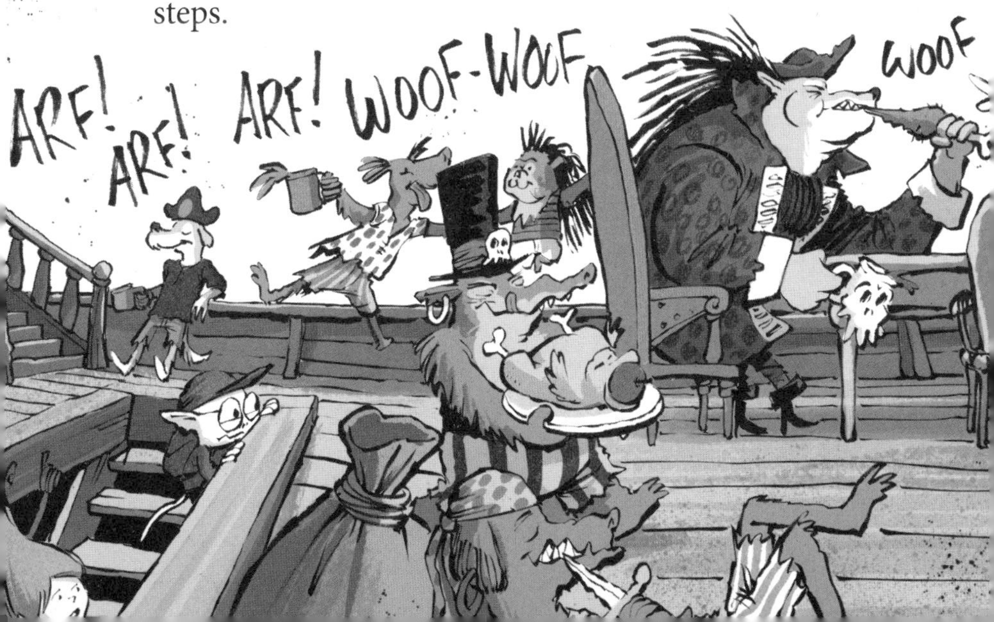
ARF!
ARF!
ARF!
WOOF-WOOF
WOOF

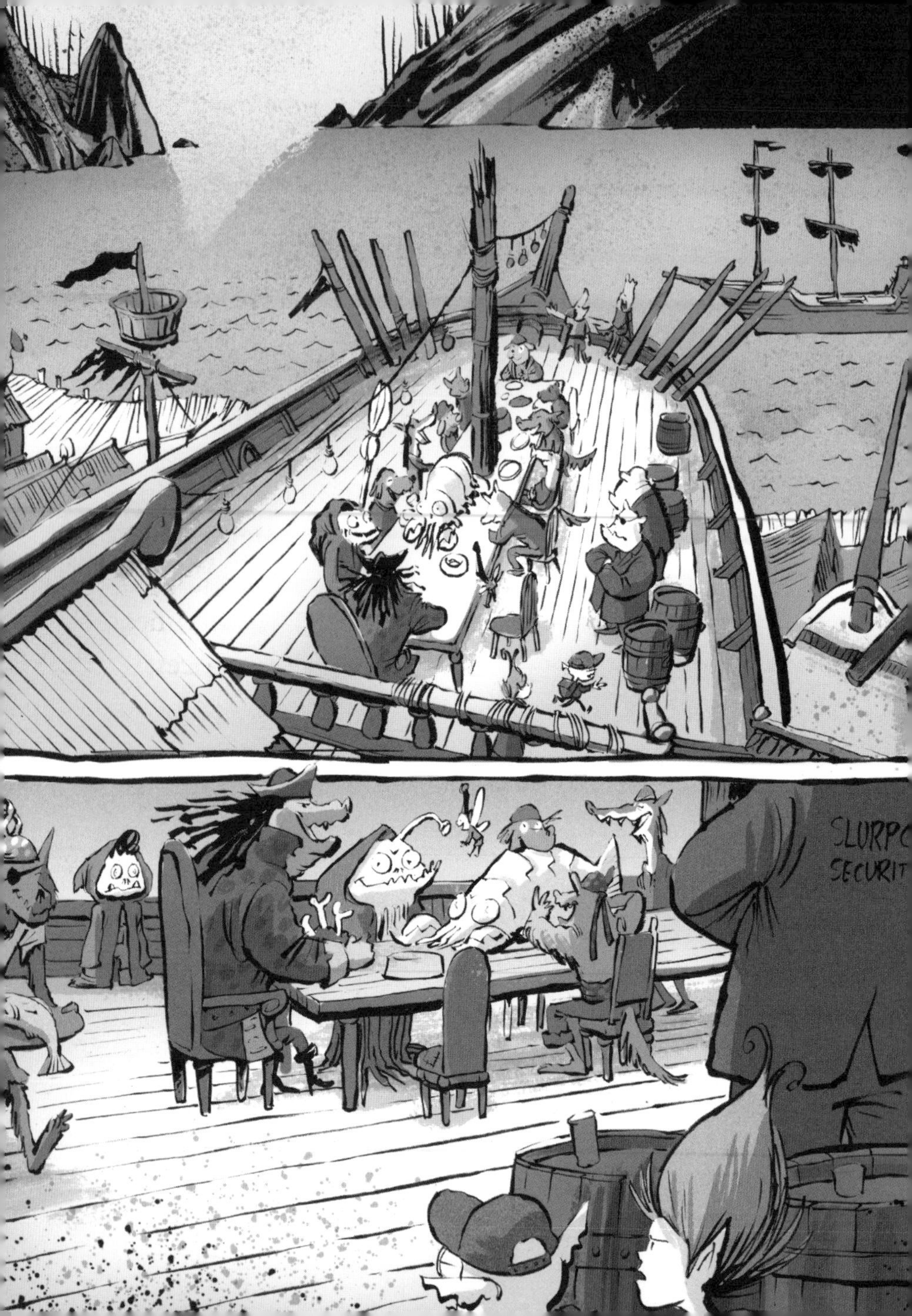
SLURPO
SECURIT

Whether because of Pequod's mind-control powers or the delicious feast, Stitch and his goons didn't notice us. Gwena and her brother and father stood near Hilsa, still as statues. From where I was hiding I could see Gwena's face under her hood. She stared blankly at the ship's wooden deck. It was clear Hilsa had her under his control. Breaking her free of that control was the key to getting us home. If Hilsa couldn't use his conduits, then he couldn't control Pequod. And that left Pequod free to, in his words, *settle things once and for all.* As I sat squished into my hiding spot with Aleetha, I really hoped settling things didn't mean crushing innocent goblin detectives in the process.

Captain Stitch thumped his fist on the table and got to his feet.

"Quiet down, you filthy dogs!" One by one the pirates stopped their yapping and faced their captain. Stitch raised a mug filled with frothy liquid. "I'd like to propose a toast!"

The kobolds howled with approval and grabbed their mugs. Stitch turned to Mirella Ballaworth, who buzzed above her seat, quietly sipping from a thimble-sized mug. The SlurpCo executive smiled uncomfortably under the gaze of so many pirates.

Behind her, the SlurpCo security guards stood ready for any pirate treachery.

"To Ms. Ballaworth from SlurpCo!" Stitch continued, mug raised high. "A blaze fairy who knows a good deal when she sees one. With my genius and SlurpCo's business skills, we're going to be hauling in heaps of loot for a long time!"

The kobolds exploded with howls, barks and cheers. Kobolds jumped to their feet and danced on the table. Soon the whole table was a cacophony of singing, shouting and laughing.

In the chaos, no one noticed the water churning in Howler's Bay. The waves grew larger by the second, rocking the ships anchored in the harbor.

Then Deekin wiped his crooked snout, looked out over the harbor and frowned. "Er, Captain. What's going on down there?"

Stitch turned in time to see a wall of water burst up from the bay. Behind the wave, a tentacled terror rose up.

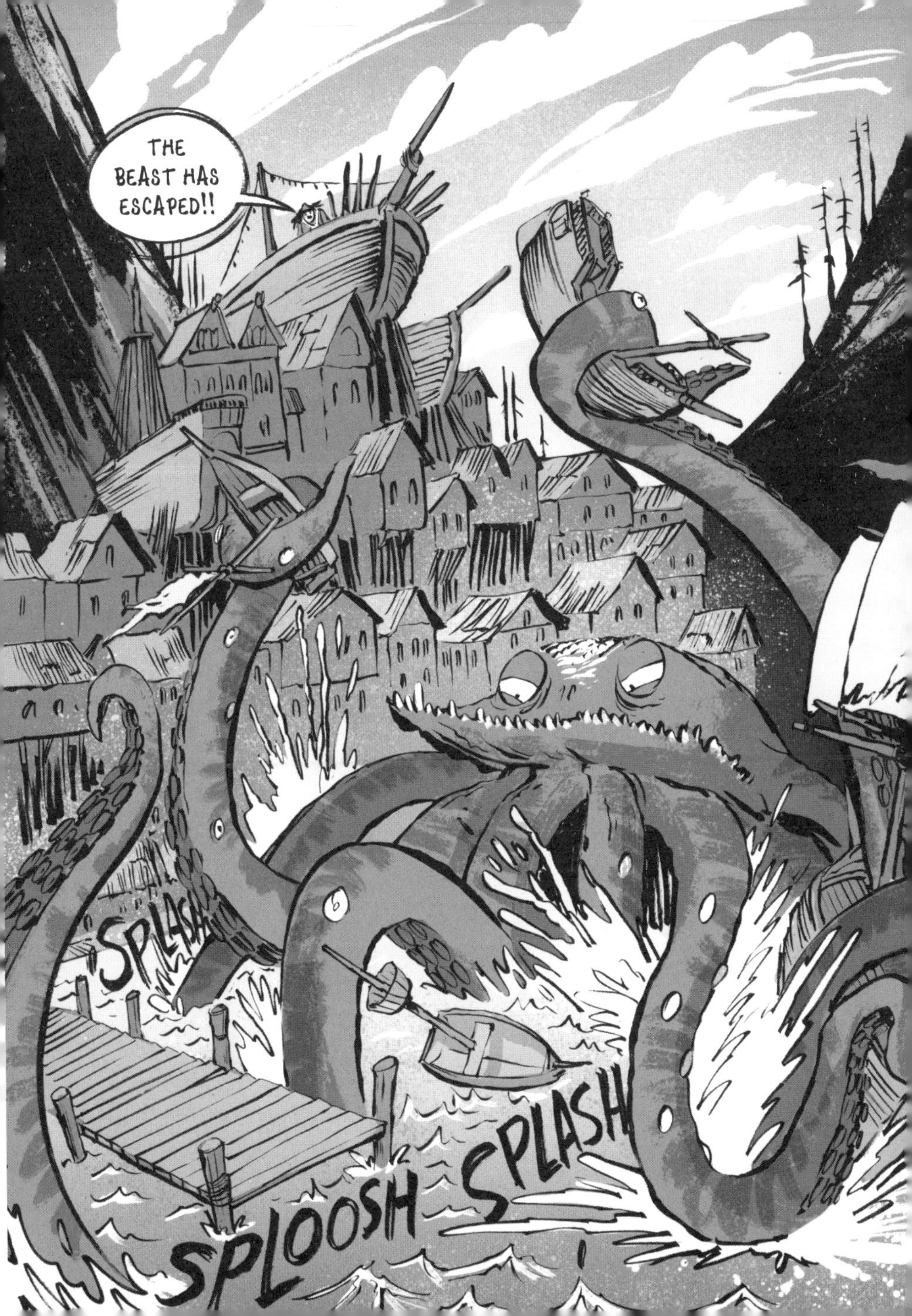
THE BEAST HAS ESCAPED!!
SPLASH
SPLOOSH
SPLASH

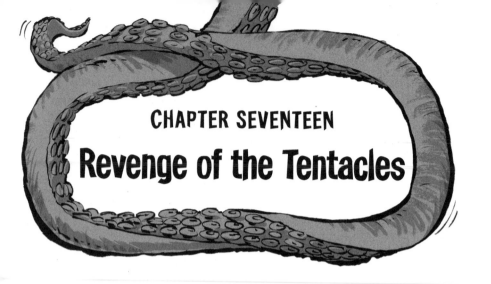

CHAPTER SEVENTEEN
Revenge of the Tentacles

Chaos of a different kind erupted on the deck of Stitch's mansion.

The kobolds' laughter and singing turned into screams and shouting as Pequod smashed the pirate ships anchored in the harbor.

"Party's over, lads!" Stitched hollered over the noise. "Get back to your stations and stop that beast!"

"That's our signal!" Aleetha jabbed me with her elbow. "You know what to do."

She scrambled out from her hiding spot and into the crowd of panicked kobolds. I followed, half a step behind her. Around us, the pirates ran in all directions as they raced to follow their captain's orders.

I had to hand it to Pequod. The meglohydra knew how to create a distraction. His tentacles were causing mayhem on the water and on the land. He had plucked one of the smaller pirate ships from the water and was shaking it like a baby's rattle. Two other tentacles swept through the streets of Howler's Bay, crushing buildings and flattening shops. Monsters poured out of the buildings, escaping the giant creature's revenge.

Aleetha and I hurried to the front of the ship, where Stitch watched the destruction unfold with Hilsa at his side.

"Your pet is destroying my town!" Stitch screamed to the wave mage.

"Not for long," Hilsa growled. The wave mage slammed his shell-encrusted staff onto the wooden deck. "Conduits, stand ready."

Gwena, her brother and father moved to Hilsa's side like mindless robots. Hilsa was preparing to use them for his magic. We had to get Gwena away from Hilsa before he could draw on her power to control Pequod. If we could disrupt Hilsa's spell, Pequod could continue his rampage. I charged at the three conduits with Aleetha at my side.

We'd gone only a few steps when a dark, furry shape leaped in front of us.

"What are you two city rats doing up here?" Deekin snarled his crooked snout, drawing his sword. The kobold's curved blade sliced through the air a scale's width from me.

Stitch turned at the noise behind him and moved to join his first mate. "Fizz Marlow, the goblin who wouldn't quit. I'm impressed by your determination."

"Tell that to my math teacher," I snapped.

"How about we do a little division right now, and I slice you in two?" the captain growled.

At the same moment, Stitch and Deekin both swung their blades. I dove one way, and Aleetha the other. I felt the rush of air as Stitch's sword narrowly missed my tail. I scampered along the ship's deck, with Stitch only a step behind.

The captain's sword swiped at me as I ran. Each strike came closer than the last. It was only a matter of time before he took my tail as a trophy. I was scrambling up some rigging when movement on the ground below caught my eye.

Goblins were pouring into the streets of Howler's Bay. Tank had freed the villagers of Fishers Hollow and was leading them down to the shipping containers on the docks. Some had already climbed onto the containers loaded with SlurpCo products, broken open the doors and started tossing MagTech-chipped toasters, vacuums and other appliances into the harbor. Mirella Ballaworth buzzed down from where she'd been hiding and flew next to Stitch's ear.

"Stop those goblins!" She pointed to the green swarm below. "Or our deal is off!"

Stitch shook his sword at me. "This ain't over, Fizz Marlow."

The pirate captain stormed off to deal with his precious cargo with Mirella still buzzing in his ear. On the far side of ship, Aleetha was doing a good job of avoiding Deekin's swinging sword. Far below, at the shipping containers, Stitch's pirates and Mirella's SlurpCo guards moved in on the looting goblins, only to be swept aside by Pequod's massive tentacles. Having a meglohydra on our side was definitely helpful.

Not far from me, Hilsa had his conduits in place. Gwena and her brother and father stood stoically in a line, not moving. The wave mage held his staff aloft, preparing to bring Pequod back under his control. If he was able to cast his spell using the conduits, he'd regain command of Pequod, and our little revolt would be crushed. I had to get to Gwena first and disrupt Hilsa's spell.

I scrambled down the rigging and charged toward the wave mage and conduits. By this time most of the kobolds were on the ground, trying to squash the goblin uprising in the streets. My path was clear. Hilsa's words of magic grew louder as I got closer. I took a final step and leaped into the air, ready to tackle Gwena.

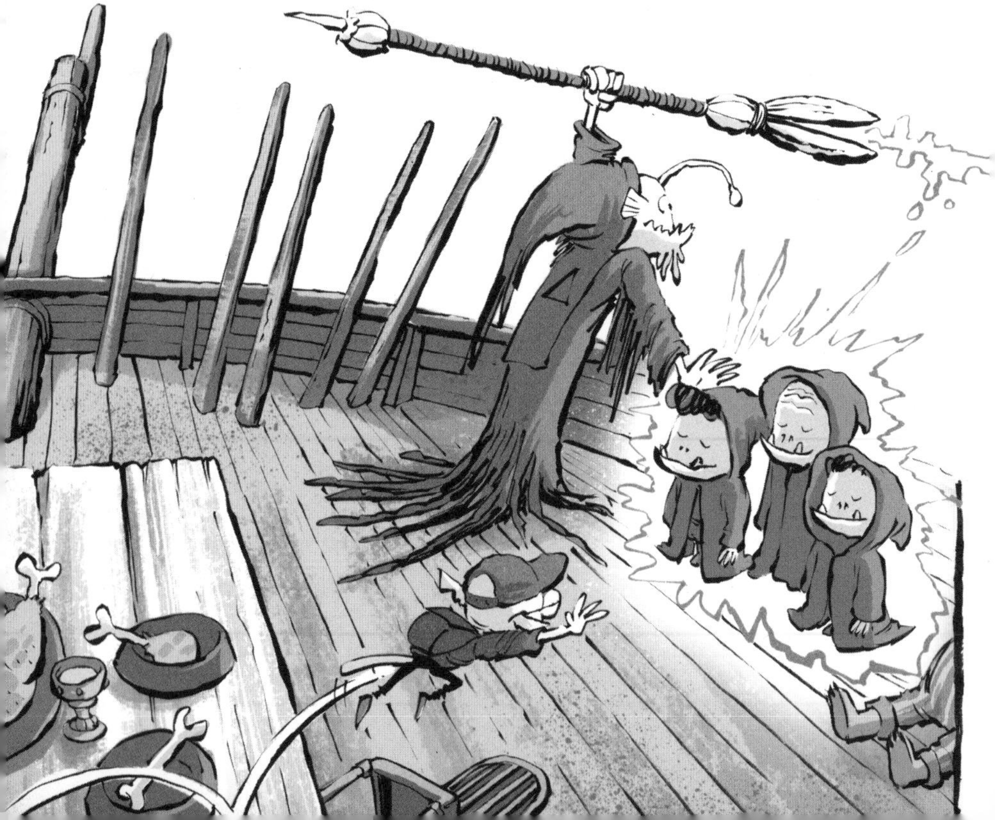

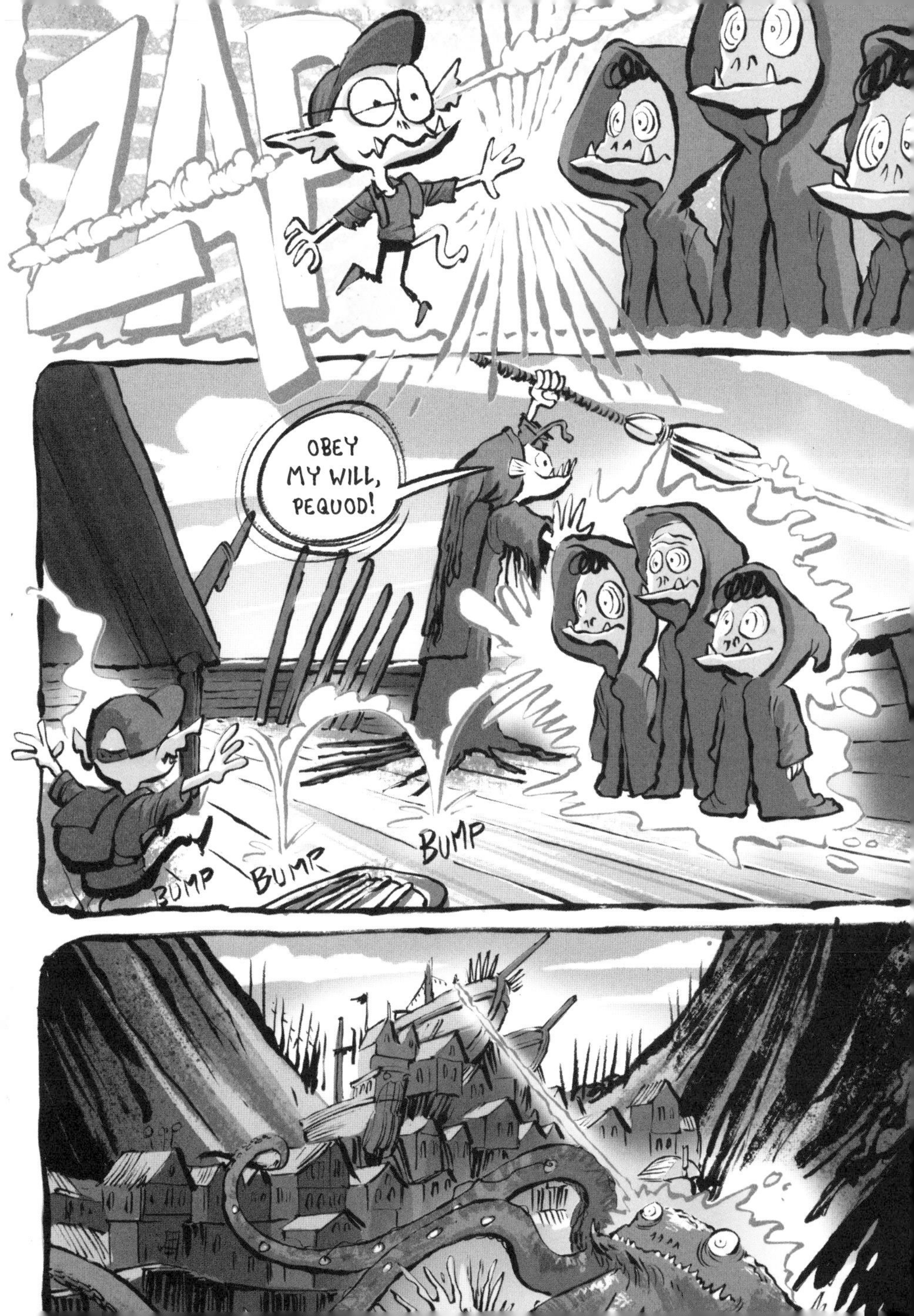
ZAP
OBEY MY WILL, PEQUOD!
BUMP
BUMP
BUMP

The jolt of magic rattled my scales and sent me crashing onto the wooden deck. Hilsa's spell soared through his conduits and across Howler's Bay, where it gripped the mind of the meglohydra. Pequod's tentacles went limp. His storm of destruction stopped in an instant. Relative calm fell over Howler's Bay. Kobold pirates emerged from their hiding places and into the streets. The SlurpCo guards picked themselves up, regrouped and turned their attention to the goblins still looting their valuable cargo. They charged at the goblins, sending them fleeing in panic.

My heart sank. Hilsa had captured our biggest advantage. Only a small portion of SlurpCo's corrupted cargo had been destroyed, and Gwena was still trapped as a mindless conduit. Our rebellion was a failure. My friends and I would be doomed to spend the rest of our days in Howler's Bay, serving a fur-brained pirate and his band of muttheads.

"Get up, Fizz!" Aleetha's voice cut through my misery. She crouched under Stitch's feasting table. I scurried to her and slid under the table. "We're running out of time," Aleetha said when I got to her. "Hilsa will have Pequod back in his tank soon.

Then Stitch and his pirates will round up the Fishers Hollow goblins."

"And that will be the end of our little rebellion," I muttered.

Hilsa stood at the edge of the ship's deck, his staff raised high and his back to us. The wave mage was fully focused on controlling Pequod in the harbor. Beside him, magic energy engulfed Gwena and her brother and father.

"I can't get near Gwena," I said. "One more zap from Hilsa's magic will melt my scales."

"I think I can break through the magic." Aleetha got to her feet like a sprinter ready to race. "I get a lot of practice getting zapped in the Shadow Tower."

Before I could stop her, the lava elf charged out from under the table and straight for Gwena. Aleetha dove into the bubble of magic that surrounded Hilsa and his conduits. As she crashed into Gwena, the air around them sizzled like someone had stuck a fork into a toaster. I guess she was right about her tolerance to getting zapped, because she didn't shoot across the deck like I had. Instead the magic around the wizards vanished. With his magic gone, Hilsa spun to face Aleetha. She lay on the deck, dazed and confused. The wave mage pointed his staff at my friend.

"The staff!" I jumped to my feet, banging my head on the underside of the table. But that didn't stop me from doing what I suddenly realized I had to do.

Pequod's words from only a few hours earlier ran through my mind. The staff gave Hilsa his ability to turn Gwena into a conduit and control Pequod. If I could get my claws on that staff and not get fried, then Hilsa's magic would be gone for good. Maybe. I raced across the deck.

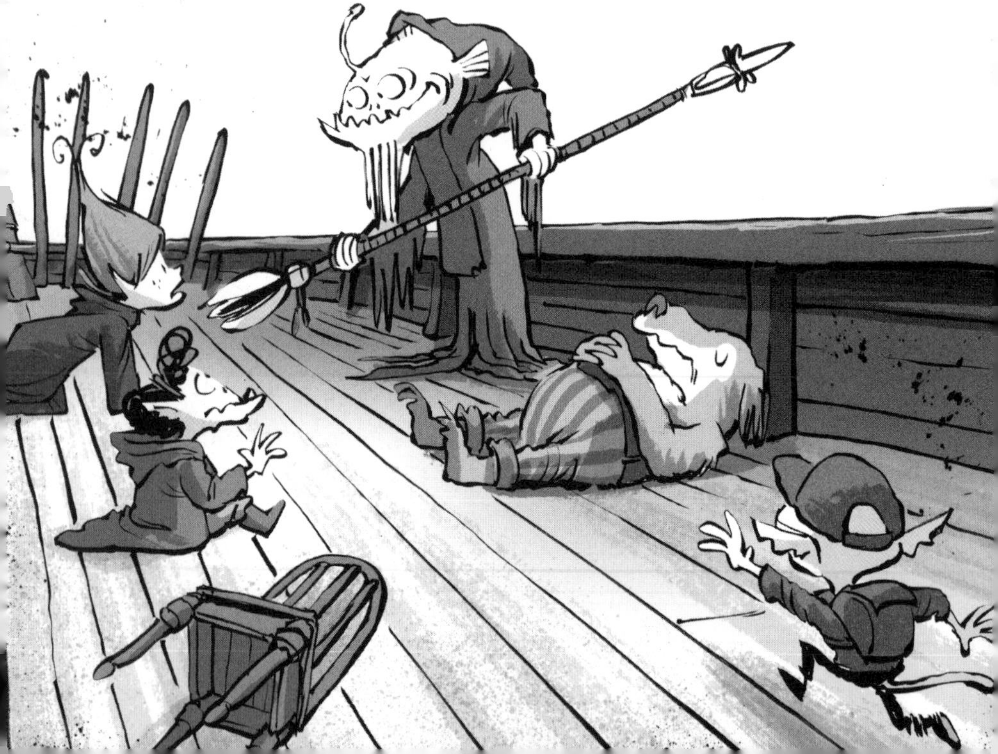

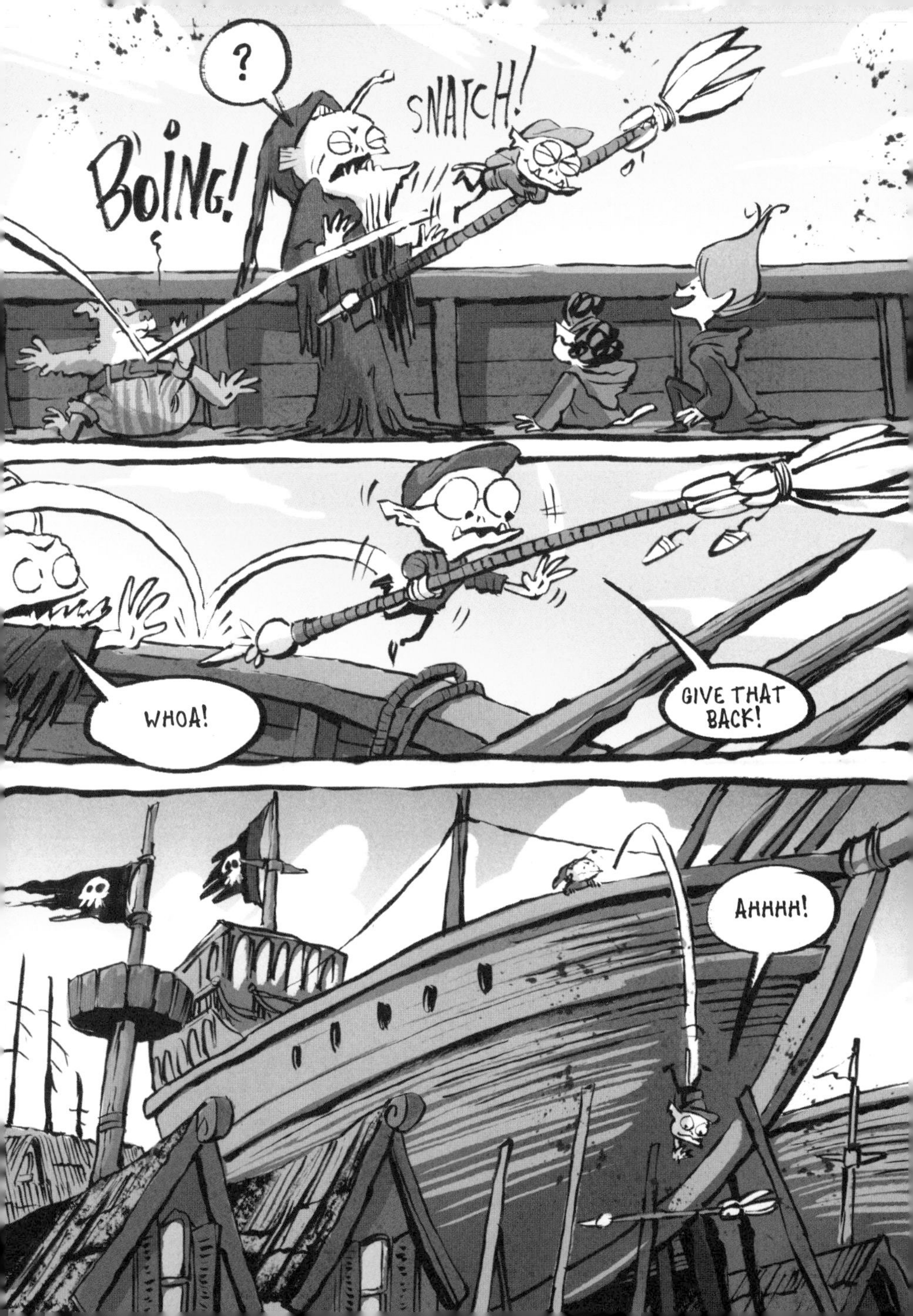
?
BOING!
SNATCH!
WHOA!
GIVE THAT BACK!
AHHHH!

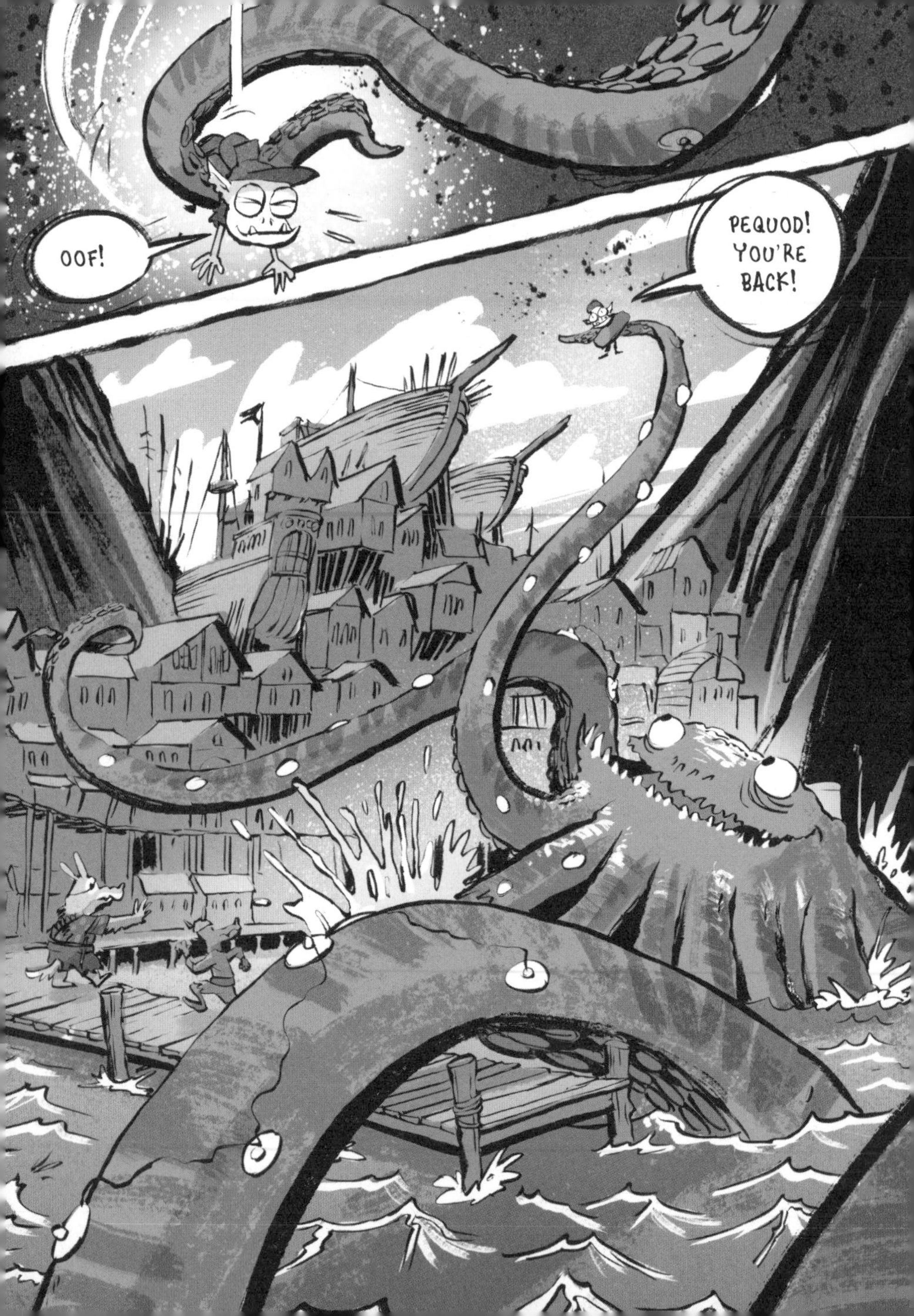
OOF!
PEQUOD! YOU'RE BACK!

The meglohydra's words filled my mind.

Thank you for helping me break free of Hilsa's grip.

Pequod carried me to safety and set me down on the ground near the shipping containers on the docks. With his staff knocked from his hands, Hilsa had lost his hold over Pequod for good.

Keep the staff safe, Fizz Marlow. I have some pirates to catch.

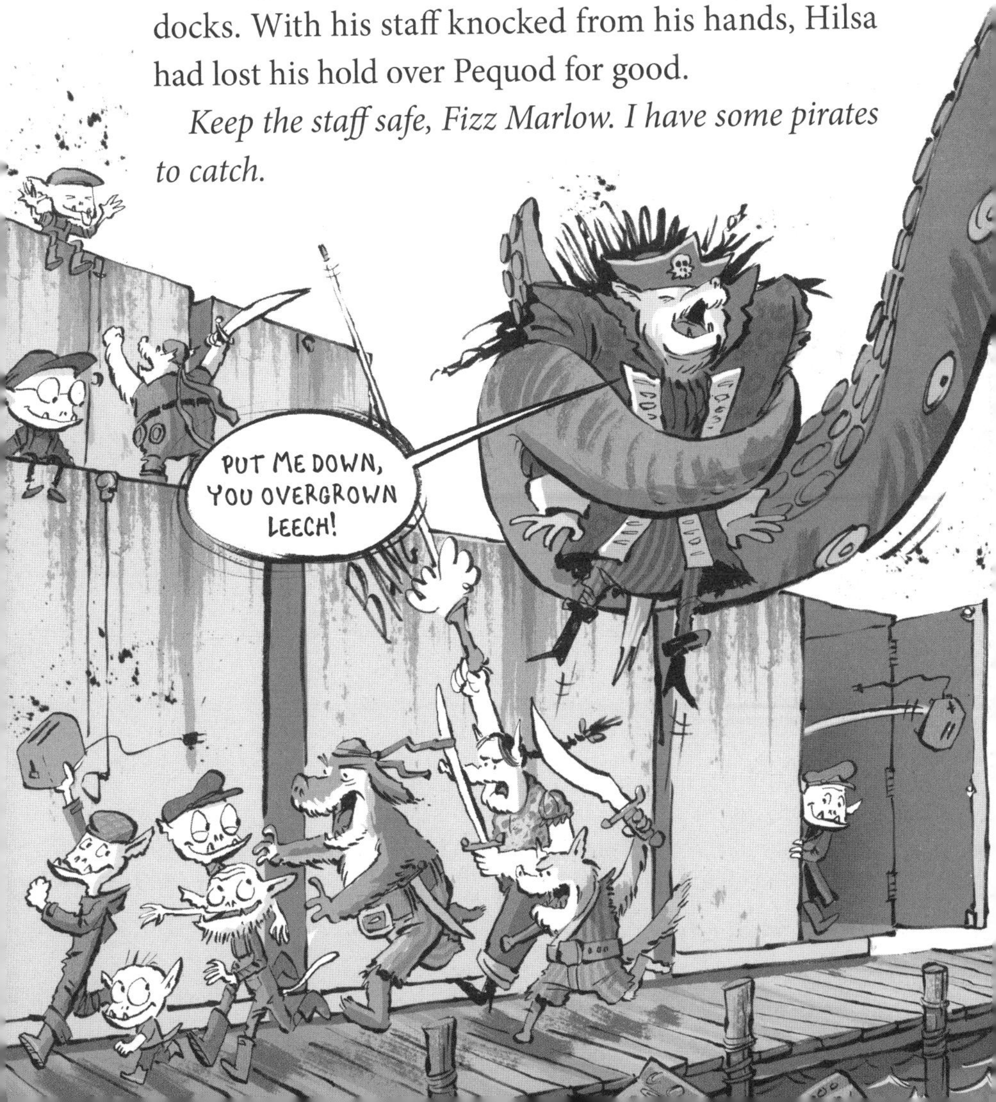
PUT ME DOWN, YOU OVERGROWN LEECH!
BANG

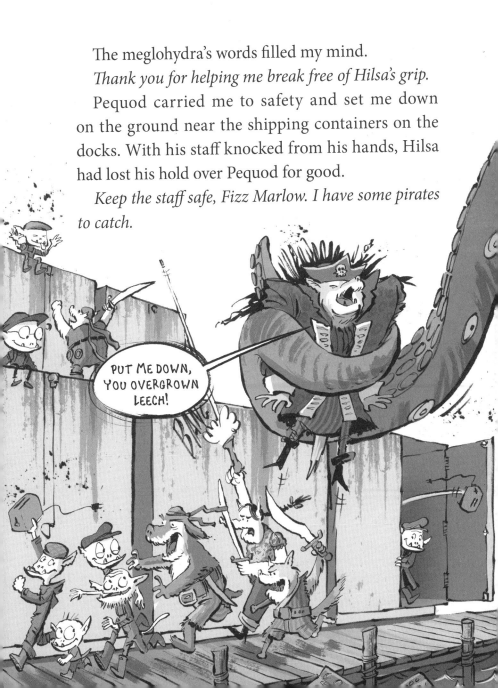

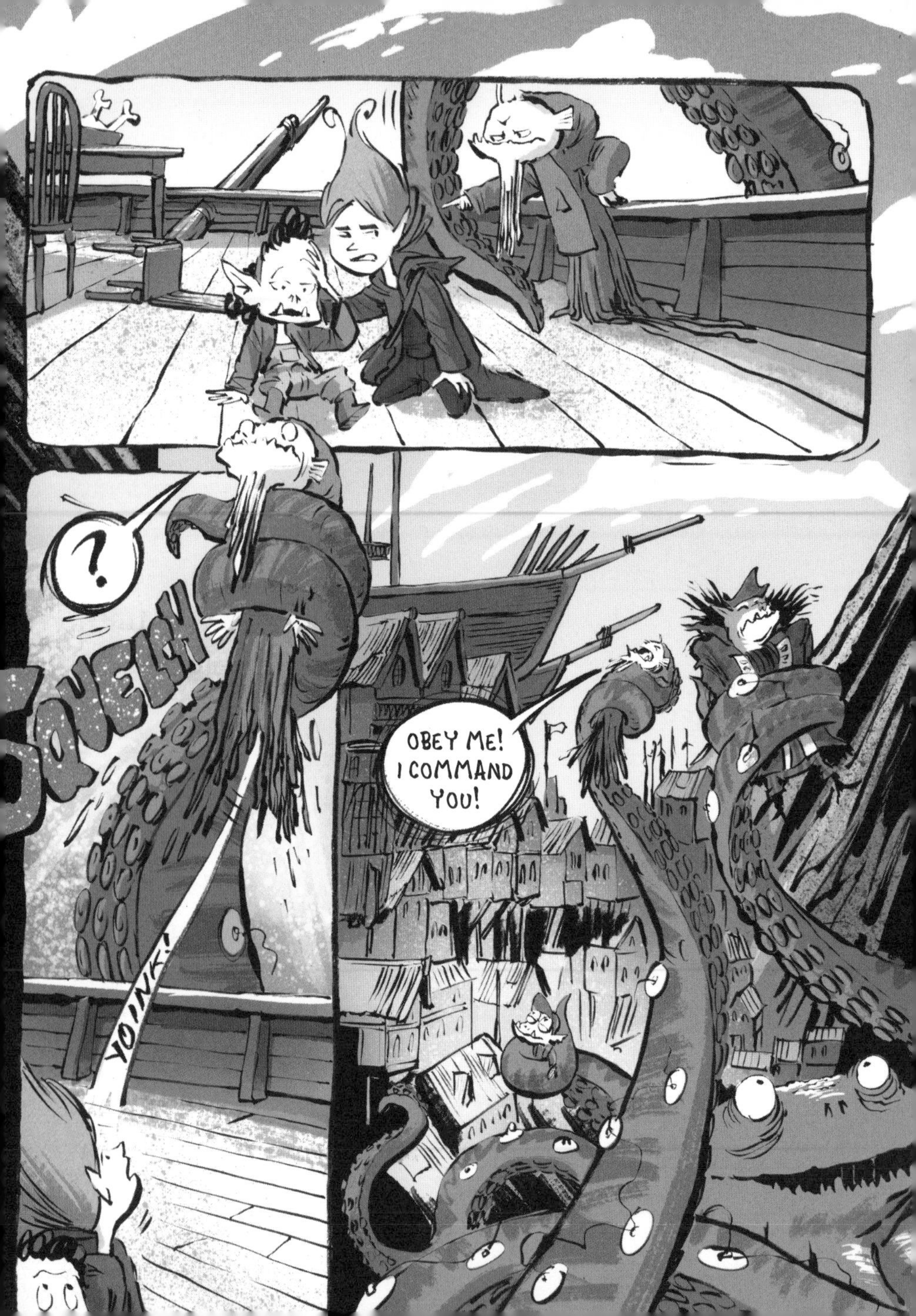
?
SQUELCH
OBEY ME! I COMMAND YOU!
YOINK!

Without his staff and the power of the conduits, Hilsa's words had no effect on the meglohydra. Stitch's howls did nothing to loosen Pequod's grip on him. On the ground, the sight of the captain and wizard dangling in the air sent panic rushing through the kobold pirates. Chaos gripped their fur and sent them fleeing Howler's Bay like slagrats fleeing a flood. The kobolds weren't the only ones leaving town.

Realizing the battle was lost, the SlurpCo security guards dropped their batons and fled. They ran past the Fishers Hollow goblins and retreating kobolds, desperate to get back to their ship waiting on the other side of the island. From the top of one of the shipping containers, a tiny voice rang out.

"Get back here, you cowards! SlurpCo's products must be saved!"

Mirella Ballaworth buzzed in angry circles above the shipping container. Her guards ignored their boss's commands and continued to flee the harbor. Mirella watched them go with growing despair. Then she noticed me watching from the ground, and despair turned to anger.

"This is all your fault, Fizz Marlow!" she hissed. "You will pay for crossing SlurpCo!"

Mirella swooped down on me like a rock fired from a slingshot. She might have been smaller than my backpack, but I knew she could pound me into a goblin pancake. I stood frozen to the spot. I managed to get Hilsa's staff in front of me, but without a crash course in becoming a wizard, I knew it would be about as useful as a bag of wet cookies. The blaze fairy zoomed closer, her little fists clenched. A second before impact, a dark square flew out from the top of the shipping container. It landed on Mirella's back, wrapped around her wings and brought her crashing to the ground.

A ponytailed head poked out from the top of the container. "Did I get her?"

"Tank!" I shouted. "Nice shot."

Tank climbed down from the shipping container. She rushed to where Mirella lay, fighting frantically to free herself from the blanket Tank had tossed. "Help me, or she'll wriggle free."

As we wrapped up the struggling fairy, I spotted the familiar SlurpCo logo on the blanket.

Tank grinned. "Who knew their electric tail-warming blanket could be a fairy catcher too?"

The last of Stitch's pirates fled to their ships, and the streets of Howler's Bay filled with something I never thought I'd see: goblins dancing in the light.

CHAPTER EIGHTEEN
Home for a Rest

P equod's tentacles wrapped around me in a damp
hug.

It wasn't as gross as it sounds. In fact, I'd never been happier to be in the clutches of a deadly meglohydra the size of a battle-bot stadium. Two tentacles over, Tank and Aleetha were also held in Pequod's grip. They were both smiling as much as I was. Pequod's other passengers weren't so happy. Stitch, Hilsa and Mirella were each wrapped tightly in Pequod's tentacles. They continued to struggle against the meglohydra's grip, refusing to admit their ship-stealing, mind-controlling, money-making scheme was finished for good.

"Are you monsters ready to travel?" Gwena called from the water's edge.

The goblin had ditched her dark robes for her regular fishing clothes. Gwena was no longer Hilsa's conduit, but she wasn't a simple fisher-goblin anymore either. In her hand she held the shell-encrusted staff formerly owned by Hilsa. After her father and brother recovered, Gwena had learned from them the truth about her family's special powers. They had the rare ability to combine magic and technology with powerful effects. It had been in their family for many generations. Her father had tried to keep their abilities a secret and live a normal life, but Hilsa had other ideas. When he learned of their powers, Hilsa came to Hook Island and teamed up with Captain Stitch. Together they captured the goblins to use their unique powers to fuel their own greed. Although Gwena's father and brother had no interest in pursuing their strange abilities, Gwena was hungry to learn more.

One of Pequod's remaining tentacles reached down to the shore and scooped up Gwena. She waved goodbye to her family and the goblins of Fishers Hollow, who had gathered on the beach to say farewell.

"Are you sure they're expecting us?" Tank asked from her tentacle.

They will be there. Pequod's words sounded in our minds. *I was able to send them a message and tell them of our arrival.*

"How is that possible?" Tank asked. "I thought the equipment in the lighthouse couldn't send signals into Rockfall Mountain."

My mind is much more powerful than some jumble of wires in a tower. Pequod's words bubbled in what I guessed was laughter, then became more serious. *Gwena, I am ready when you are.*

Gwena, still held tightly in Pequod's tentacle, raised the shell staff over her head and spoke words of magic. I'd seen Hilsa do the same thing only the day before, but this time I wasn't filled with fear. Gwena drew on her power and the power of the staff to activate the density-inverters. The discs began to glow just as they had when the meglohydra made the *Wave Dancer* vanish. Now it was our chance to disappear.

In an instant, the waters of Fishers Hollow were gone. In their place appeared another body of water I'd thought I'd never see again.

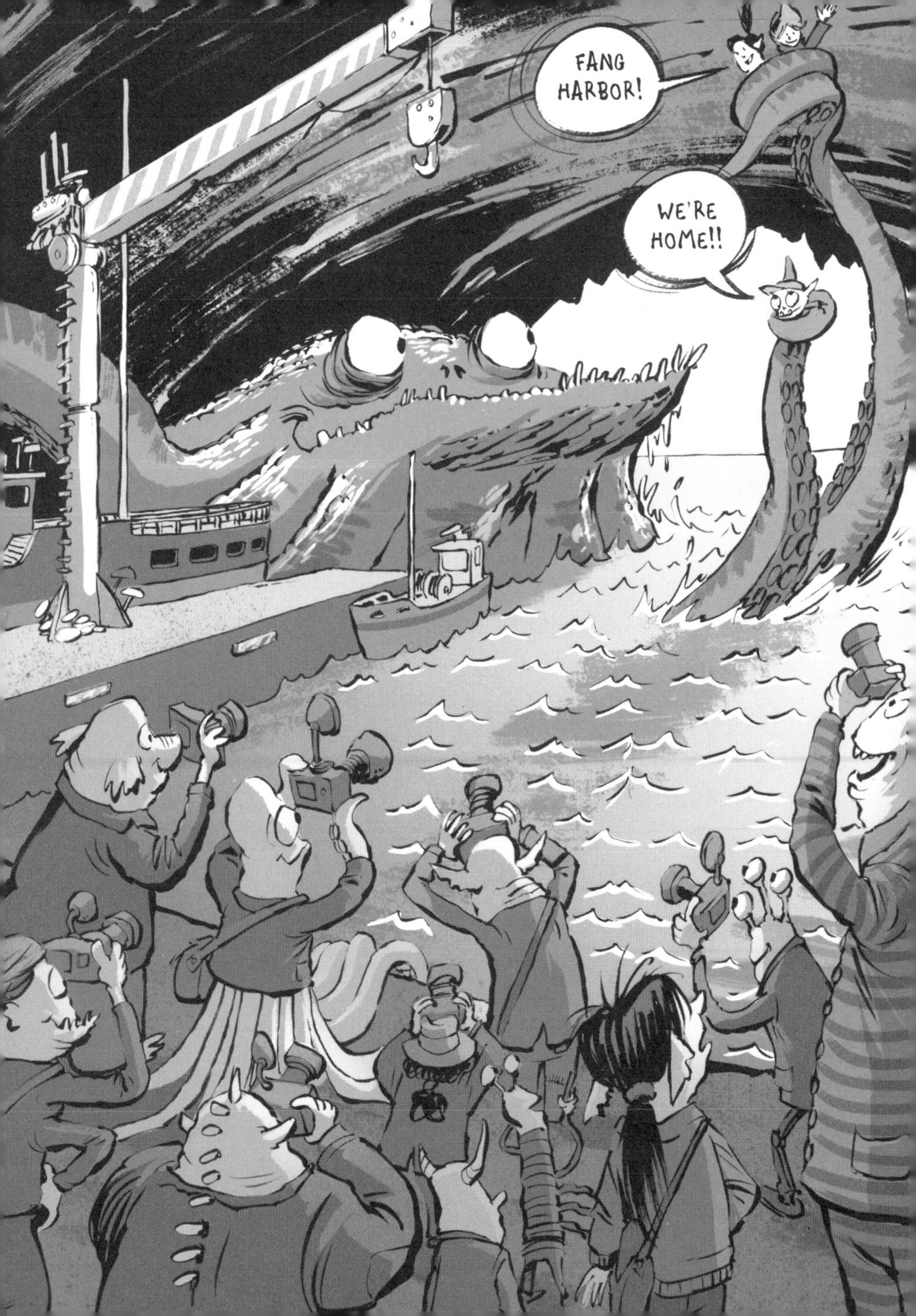
FANG HARBOR!
WE'RE HOME!!

The crowd on the pier cheered when we appeared. A few days earlier they would have run away at the sight of a meglohydra in their harbor. But now they welcomed us like heroes, which we totally were. Pequod's message had warned Officer Hordish and the Slick City Police Department that we'd be returning with the ship-stealing culprits in tow, or, rather, tentacle. The ogre must have spread the word, because it looked like half of Slick City, including all the media, had turned up to welcome us home.

The cheering grew louder when Pequod lowered us onto the pier. The meglohydra seemed to be enjoying the attention. He delighted the crowd by waving his massive tentacles in the air and splashing them in the water, creating large waves. Hordish's officers had no time for fun. They immediately grabbed Stitch, Hilsa and Mirella. As they led the culprits away to waiting police cars, Detective Hordish stepped out from the crowd and stomped over to us.

"I don't know how you did it," Hordish grumbled, "but it looks like you runts saved Slick City."

"Again," I added. "We saved Slick City *again*."

Hordish looked at me like I was bug that needed to be stomped. "Don't get cocky, kid." His glare quickly collapsed and a grin crossed his warty face. "But you're not wrong. Good work *again*, detectives."

The ogre turned and marched back to where his officers were struggling to push a buzzing Mirella Ballaworth into the back of a police car.

Tank's ears had jolted upright. "Did he just call us detectives?"

"He certainly did," Aleetha said. "I think the old grump is warming up to us."

A rail-thin lava elf stepped from the crowd. His red robes marked him as a wizard from the Shadow Tower.

"Aleetha Cinderwisp," the wizard said. "Have you brought the new student the meglohydra spoke of?"

"Professor Phandon!" Aleetha immediately stood at attention. She pulled Gwena closer to stand at her side. "This is Gwena. She wishes to learn the arcane arts. I think you will be very impressed by what she can do."

Gwena bowed her head to the wizard. Professor Phandon looked the young goblin over as if she were something he'd found under his fingernails.

"We have never admitted a goblin to the Shadow Tower," he grunted. "But if she can harness the power of magic and technology, she is welcome."

Gwena's eyes lit up. "Thank you, professor."

Professor Phandon looked at the cheering monsters around him and smirked. "You may travel with Aleetha to the Shadow Tower when you are finished your celebrations."

The wizard stepped back and vanished before our eyes.

"How did he do that?" Tank gasped.

Aleetha rolled her eyes. "Do you really have to ask, Tank?"

Two monsters pushed through the crowd, and my heart did a backflip.

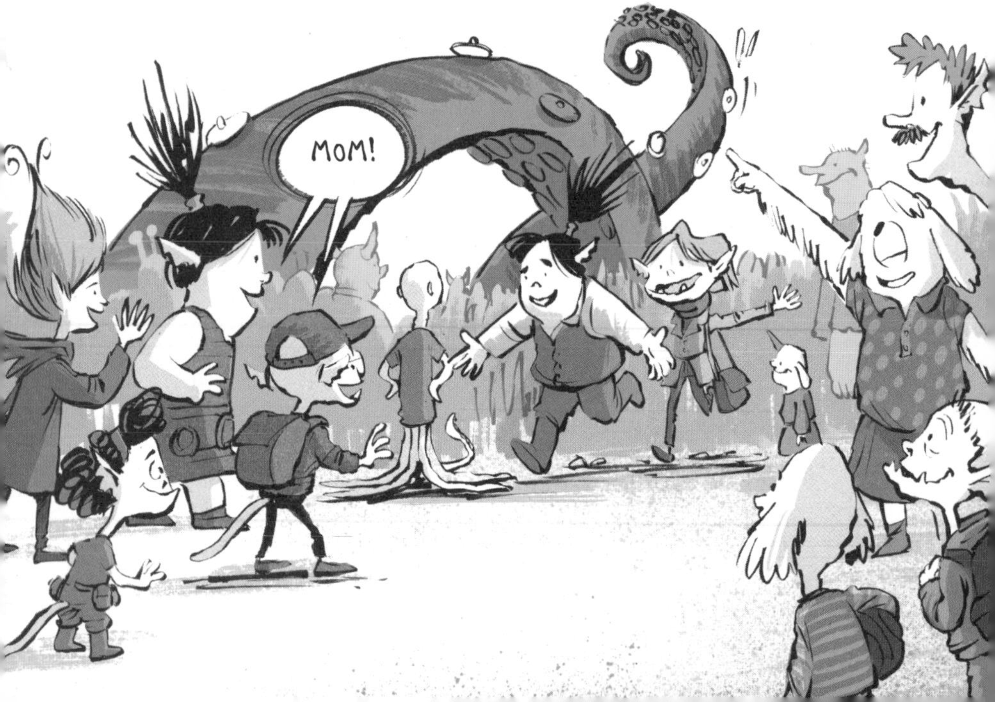
MOM!

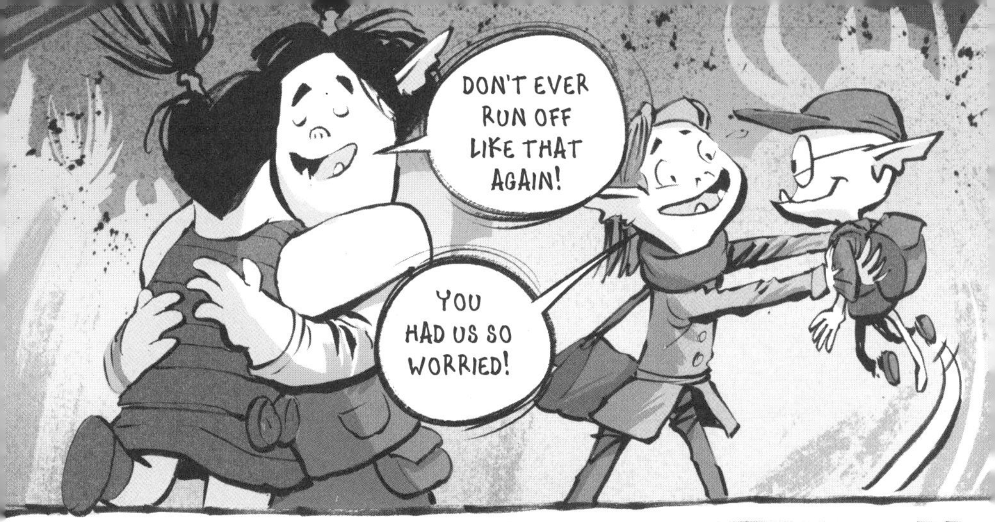
DON'T EVER RUN OFF LIKE THAT AGAIN!
YOU HAD US SO WORRIED!
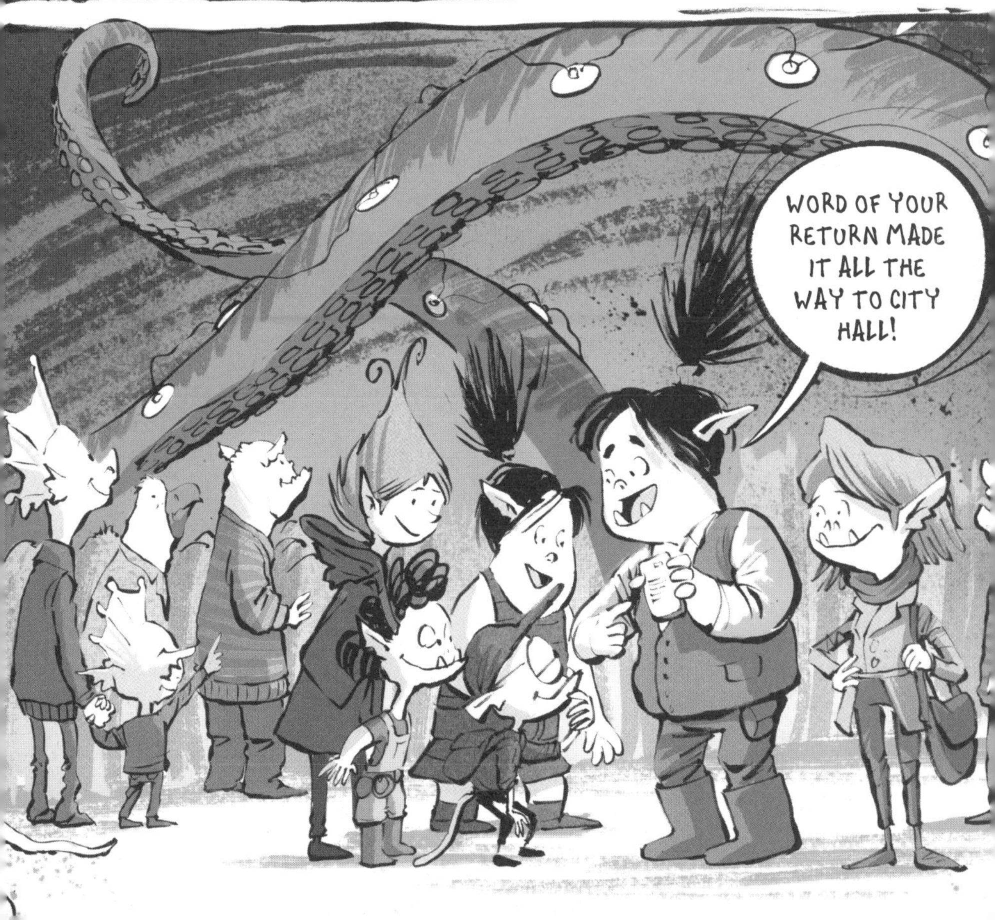
WORD OF YOUR RETURN MADE IT ALL THE WAY TO CITY HALL!

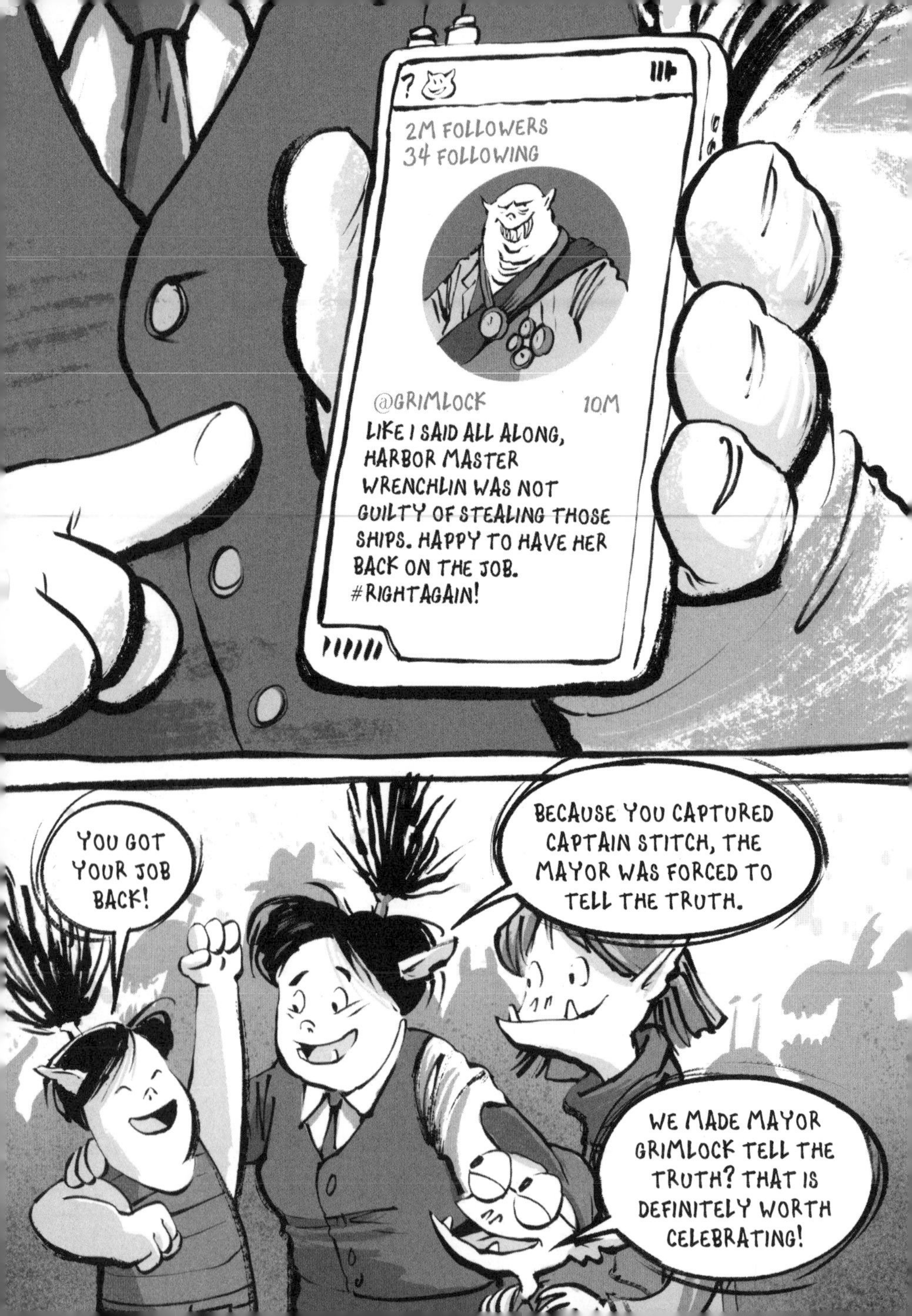
2M FOLLOWERS
34 FOLLOWING
@GRIMLOCK 10M
LIKE I SAID ALL ALONG, HARBOR MASTER WRENCHLIN WAS NOT GUILTY OF STEALING THOSE SHIPS. HAPPY TO HAVE HER BACK ON THE JOB. #RIGHTAGAIN!
YOU GOT YOUR JOB BACK!
BECAUSE YOU CAPTURED CAPTAIN STITCH, THE MAYOR WAS FORCED TO TELL THE TRUTH.
WE MADE MAYOR GRIMLOCK TELL THE TRUTH? THAT IS DEFINITELY WORTH CELEBRATING!

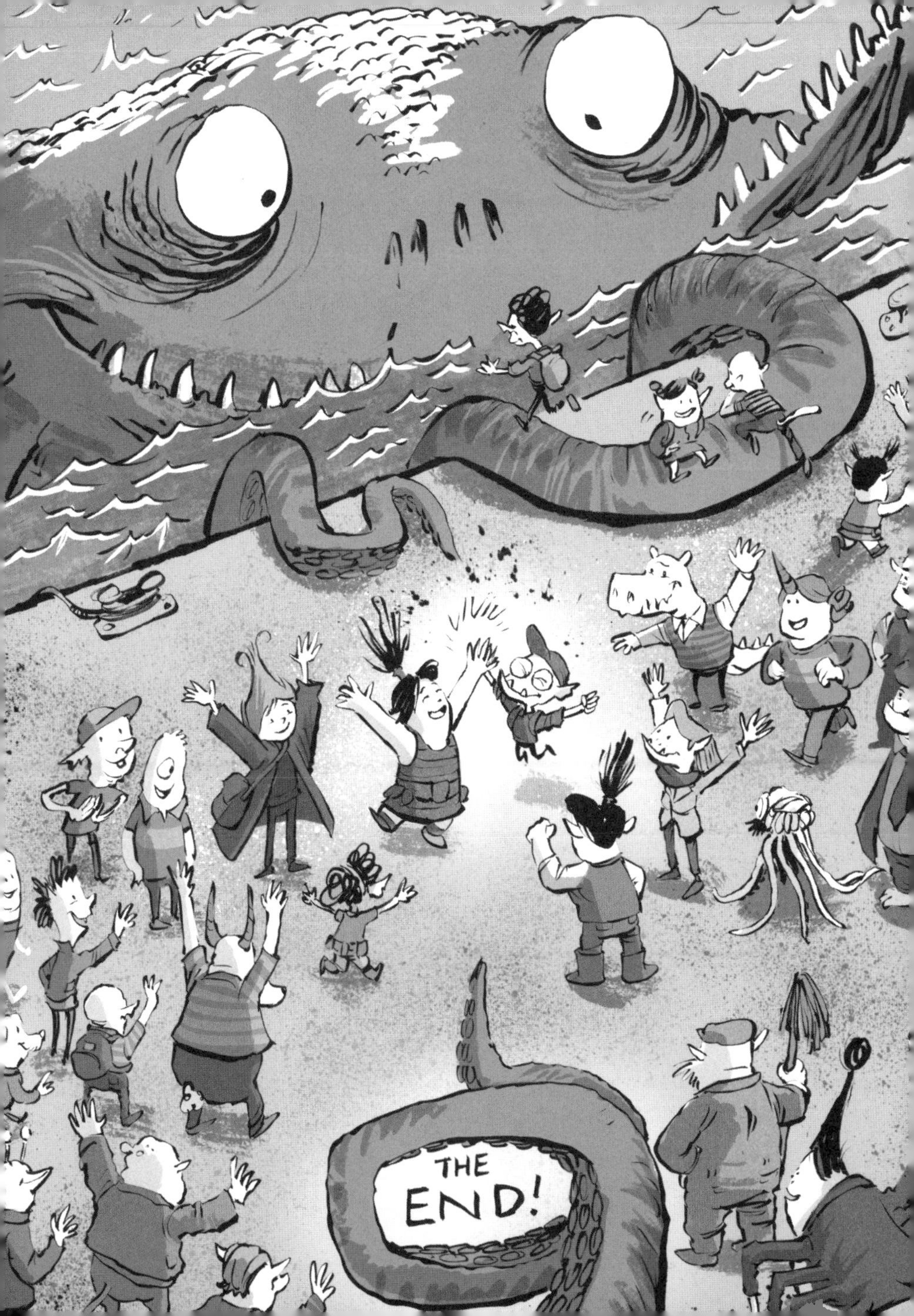
THE END!

LIAM O'DONNELL is an author and educator who has created over forty books and graphic novels for young readers, including the Max Finder Mystery, Graphic Guide Adventures, West Meadows Detectives series. He was born in Northern Ireland and came to Canada when he was five years old. He studied media at Ryerson University and has worked on film sets in Canada, Ireland and the United Kingdom. Liam lives in London, Ontario. For more information, visit liamodonnell.com or follow him on Twitter @liamodonnell.

MIKE DEAS is an author/illustrator of graphic novels, including Dalen and Gole and the Graphic Guide Adventure series. While he grew up with a love of illustrative storytelling, Capilano College's Commercial Animation Program helped Mike fine-tune his drawing skills and imagination. Mike and his wife, Nancy, live on Salt Spring Island, British Columbia. For more information, visit deasillustration.com or follow him on Twitter @deasillos.

Don't miss the first four books in the Tank & Fizz mystery series!

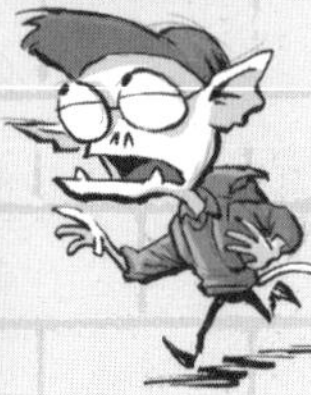

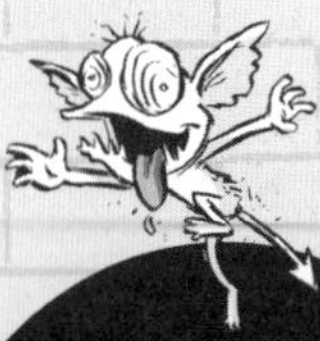

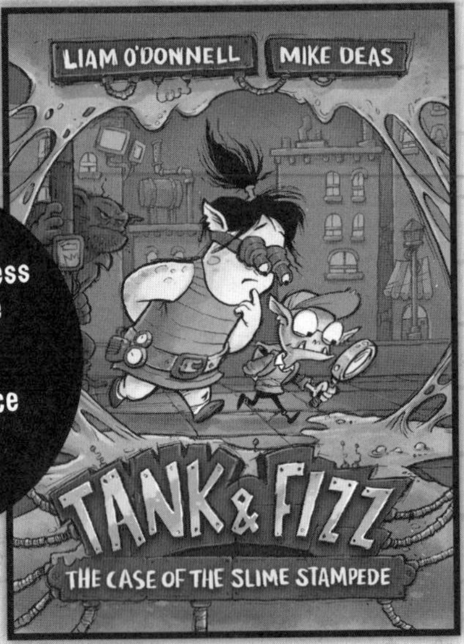
LIAM O'DONNELL
MIKE DEAS
TANK & FIZZ
THE CASE OF THE SLIME STAMPEDE

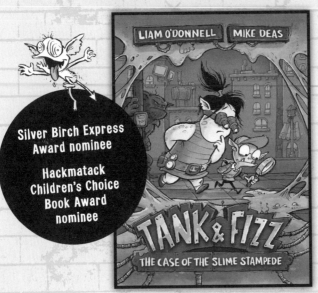

Silver Birch Express Award nominee

Hackmatack Children's Choice Book Award nominee

9781459808102 • $9.95

The cleaning slimes have escaped, leaving a trail of acidic ooze throughout the schoolyard. Can detective duo Tank and Fizz solve this slimy mystery?

"Young readers will slurp up the gumshoes' gooey first exploit with relish."
—*Kirkus Reviews*

"Something slimy is running amuck in Rockfall Mountain and it isn't the cleaning slimes. This chapter book brims with reader appeal."
—*School Library Journal*

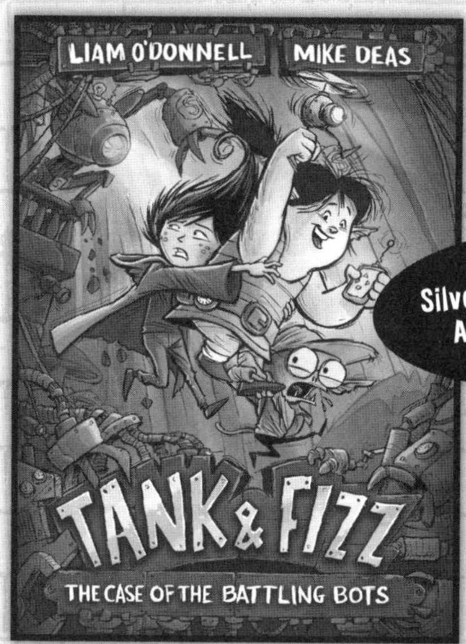
LIAM O'DONNELL
MIKE DEAS
TANK & FIZZ
THE CASE OF THE BATTLING BOTS

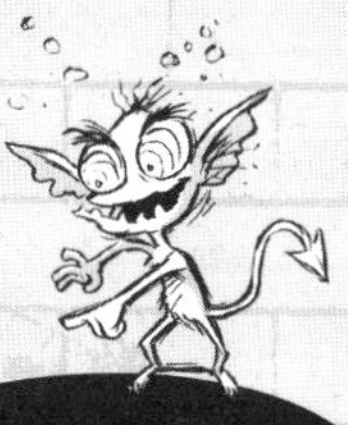

Silver Birch Express Award nominee

9781459808133 • $9.95

For monster sleuths Tank and Fizz, proving Rizzo Rawlins intends to cheat in the upcoming Battle Bot Cup should be a piece of cake. But a trail of corrupted computer code soon leads the detectives all the way to a mysterious hacker known only as *the Codex*.

"High-energy high jinks in a multicultural, or at least multispecies, setting."

—Kirkus Reviews

"A perfect mix of monstrous and silly."

—The Bulletin of the Center for Children's Books

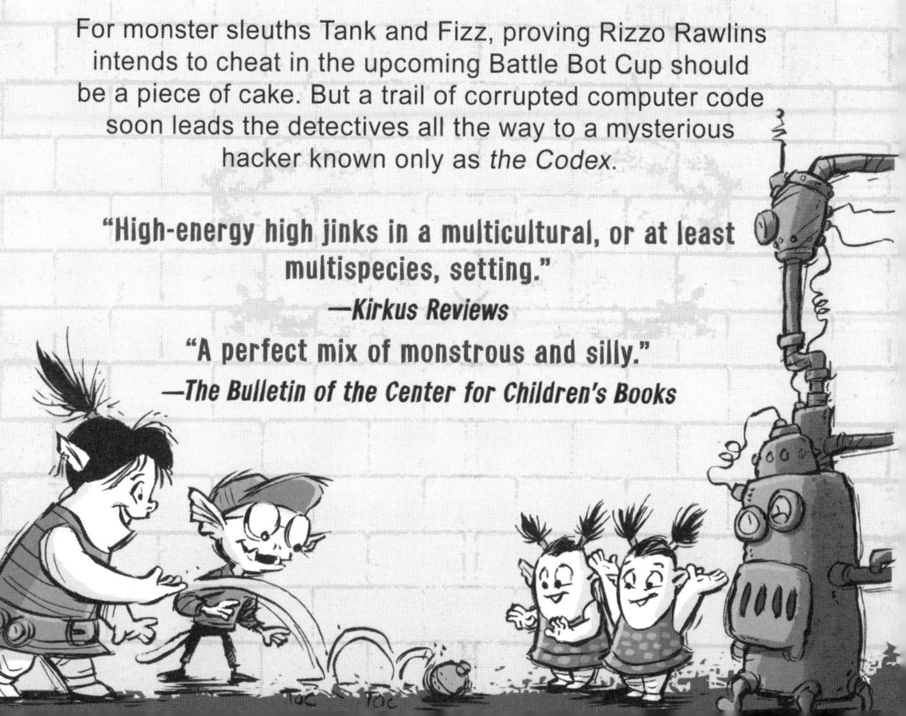

TANK & FIZZ
THE CASE OF THE MISSING MAGE

LIAM O'DONNELL MIKE DEAS

9781459812581 • $9.95

When mysterious figures start making off with the professors
at Shadow Tower, wizard-in-training Aleetha needs the help
of supersleuths Tank and Fizz to find the missing mages.
Using their detective skills, a pinch of magic and a trickle of
technology, the friends explore Shadow Tower and stumble
into a battle that's been brewing for decades.

"An action-packed detective story set in a land of
monsters and magic."
—*School Library Journal*

"Fast paced and fun to read."
—*School Library Connection*

9781459812611 • $9.95

While on a school field trip, Tank and Fizz witness a crime that brings them snout to snout with the ancient dragon Firebane Drakeclaw. Thieves have stolen the Crown of Peace, which keeps the monster clans of the Dark Depths from fighting. Now the detectives must track down the thieves and find the crown or their whole class will become dinner for one very hungry dragon!

"It's a rollicking romp...rich in diverse species and distinct characters."
—*Kirkus Reviews*

"[An] adventure story with constant twists and turns."
—*Resource Links*

www.tankandfizz.com

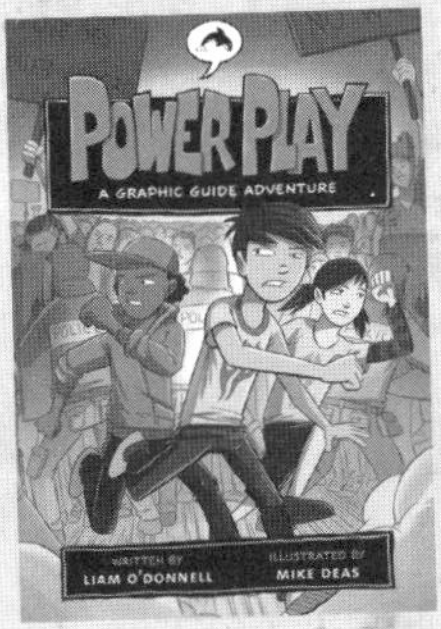
POWER PLAY
A GRAPHIC GUIDE ADVENTURE
WRITTEN BY
LIAM O'DONNELL
ILLUSTRATED BY
MIKE DEAS

9781554690695 • $9.95 pb

"Rich in detail and chromatic with atmosphere."
—*Kirkus Reviews*

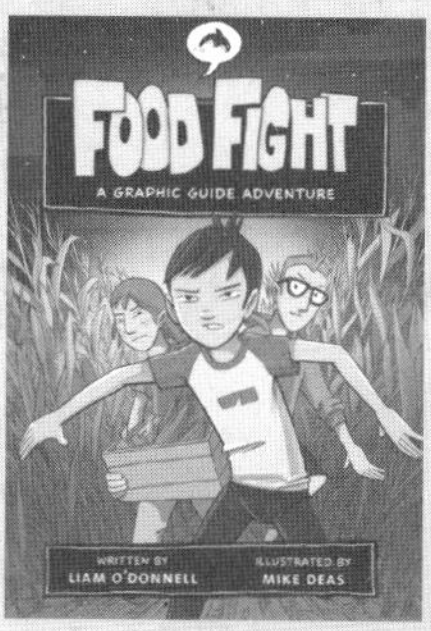
FOOD FIGHT
A GRAPHIC GUIDE ADVENTURE
WRITTEN BY
LIAM O'DONNELL
ILLUSTRATED BY
MIKE DEAS

9781554690671 • $9.95 pb

JOE SHUSTER COMICS FOR KIDS AWARD NOMINEE

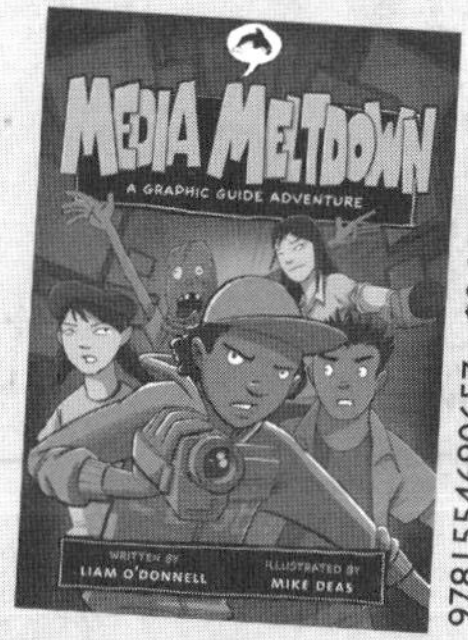
MEDIA MELTDOWN
A GRAPHIC GUIDE ADVENTURE
WRITTEN BY
LIAM O'DONNELL
ILLUSTRATED BY
MIKE DEAS

9781554690657 • $9.95 pb

"Colorful and fast-paced."
—*School Library Journal*

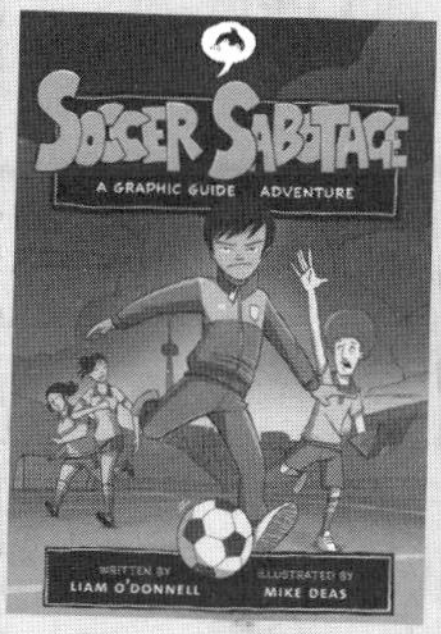
SOCCER SABOTAGE
A GRAPHIC GUIDE ADVENTURE
WRITTEN BY
LIAM O'DONNELL
ILLUSTRATED BY
MIKE DEAS

9781551438849 • $9.95 pb

JUNIOR LIBRARY GUILD SELECTION

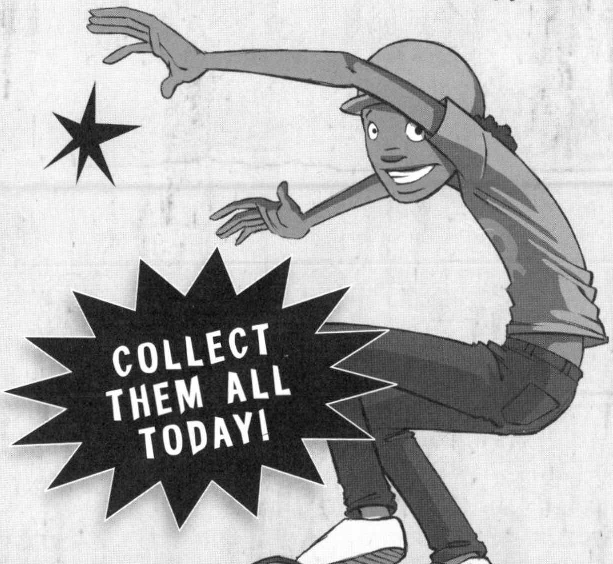
COLLECT
THEM ALL
TODAY!

ORCA BOOK PUBLISHERS

orcabook.com

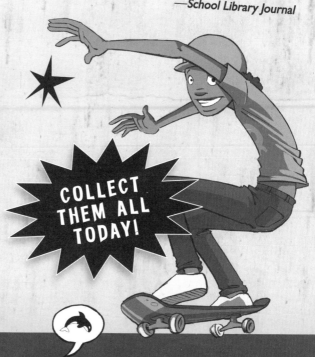